SKY
OF
THORNS

FLEUR DEVILLAINY

For permission requests, contact Alstroemeria Publishing/ Fleur DeVillainy at info@alstroemeriapub.com

Alstroemeria Publishing is the entity under which author Fleur DeVillainy independently publishes under.

Hardcover: 978-1-959356-07-3| Paperback: 978-1-959356-08-0 | Ebook: 978-1-959356-09-7

Library of Congress Control Number: 2023920226

First Edition 2023

To everyone who spent their whole life
waiting for a unicorn.

I see you. - *Fleur*

PROLOGUE

As the eve of Bolide approaches, Sybil Vandeleur, one of the last unicorn shifters on the continent of Craeweth, sits alone in the tranquil night. Tomorrow, the sky will fill with a cascade of stars, streaking across the darkness like fireflies. The robust scent of hearths cooking many delicacies will permeate the air as the village celebrates the holiday. It's a time of joy and camaraderie when the people of Kallistar come together to celebrate their shared harvest and blessings of the year.

Bolide is a time of change when the stars rain like heavenly fire. The flames turn to ash, and from the ashes, hope arises: a promise that never fades. The days grow shorter as the nights grow colder, but the earth still holds the promise of spring, even with fall fading into winter.

As Sybil sits there, lost in her thoughts, she senses a strange energy stirring within her. It's a feeling she's never experienced before, a subtle but persistent thrumming that seems to emanate from her very bones. She tries to shake it off, telling herself that it's just her imagination, but it only grows stronger with each passing moment.

Suddenly, a shooting star streaks across the sky, blazing a trail of light and color that takes Sybil's breath away. She watches in awe as it disappears into the horizon, leaving behind a trail of shimmering sparks that seem to dance in the air. Little does she know that her life will change irrevocably from this moment onward.

SYBIL

The sound of a twig snapping jolts me awake. The windows rattle as a howling burst of wind beats relentlessly against the panes, its force almost palpable. My heart pounds in my chest as adrenaline floods my veins. Instinctively, I reach for the dagger that I keep hidden under my pillow.

"It's probably just the coming storm," I whisper, trying to settle my racing heart. I'm just on edge. A loud snore above me draws my attention to Lemon, my ferret, in his hanging nest. With a sigh, I shut the book I fell asleep reading, setting it down on the floor beside me. After snuffing out the candle, I lay my head on the soft pillow and pull the blanket over my shoulders.

My eyes are just beginning to close when I hear the scrape of metal as each of my locks disengages.

Click. Click. Click. Click. Click.

The door swings open, and a shadowed figure steps over my threshold. As I try to get up, a tingle of magic, like a gale of wind, pins me down to the bed. Despite this, my eyes remain wide open, refusing to blink.

"Sybil Vandeleur," a deep baritone voice murmurs.

As a scream threatens to escape, my body spasms in my

1

failed attempts to move. My breaths come in ragged gasps, making me dizzy and light-headed. Cold fear coils in my gut.

In the glow from the dying fire, an icy blue gaze meets mine. A metallic taste fills my mouth as I will my body to fight the magical hold on me. I glare back, both fear and determination flooding my veins. Magic rolls beneath my skin, an uncomfortable need to metamorphose battling with the magic that holds me down. I take a steady inhale and reach deep inside, willing my body to shift into my equine form.

"Not so fast, little unicorn," he says as he strides to my side, clamping an iron bracelet over my left wrist. My magic immediately diminishes down to a spark. With a lift of his hand, the wind magic pinning me down relaxes, and I tense even more. The stranger pulls me to my feet, towering at least a head over me.

"Wh—who are you and wha—what are you doing in my house?!" I stammer, attempting to move so I can push away from him.

He roughly grabs the back of my head and brushes aside my hair with his free hand. With a calloused thumb, he traces the six-sided star mark in the center of my forehead. The movement sends an odd humming sensation throughout my body as a deep woodsy scent mixed with leather fills the space between us. Realizing how close his movement brought his body to me, I jerk, trying to pull out of his grasp.

"Who I am is none of your concern. As for why I am here," he pauses, grasping my wrist tightly while tying them together, then pulls me roughly to my feet. "The King and Queen of Shadowvale sent me on a mission to retrieve you and bring you before them."

My heart drops.

Shadowvale? That is hundreds of miles north of here. A kingdom mostly of witches and wizards that are rarely spoken of. Kallistar hasn't had many relations with Shadowvale since

2

the war ended over a hundred years ago. Few people dare trespass through the looming forest that separates us from the Northern kingdom for fear of the shadow monsters.

"Release me!" I yell, kicking out at him. A flicker of motion in the doorway precedes five more shadowed figures crowding around the towering male before me.

"I said, let me go!" I glare, gritting my teeth.

He pulls my wrists again and I stumble towards the door. Digging my heels into the floor, I try to buck my body away, which only elicits a growl from the male as he turns to look at me.

"There must be some kind of mistake." I object again, looking frantically around the room for anything that might help me. Fear, like cold lead, settles in the pit of my stomach and sweat perspires along my skin. I'm not a fighter, so I resort to using my words–the only thing I can use.

"Yes, my name is Sybil, but I don't think I am who you are looking for. I'm just a local healer. Half-trained at that." I attempt to clarify, because this must be a huge mistake. "I am no one of importance, nor have I done anything for or against the kingdom of Shadowvale. I have never even ventured outside this small village. You have the wrong person!"

Lemon chatters quietly behind me, but I do not dare to turn my head and draw attention to him. Instead, I look into the male's cold blue eyes and plead, pulling at my restrained arms. "Please, let me go. I have little to offer, but if it's gold and silver you want, I have a small savings in that healing salve tin. Just take it and leave me in peace." Tears prick at my eyes, blurring my vision, as I look towards the shelf where my savings sit in an old dented silver tin.

In a deep rumbling voice, he declares, "you cannot buy your way out of this." He nods to the figure behind him, who shakes the tin, causing the silvers and coppers I had saved to restock the pantry before winter to quietly clink together.

"We are not here for your money, however little you possess," he continues.

My fear turns to anger.

I knee him in the groin and twist, scrambling over the bed behind me and frantically grab for my dagger. In my elated freedom, I stupidly pause. It's enough for the man to grab a fistful of my hair and yank me back. Crashing into his hard chest, he snakes his arms around me, pinning my arms to my sides. His breath is warm against my ear as he growls. "Do not try to escape, Shifter. We have a long journey ahead of us and trying to thwart me will do you no good. Now, be a good girl." He reaches onto the bed, grabbing the dagger exposed in the blankets from our struggle and tucks it into his belt loop.

"I have a name, and I don't feel like going anywhere with you," I spit out, struggling against his hold, my body shaking.

He shoves me roughly towards the open front door before turning to the guards. He looks over at me then at his accomplices, ordering their next moves. "Grab whatever supplies or evidence you can find and load them onto the horses." I narrow my eyes in anger, quickly resolving to find ways out of this scenario forced upon me. "I've got the girl. I'll meet you at the forest pass."

Out of the corner of my eye, I spot Lemon slinking along the edge of the bookcase. He has a small leather pouch around his neck where I usually keep our family ring; the one item returned to me upon my parents' deaths. That little rascal must have grabbed it from the shelf. How did he know how much it means to me?

Lemon scampers along the floor in the shadows, then under my skirt up to his pocket. Lemon trembles as he curls into a tight ball. Even though I can feel his terror, his familiar warmth is a comfort to me as the stranger pushes me into the dark.

The chilly night air creeps along the exposed skin of my arms as the male directs me towards a cluster of trees only paces away from my house. Shadows weave between their trunks and my body shudders involuntarily.

"Aramis." One of the males calls out from the doorway,

tossing a dark bundle towards us. My captor turns and catches it with ease, shaking out what appears to be my heavy woolen cloak. He slings the fabric around my shoulders and roughly fastens it at my neck before proceeding to guide me forward again. Our walk takes us past my small garden, turning brown with the change in the season. The shapes of the plants are barely visible in the dim moonlight as we trek through the glen and towards the forest edge. The night is still, apart from the soft melody of crickets chirping and a gentle breeze.

"Don't knock it off. Freezing before you get there would be rather useless," he says callously.

"I would be perfectly fine with no concern of freezing to death, had you and your cronies not broken into my house, ransacked my property, and tied me up." I attempt reasoning with him once more. "Now, Aramis, this is a big mistake. You. Have. The. Wrong. Person." I enunciate each word vehemently, as I stare him down, gritting my teeth and clenching my fists tightly. Twisting my wrists, I try to slip through the knots, which only seem to tighten. "Goddess damn you!" I dig my heels into the ground and shove my bound fists into his back.

"I don't make mistakes," Aramis asserts coldly as he turns around to face me, his height towering over my slight frame. "You are exactly who they tasked me to retrieve. Now, we can do this the easy way, and you can cooperate, or we can do it the hard way." Another thrill of shock goes through my body as he stares at me with a mocking leer.

"I am not leaving my home." I take a step backwards as he takes one towards me. I frantically try reaching out for my magic as I continue to back away. Shifting into a unicorn would nearly guarantee my escape. The tingle of magic pulses under my skin before it abruptly goes still. I look down at my wrist, at the iron cuff. I can't shift. My mind races as I contemplate my options. I can find my way in the dark with my eyes closed. I spent my entire childhood exploring the glen and woods, practicing my power to shift forms and guiding myself home by the stars. However, I don't know how far this male's magic extends and if I'm able to get far enough away before he could pin me again. The sound of quiet nickering stops me in my steps. Hot air blows across the back of my head as the large, dark shape of a towering war horse leans over my shoulder.

Aramis reaches out a hand and rubs the velvety snout before turning his attention to me, a broad grin on his face at the sight of my terror. He eyes me like I'm something that both repulses and fascinates him. "Afraid of a horse?" he snorts. "His name is Percy."

"I refuse to go anywhere with you," I spit out with anger, eyeing him and then the horse. "Not to mention the indignity of such a ridiculous act. A unicorn riding a horse? It's unacceptable. Abominable." I take a step to the side and an unexpected gust of wind hits me, causing me to lose my balance and stumble back into the stallion behind me.

"So, you're really a unicorn..." His expression is a mask of disgust, but his eyes hold a glint of curiosity as they scan my face. He pulls his hand away from the horse and runs it through his blonde hair, making it look mischievous and unruly. "I've heard your kind are proud, untamable creatures. That you are impossible to capture." The corners of his mouth pull into a smirk as he whispers, "or conquer. Looks like those tales were wrong."

"Ha!" I scoff, rolling my eyes. "You know nothing about me or my kind."

"We ride," Aramis commands, ignoring me. "Now." Before I can protest, he slides his hands under my cloak, around my waist, and hoists me on top of the horse's back, then pulls himself up behind me. I'm so useless in this human form. Holding the reins in his right hand, his other clamps tightly around my midsection. Lemon squirms in my pocket and I pray he doesn't notice. Aramis guides the horse northward and starts off at a trot.

"Let me go!" I yell, only resulting in another chuckle from my captor as I struggle under his grasp. Realizing the futility of my efforts, I try to calm my breathing and reassess the situation.

Why does he care that I'm a unicorn shifter? What would the king and queen of Shadowvale possibly want with me? Yes, we are known for our skills at healing, but I'm only an amateur healer from a small town in Kallistar. Surely, they have hundreds of healers with a better reputation than me? And if they just needed my healing services, all they had to do was ask. I would have come willingly.

The sound of hooves beating the ground brings me out of my thoughts as a group of riders approaches us from behind. My body tenses and I twist my wrists, trying to free them, but the rope tightens painfully once again. A warm chuckle near my ear has me slamming my head backwards, and I hear a satisfying grunt before his arm tightens around me.

A chuckle off to my right side drags my attention to another one of my captors. He removes his hood, revealing his gold-flecked brown eyes, tanned skin, and hair rich as dark hot chocolate.

"Ye sure yer doing okay there, Aramis? It looks like ye have yer hands full. I could keep her contained for the journey," he says with a light brogue accent, laughing warmly before winking at me.

"I am not an animal. I don't need containing," I seethe through clenched teeth. The minute I get my horn back, he will regret his actions. My words aren't the only sharp thing I'd like to stab him with. I scowl as I narrow my eyes towards the male.

"Don't test me, Nero," Aramis scoffs to his companion, clearly unconcerned. "She just needs to understand she cannot escape me."

"Umm, hello?" I say, continuing to wiggle and twist. "That 'she' you are talking about is right here. Just tell me why you abducted me!"

"Stop—moving—so much," Aramis's voice deepens slightly, his body tensing behind me.

"Or what?" I question, bitter laughter escaping from my mouth. "You'll kidnap me, block my magic, let your goonies ransack my house and force me to travel hundreds of miles against my will?" As I speak, my cheeks heat in embarrassment. I can feel the firm bulge between our bodies, my thick cloak doing little to conceal it, as I realize the effect my movement has on him.

"That is enchanted rope," he replies coldly, ignoring my retort. "The more you fight it, the tighter it'll become, cutting off circulation to your hands. I don't think a healer would want to lose her most precious asset, would she?" He clears his throat before slightly loosening the arm holding me, stroking a finger along the rope before continuing. Immediately, the material relaxes, no longer from cutting into my skin.

Aramis turns in his saddle to speak to Nero, who rides to our right. "If we take the path up through the mountain pass, we can stop and make camp until morning once we've reached the first clearing."

The wind bites into my cheeks as we pick up speed. I shiver and try to pull the edges of my cloak tighter around me as best I can, but the bitter cold seeps through the weave of the fabric. The only warmth radiates from the male behind me, but I hold my spine stiff to avoid as much contact as I can. The trees blur as we race past them along the path.

I don't want to give up hope, but I can't see any way out of my situation. Despair claws at my heart, while a bitter mixture of uncertainty and fear coats my tongue. Briefly closing my eyes against the hopeless feeling, I let my mind wander to tomorrow's festival.

Staring into the night sky, a flash of dancing gold, purple, and burgundy light streaks through its velvety darkness, leaving a burning trail in its wake—an infinite streak of beauty. It was just a taste of what tomorrow's sky would offer. In all my life, and all the tales and books I had read, I had never once heard of one of the glorious stars falling before its time during Bolide.

What did it mean? Is this an omen of unfortunate events to come?

ARAMIS

My hands grip the reins so tight, my knuckles blanch white. I am annoyed. Beyond annoyed—I'm pissed. This is a waste of my time. When my father and his wife sent me on this mission to detain a rebel shifter who evaded capture, I thought we'd be going after a hardened criminal. I did not expect to break into a young female's cottage and abduct her in the middle of the night. My eyes glance to her form shivering under her cloak before me. She's finally fallen into silence as we continue North towards Shadowvale. I'll be glad to deliver her to my father and return back to my real mission. My people and their protection.

As a shadow of moonlight slices through the trees, her petite form tenses. "Where are we? Why have you taken me? What does Shadowvale want with me?" She demands, twisting around in the saddle to face me.

I purse my lips in agitation, debating my choices. Of the questions I can answer, our location is the safest. All I was told was to get the rebel to my father's court so she could account for her crimes.

"What the kingdom of Shadowvale wants with you— well, it's—" I clear my throat. What does the Kingdom of

9

Shadowvale want with her?

"At a loss of words now, Aramis?" the shifter quickly cuts in. "I don't even know who the King and Queen of Shadowvale are these days? Is it still King Mattheo and Queen Elanora?" she adds, frustration lacing her words.

"Well, actually," a young voice cuts in, one I had expressly told not to address the prisoner, "King Mattheo and Queen Elanora reigned Shadowvale until 350 years ago, when they tragically died of the vermillion fever. After them, their son King Lysander took the throne and married Queen Rosalind, but unfortunately—"

"That's enough with the history lesson, Edmund. We are almost at the clearing," I say curtly. "We will let the horses rest and then continue on our way to Shadowvale."

The shifter turns to the boy riding on our right and gives him a smile that makes my breath catch. "Thank you for the history lesson, Edmund. At least now I know who ordered my kidnapping," she then moves around in the saddle once more, making me flinch. My body stiffens and I curse the way this fool of a girl is twisting around as we are cantering through the forest. She's likely to break her neck if she falls off at this speed. So I keep my arms steady, caging her against my chest but careful enough to leave some distance between our bodies. I can't stand being this close to a shifter, not after what happened to my mother. Not after the destruction the rebels have caused to Shadowvale, trying to tear down my family's legacy, everything we built and strive for.

But, when Nero volunteered to contain her for the trip back…

My gut had clenched at his words. I need to keep her close. I cannot risk failing this mission by leaving her under someone else's protection. And what did she think she was going to accomplish–wriggling in my lap like some goddess forsaken siren? I would not touch shifter scum even if my life depended on it. But she is my responsibility and if she really is as dangerous as the court seer has predicted, then I have to put my pride aside and not let it get in the way of duty.

"That does not answer my question of why I'm in this situation," she replies after a moment. The strain is palpable within the silence, but I choose to continue ignoring her. I don't owe this prisoner a single answer. "Also," she continues, "I am hungry and thirsty." Her stomach gives out an audible rumble in protest.

"If you can not be quiet for five more minutes," I snap, my anger and temper getting the better of me, "You're going to find yourself gagged and trussed over the back of my stallion until we get there. Do you understand?" She huffs with anger, body tensing, but remains quiet. Goddess above, are all unicorns this needy and insistent?

We continue on towards the clearing and the silence is finally a welcome reprieve. My men and I pushed hard over the last two weeks on this mission, careful not to raise suspicion or be seen by Kallistar guards. Luckily, the goddess was on our side as we did not encounter any of the shadow beasts on the trip south, nor patrols that would have questioned our presence in this kingdom. I only pray we are as lucky as we were on the way back home.

Realizing the intensity with which I have been holding the reins for the last couple of hours, I stretch my hands one at a time. My neck and shoulders are stiff and there is a heavy weight pushing on my chest since the moment we left the shifter's cottage. I would be lying if I said that I accepted this mission lightheartedly. Secretly capturing a citizen of a neighboring kingdom on very vague grounds feels unjust. But if the risk is allowing this shifter to aid the rebels in destroying Shadowvale, I have no other choice but to trust Queen Tricella's orders. We might not like each other, but we both have the safety of the kingdom at heart.

A whistle rents the air as Nero points towards a break in the trees, and I sigh with relief. We all could use a quick rinse in the small crystalline pool that lay at the edge of the clearing and the horses need to rest before we push onward. If we minimize our stops, we could shave a day or two from the journey back.

I dismount, leaving the girl high up in the saddle, before patting my stallion on the neck. He shakes his head at my touch before nudging me with his snout. I pat him once, but he snuffs loudly, nipping at my fingers. Is he agitated with me?

"Later boy," I whisper, then turn towards the others. "Make haste, we won't tarry more than a few hours. I want a fire set up. The horses watered and brushed down, food prepared. Sven, Charles, you're both on first watch. And Edmund, try not get into trouble please," the men laugh at the remark, and Charles affectionately elbows Edmund, who is struggling to unload his bags.

"What aboot the prisoner?" Nero asks by my side, glancing behind me.

"What about her?" I grunt, turning my head. Her features have taken on a weary, glazed look. Her body begins to lean to the side as she stares towards the water, her tongue darting up to lick at her lips, dry and cracking from the cold winter wind.

What is she doing!?

"Shit." Instinctively, I cast out my powers as her eyes roll into the back of her head and her body slips like a doll from the saddle. I barely cushion some of her fall with my wind, the brunt of her weight hitting the packed forest floor with an audible thump.

"Boy, those are quick reflexes," Nero whistles at my side as he walks closer to inspect. Moving the woman's unconscious figure into a more comfortable position, he carefully adjusts his cloak under her head. "Looks like she passed out, but she's breathing."

"She's lucky we need her alive." I storm over to my horse and start unloading the saddlebags.

Nero follows suit, but his glance keeps going back to the girl. "She's not that bad looking for a shifter."

"Nero, you fuck anything that walks," I scoff with amusement, leading the horse over to the pool to drink.

"Hey now, I have some preferences," he replies indignantly.

"What? Alive and breathing? With a second serving of dinner?" I chuckle, punching him lightly in the arm.

Nero rolls his eyes at me. "Ye know, asshole, I actually hope to find my mate one day." His words trail off as he glances down at Sybil's form on the ground.

"You can't possibly think–" My lips twitch in annoyance as I stare blankly at my friend. "That would be a cruel twist of fate to be mated to one of their kind."

"Of course no' a shifter, Aramis. But I can appreciate beauty when I see it, regardless of its kind" He turns away from me and pulls out a flask, taking a deep swallow. "But, I do hope to one day have what my parents shared. My mother used to tell me stories about the day she met my father and the instant pull she felt towards him. As if fate had tied a string between their two life forces, an eternal invisible bond." An instant tug. I shift my thoughts away from that notion.

"I didn't know you to be such a romantic," I scoff, but a smile turns on the corner of my lip. Mates are rare. You could go hundreds of years and never find one another. From the stories I've heard, my own mother and father were fated mates. Until he lost her at the hands of those fucking shifters. He's become a shell of the man he once was when they killed her. My hands clench at my side, anger rising in my chest.

The shifter attacks had become a growing problem in Shadowvale in the last fifteen years. Towns ransacked and destroyed, innocent women and children lost in the madness of it all. And all because they no longer feel protected by the peace treaty that was introduced to ensure mages and shifters coexist peacefully in the kingdom of Shadowvale after the Armaghdale war. The day I lost my mother I swore that, as the crown prince, I would never let another Shadowvale born child suffer the same pain I have endured. So I have taken it upon myself to find a way to stop this carnage for my people and my kingdom. I glance at the seemingly innocuous shifter laying on the ground and try to silence the voice in my head. But what about the missing shifters? It whispers. How can she be the one that will destroy Shadowvale? It asks all questions I don't have answers for.

Nero follows my gaze and crouches over her still form, brushing her chestnut hair from her face. "Oh great, she's bleeding."

Instinct overrides my senses as I look at her, my jaw clenching in concern when I see the blood sticking to her hairline. As I approach them, my lips twitch with a sneer when the worry grows stronger. She better not die on me after all we've been through to retrieve her. I lean down to inspect further, but don't touch her.

"They want her alive, " I grunt, annoyed as my heartbeat keeps racing. I step back from the shifter, feeling the need to move so that I can get her out of my sight as soon as possible. I look back at Nero, who's waiting for my instruction. I sigh, exasperated. "Do what you must. Make sure she is safe."

SYBIL

Whispered voices breach the edge of my consciousness as warm flickers of firelight play across the skin of my face.

"She will be fine. She's breathing," Aramis comments nonchalantly. I keep my eyes shut and my breathing in check to make sure they don't realize I am awake. A pounding headache is overwhelming my senses, but I try to keep my ears peeled.

"We pushed her too hard. She's too delicate, and no' used to the rough pace. Females." Nero argues, and it seems as if the last word was said with exasperation.

Well, at least Nero gets it.

"You know we are on a deadline. The shifters must be stopped or Shadowvale will be ruined," Aramis replies matter-of-factly with a cold, hard tone fitting of his soul. What does he mean by Shadowvale will fall from ruin if the shifters aren't stopped? What is going on in their northern kingdom?

"Look at her Aramis," Nero protests. I imagine his arms waving around me, trying to get Aramis' attention. I'm surprised he even cares as much as he does. "Do you really think she's organizing the rebellion and orchestrating attacks? She appears to be rather weak for a leader; she can't even make a short journey. This shifter is nothing but a weak bairn as far as I am concerned."

"Nero, it doesn't matter how old or young one is. Don't let these shifters fool you, we don't know how strong she is in her creature form." Aramis answers, nonplussed. "And you've heard the story of her parents, what they did and destroyed."

"The only things we ken are rumors." Nero continues to dispute Aramis. "We searched the entire house from top to bottom for evidence, and we found nothing but ointments, herbs, and copious amounts of books. Everything I'd expect to find in a healer's household. Nae signs of the rebels or their plans. No signs of anything even slightly suspicious."

My parents? They have heard of my parents?

"She must have been hiding the evidence. We can't have come all this way just to retrieve some silly girl.' Aramis retorts, his voice full of disbelief and a fury that's disproportionate to the situation. As the two men bicker, I begin to slowly exhale, counting to ten, and running through a wellness check of all my moving body parts. I slowly open my eyes and see Aramis' hateful gaze boring down on me. Not wanting to give him any power over me, I stare back just as intently. Why would I shy away from him if I have nothing to hide?

Aramis snorts, noticing that I'm conscious. "Looks like our damsel in distress is finally awake." Aramis's voice is loud above me, interrupting the guards' conversations happening around the fire. I attempt moving towards the sound of the voices, but a small cry of pain leaves my lips. Every muscle in my body aches, and my temples keep throbbing as I push myself to a sitting position. Reaching up to touch the source of my pain, I am surprised when my fingers do not come in contact with drying blood. I prod the laceration, which is shallow, but it appears as though someone cleaned away any blood. I don't bother asking who did it, only noting that maybe it's a kindness I can take advantage of, should I need it.

I try to recollect my last memories before everything went black, but my mind fails me. What happened?

One of the younger guards' with a mop of dirty brown hair and kind green eyes leaves Nero's side and shoves a canteen into my face. I chug the water with enthusiasm. But my wretched body betrays me the moment I finish half of the bottle and I immediately turn away, retching the precious liquid into the dirt. I should have known better. Next time, pace yourself, Sybil.

"Whoa, steady there. Ye had a nasty fall and hit yer head." Nero crouches in front of me, studying my face. "Ye need to take it slow. Have ye not ridden a horse before? If you injure yourself, it won't do ye, or us, any good."

"What do you think? Of course I've never ridden a horse. I'm a unicorn." I scoff, then snort with laughter. Honestly, the idea is laughable, and incredibly insulting. "What use would I have to ride a horse? Plus, I've never had a reason to leave my village." I scrub the back of my hand across my mouth before gingerly taking a small sip of the water. Well, I would have had one reason, had I heard from Nova Esther, the renowned healing academy of Kallistar. My parents had been professors there before I was born, training aspiring healers in biology, herbology and the healing powers of magic. They were esteemed unicorn healers, some of the best Nova Esther had ever seen, and not a day goes by where I don't miss them with all my heart. After their death, I swore I would join the academy to continue their legacy and become a great healer for Kallistar, my kingdom. But Nova Esther never responded to my letters, and I was too afraid to leave my home and embark on a journey full of unknowns. Countless times, I had packed my bags and reached the edge of Bellenau with Lemon in tow, desperate to make the most of my life, only to return to my family home. Too anxious to abandon the comfort of what I knew and to leave all the memories of my parents behind. So

I stayed in Bellenau, helping the villagers with the few skills my parents had taught me, wondering if that adventure I had always longed for would eventually come and get me.

Turns out, it did. But I wasn't wholly convinced this was the adventure I had dreamed about.

Nero offers me a piece of bread he's torn off once he sees I won't hurl again. I take it gratefully as my stomach grumbles loudly and gingerly nibble at its edge.

The smell of meat permeates my senses as I survey the camp. One guard turns a makeshift spit with two small creatures cooking over the flames. My stomach growls as I watch the fat sizzle and pop as it hits the flames below. While I preferred a variety of vegetation to my diet, adequate protein was required for all shifters due to the vast energy expenditure required to change forms. I try not to move as Lemon squirms around in my pocket before poking his nose out to sniff the air. Aramis reaches into the fire and grabs a single stick, and I take the moment to shove Lemon's head back into the recess of the fabric. Aramis swiftly rips off the leg of the poor creature and hands it to me.

"Eat. We will rest here for another hour, then we will be off again." His eyes look over my shoulder, refusing to make contact. Bastard. He could at least have the decency to look at me when he offers me food. "I suggest you relieve yourself."

Does he think I signed up for this? I scoff internally.

I will my body to shift and take over my form—just to see if I can, but nothing responds to the pull. I bite my inner cheek in frustration, glaring at my captor. If only I knew any kind of defense to save me from this mess. I need to be smart if I want to get out of this mess. I might not know a lot about self defense, but I have my wits.

After staring at Aramis' outreached hand, hunger wins over my resolve, and I reluctantly take the meat. I tear off a small piece and shove it nonchalantly into my pocket where Lemon immediately grabs it and stuffs it in his cheek, making small noises of contentment. I stare at the food in my hand, amazed I'm about to eat with my kidnappers. Who, to my disgust, discusses my parents like they're criminals. I tear off another small piece for Lemon in protest, then sigh. What good will an empty stomach do? I take a bite, emitting a small groan of pleasure. Food is my comfort language, but consenting to eat this meat does not mean I trust them.

I eat faster than I care to admit—starved for the nutrients that will support me through this journey. There's not enough for a second helping, so I try to savor every bite. The dizziness settles, and my mind is less foggy. Aramis and his men sit on the other side of the fire and ignore me, comfortable in their conversation. Flashes of the conversation I overheard between Nero and Aramis come back to me. The accusations of me partaking in a rebellion is ludicrous. Shifters have been living peacefully amongst most kinds all over Craeweth. Or at least that's what I heard from the traveling fae, humans, and other shifters that cross Bellennau from time to time. News of a rebellion would have surely reached the village if it was true, wouldn't it?

"And what exactly makes you think that I'm part of some rebel group?" I question, keeping my tone light, friendly even. I attempt to make eye contact with Aramis, Nero—anyone as I continue reluctantly look at the now bare bone in my hand.

No one deigns to respond, and I'm ready to scream my frustration at them. Who the hell are these men, and why are they acting like I don't exist when they sought me out for capture in the first place? My blood boils under my skin. Fine, the more they ignore me, the more I can work it in my favor. Every inch of me aches with bruising as I push myself off the forest floor and head towards the pool of water at the border of the clearing.

I reach into my well of magic once more, almost screaming

when I can feel the depth of its suppression. Kneeling at the water's edge, I can see my reflection in its silvery surface from the light of the full moon above. Dark circles bloom under my eyes, cheeks wind chapped. I dip my hands into the frigid water and splash my face, clearing my head. Careful not to let anyone see, I allow Lemon to come out from the pocket he is hiding in so he can have a sip of water. "We need to find a way to escape" I whisper to my ferret as he merrily dips his paws in the pond.

"Talking to yourself now, are you?" Aramis's sarcastic voice interrupts my thought and sends Lemon running back into his hiding spot. His figure towers behind me, his head curiously tilted to one side, studying me.

"I wouldn't have to if you'd give me some damn answers," I respond as I push myself up and clear the dirt from my dress. "Rebels?" I shout, "You think I'm... a rebel? And my parents?" I scoff in amusement.

Aramis moves towards me, his hands gripping my wrists and forcefully tugging, making me stumble and nearly topple into him. Whispering in a language I can't decipher, the rope unties, sliding across my skin before it falls loosely into his palms. He sneers with disgust as he releases me, shocking me when he grabs my chin, the rough calluses of his finger and thumb scraping across my skin. The hardness of his fingertips is just as rough as my hands, and the similarity is too much to bear.

"I am going to say this one last time, " he replies gruffly. "Stop demanding answers you won't receive. We've wasted time waiting for you to wake up since you've been out for nearly six hours."

I raise my brow in disbelief. Taking a step back, I abruptly move my face to get his hand off of me. But Aramis follows my lead and steps uncomfortably close in my body space to continue his tirade. His seething anger curls around me, and I shiver with discomfort. "This journey to Shadowvale will take us a fortnight, if we travel in fit weather. These horses that you scoff at are true-bred stallions from the Brimdwell mountains and will make the journey without tiring."

What, I'm supposed to be impressed with that?

I glance at the horses, who are, in fact, fine specimens. The horse Aramis forced me onto acknowledges my glance. He snorts with derision, and I scoff. Yes, we're on the same page.

Aramis puts his fingers on my face once more and makes me look at him. "I don't know if your little fainting episode was a terrible attempt at escaping, but we carry on. " My body recoils from his touch, but he holds tight. "Now, I expect you to be a good little unicorn and ride well with us—on a horse—because we cannot afford to waste more time." His hand falls from my face and we both take a step back, conscious of how close we were.

"We wouldn't need to waste time putting me on a horse," I muster, full of my own rage. "If you let me transform—"

"That is out of the question." Aramis yells, and my body stiffens at his hatred and the way he steps back into my space. I'm so angry that I nearly attack him with outrage. But my head begins to pound, reminding me that I'm in no fit state to move against him. As outrageously enraged as I am at Aramis, I've gleaned important information: this is taking a fortnight.

And the horses are from the Brimdwell mountains. I furiously catalog all the maps in my head that I studied with my father. One of the most prominent peaks in Craeweth, located in the northeastern corner of Shadowvale, these mountains were famous for their steep inclines and the perpetual snow that covered them throughout the year. This means that if I manage to steal one of the horses I can rely on it taking me far away from these brutes until I can get this goddess damned cuff off my wrist. The handsome lines of his face are callous and cold. He turns on his heel and almost walks away until he decides there is something else worth saying. "As for what will happen to you, that is up to the king and queen to decide, so stop fucking asking." His tone offers no room for argument. "Now go and relieve yourself. Don't wander too far, or try to escape. I don't need to touch you to hold you captive, and you don't want to know what happens if you try escaping." I wrap my arms around my torso as Aramis makes his way towards the horses.

"Ugh! You are so abhorrent!" I growl between clenched teeth, but loud enough for him to hear. Aramis turns around to lock eyes with mine and we have a battle of wills until another curl of wind sweeps against my hair, causing my breath to catch. Then another gust pushes me back and I fall, landing on the ground with a thump. Aramis smirks, and I huff with anger as I push myself back on my feet, standing tall, heat burning my cheeks. I turn on my heel and head beyond the edge of the forest, opposite the pool of water. I can hear the males chuckling behind me. One of them mimics my outrage and stumbling, and I have half a mind to tell them where exactly they can put their spoons. As soon as the shadows of the forest start blocking out the flickering light of the fire, Lemon climbs out of my pocket up to my shoulder and nuzzles my cheek.

"Oh, Lemon." I sigh, running my fingers through my tangled dark brown hair. "What are we going to do?" He whimpers and climbs down my arm to inspect the simple iron bracelet that I was absently spinning around my wrist. He looks back up at me with concern.

"I know, boy. I don't know what it is, or why it's dampening my powers." I sigh, furious at what has been taken. "I can't heal or shift. My power is like a dead weight in my chest." Lemon nudges at the cuff once more with his nose, places his paws on it, looking for a release catch, but fails. He chitters with annoyance. I smile ruefully at his indignation, feeling it

22

in my bones. "Don't worry—we're going to escape somehow. I promise you." I sigh and lay my hand on the tree next to me, bracing my weight when the familiar texture of moss brushes my fingertips.

Moss! It prefers to grow on north-facing surfaces because it favors the darker, more humid environment. I squeal in delight as one of my mother's lessons springs to mind. It isn't a solution, but at least, it gives me a sense of direction.

And where there is moss, there should be yarrow.

I search the ground away from the roots of the trees where the sunlight would filter in during the day. I have little time before my captors come looking for me. But just as I am about to give up, I spot what I'm looking for. The plant is small with a distinct cluster of small white flowers. They have faded and dried, but they will have to do. Settling myself on the ground, I make quick work, plucking as many leaves as I can grab and stuffing them in my spare pocket. The feathery leaves crush under my ministrations, filling my nostrils with a spicy, aromatic scent of fresh pine needles mixed with rosemary and oregano. Yarrow is one of the most common herbs for healing, and one of the first I learned how to use from my parents. This unexpected find will be able to help me with my wounds, and I'm grateful that perhaps someone is looking out for me.

I hear the crunch of feet from the direction of the camp and a deep male voice calling out my name. I lament not having more time to myself, but I gathered enough to help heal my wrists and temple and prevent infection. Standing up, I quickly look around.

Can I escape? Where can I go?

We are in the middle of the forest. My magic is dampened and my hands are bound, but this could be my only chance. I nimbly head away from the voices, weaving between the trees. My palms are slick with sweat and I pick up my pace. The undergrowth is thicker the further I move from the path and thorns tug at my skirts. Sweat beads along my brow, but I don't have time to cover up my tracks. I only hope I'm fast enough to outrun them.

"Balderdash!" I lose my balance as my foot is caught on a raised root. My body hurls down a small hill. I land sprawled at the bottom near a small stream. Panting, I make a quick mental note of my body as I gingerly push myself up to a crouch. My ankle aches in protest as I place weight on it, but nothing appears to be broken. Small scratches cover my arms and my hair is a wild mess. Lemon pokes his head out of my pocket and my heart floods with relief that I did not crush him with my fall.

The sharp crack of wood snapping echoes, and the birds fall silent. I hold my breath. The sound of my heart pounds in my ears as my gut clenches. Even Lemon stops his chattering, curling into a ball in my pocket. Moments tick by.

The moon is already high in the sky, but I pray to the Goddess that it is still too light outside for the shadow beasts to be roaming the forest. Perhaps it was only a deer, spooked by my fall.

I cannot risk waiting any longer. I have to put more distance between myself and the camp. Rinsing my hands quickly in the stream, I wince as the ice cold water stings at the fresh scrapes. A shiver of apprehension runs down my spine as the memory of last night comes back to me. The power of his wind magic pinning me to the bed, unable to move. If only I had access to my powers, I could canter faster and further through this forest. "Oh, come on," I utter as I push and twist at the iron band, trying to slip it off without luck. Sighing, I quickly glance behind before stepping over the stream and continuing.

This far away from the path, and deep into the forest, it all looks the same. My ankle aches dully with each step, hindering my progress. If I can only find somewhere to hide. I no longer

24

hear the pursuit of my captors. Have they given up their chase that easily?

I duck under a branch. Exhaustion weighs heavily on me, but I push myself. I freeze as a loud crack echoes around me. Lemon hisses from my shoulder, his claws digging through the fabric into my skin. I close my eyes tightly and inhale through my nose. I had to have imagined it. The woods creak and groan all the time at home.

"As soon as we get back home, we're packing our bags and heading to Nova Ether," I whisper to Lemon as I step over a fallen log. "I'm going to find a way to train with the great healers of Kallistar, even if I have to beg at the Queen's feet for acceptance. After everything mother did for her, it's the least she could do."

A flicker of shadow catches the corner of my eye and I pause, my breath catching in my chest.

Moments of silence tick by before I slowly continue my path. It must have been a figment of my imagination.

A deep growl precedes the scraping of claws against wood. I spin, my heart racing, but all around me the forest is empty. And quiet. It's all too quiet. I can't even hear the faint chirping of birds. I reach towards my belt, but my hand comes away empty. Damn them for taking my dagger.

I back up against a tree, my eyes darting around for any sign of movement. Suddenly, a pair of glowing yellow eyes materialize in the darkness. As I stand frozen with fear, its monstrous form materializes, causing my heart to jump to my throat. Dark shadows surround its massive frame, curling and whipping around it. The creature possesses the head and forepaws of a lion, but it has cloven hind hooves. Its barbed tail whips around, and each spike drips as it fixes its deadly gaze on me.

A shadow chimera.

SYBIL

I try to inch my way towards the tree line, but the chimera lunges at me, its jaws snapping shut inches from my face. I barely manage to dodge out of the way, my heart pounding with fear. As I breathe in, the stench of decaying flesh overwhelms me. The putrid odor fills my nostrils, making it difficult to inhale without gagging. I search frantically for anything to use as a weapon, but all I find is a broken branch. I grip it tightly, my knuckles turning white. With a sudden burst of speed, it charges at me again. I lash out with the branch, bracing myself for impact when a gale of wind hits. Its impact knocks me to the ground as the creature's massive frame is thrown into the nearest tree. The chimera howls in pain and fury as flickers of flame protrude from its open mouth, but I know it won't be long before it attacks again. As I scramble backwards, gnarled roots tearing at my skirt, Lemon slides down from my shoulder.

We have to get out of here.

My heart races with adrenaline and as I clutch Lemon to my chest, I hear the singing of steel. My head whips to the side as I spot Aramis swinging his blade as he advances towards the creature. Wind blows around him like a tornado, whipping his hair in an angry fury. I can hear the chimera's heavy breathing beside me, its paws digging against the forest floor as it turns to face his new foe.

Turning away, my instinct is telling me to run while I still have the chance. I should let that male get what he deserves. After all, if he's so high and mighty, he should be able to protect himself from the shadow beast. But the tearing of fabric, followed by a deep yell, draws my attention. Red blooms on the fabric of his sleeve, now torn and fluttering in his wind as Aramis and the beast circle each other.

He needs me.

The beast snarls, bearing its fangs as Aramis strikes with his sword once more. The blade glances off its thick hide, sending sparks flying. The creature lashes out with its claws, narrowly missing Aramis' face. He ducks and rolls, coming up behind the beast.

Better the beast you know than the beast you don't, I decide. It's wiser if I take my chances with the male before me rather than risk running into another shadow creature while I still can't access my magic.

"Hey, you ugly brute. Go pick on someone else!" I yell as I hurl the largest rock I can find towards the chimera. It bounces harmlessly off its side, but it's enough of a distraction that it swings its head toward me. With a swift thrust, Aramis plunges his sword into its side. The beast howls in pain, but its fury only grows. It charges at him, but Aramis stands his ground. Just as it's about to strike, he sidesteps and plunges his sword into its heart. The beast falls to the ground, dead. Aramis stands panting, his clothes torn and bloodied, but victorious.

"You're welcome," I say, as he tries to catch his breath.

"Thought you could get away that easily, did you?" Aramis's deep voice sends chills down my spine. He lazily twirls his bloodied sword with a flourish in the air before him. His blue eyes pierce my soul as he lifts his gaze to mine. A small scowl quirks at the corner of his lips, but it's not a friendly one.

"Nice try, little unicorn," he gestures in front of him before replying in a curt tone. "We are leaving. Now."

I sigh, as I instantly begin second guessing which beast I am better off facing.

We make our way back to the clearing in absolute silence as the first rays of morning peek through the branches above us.

As we finally reach the rest of the group, a snicker draws my attention to Nero who's standing next to the horses, our makeshift camp packed away in the saddlebags. "Ye look a little worse for wear there, Aramis. Pick a fight with the wrong beast?" he says, with a huge grin on his face.

"Shove it, Nero." Aramis snatches the reins from his friend's outstretched hand, causing the stallion to nicker and toss his head. "I didn't see you protecting my back against a shadow chimera."

Nero lets out a low whistle before hosting himself into the saddle. "And mar this shiny new captain's badge?" he gestures towards his chest. "Plus, someone had to stay and keep an eye on the horses. I figured ye could handle just one wee pony."

"This pony saved your friend's life. I'll have you know," I retort, crossing my arms over my chest.

Aramis pulls off his torn and bloodied shirt, tossing it at Nero's face. But with a flick of his wrist, Nero sets it aflame mid-air before it reaches him. The flames quickly consume the fabric in a whoosh, leaving behind flakes of ash that float in the surrounding air. Ropes of muscle flex on Aramis's back as he retrieves a clean black tunic from a saddlebag. In one swift motion, he pulls it over his head and onto his body.

"Come Sybil," he commands as he once again ties my hands and lifts me by my waist onto his stallion.

I let myself get lost in the rhythm of the horses' pace as we make our way through the forest. The trees continue to grow more dense with each passing hour. A musky scent of decomposing leaves permeates the air.

We briefly stop at a stream to refill the canteens before continuing on our way. My captors spoke amongst themselves in jovial tones when we first left camp this morning, but as the journey progresses, everyone has fallen into silence.

The longer I sit on this horse, the more infuriated I become. Hours and hours on this damn animal, with little breaks in between have me sitting on edge. The horse snorts, and I know we feel the same way. After all, horses are like kin to me. The poor creature has to carry not only me and Aramis, but also all the "evidence" they have collected from my house. I still wonder how my medical bag, my ointments and some of my clothes are going to incriminate me as a rebel. I just want to slip off this saddle and canter away, but my chances of escaping are even smaller than before.

After my failed attempt to flee my captors, Aramis's hold on me has only become more obsessive, and all eyes are constantly on me. Not to mention that I am still tied up with magical rope and bound to my human form, unable to access my magic.

Reaching into my pocket, I pull out one of the yarrow leaves. I crush it between my fingers before rubbing the poultice to my aching wrists under the cover of my cloak. The rough fibers of the rope repeatedly tightened and chafed my skin raw each time I struggled for freedom. I run a finger across the iron bracelet wrapping around my left wrist and frown as its magic tickles the pads of my fingers. There's no trick locks—no real indication of a way to break out of this bracelet. Disappointment settles further in my skin, with frustration rearing its ugly head at the top.

"What are you doing, shifter?" Aramis' baritone murmurs

against my skin, goosebumps raising on my forearms. His arms cage against me with tension, a white knuckled grip on the reins. A gust of wind shifts my hair, catching my attention and forcing me to look up. The gesture moves me closer to his mouth, and had he not been my kidnapper, it would have been rather intimate. Still... an unfurling shifts inside me and I shiver.

"Nothing." I shift my weight. My bottom and legs are numb from attempting to grip the stallion's wide girth. At this rate, I'll happily walk all the way to Shadowvale, if it means I'll never have to ride a horse again.

"What is that smell?" Leaning forward, he peers over my shoulder, his warm breath caressing my cheek. He radiates a heady scent of bergamot and cedarwood.

"Why do you care?" I clench my teeth, growing restless.

"I have a prisoner riding in front of me who smells different than before. I'd like to know why," he replies impatiently, grabbing the edge of my cloak with one of his hands and yanks it back.

"Fine." I push my arm from under my cloak and bare my wrists to him, now covered in the drying green poultice. "Happy now?"

"What is that?" He asks, wrinkling up his nose.

"It's a poultice." I reply sarcastically. "No thanks to you, my wrists are chafed raw from your magical binding rope."

"Well, if you stop moving around so much they won't tighten to the point of chafing," he snaps back.

"If you hadn't tied me up and forced me to ride day and night on the back of a horse until I couldn't feel my legs, I wouldn't shift around so much to begin with." I shout, eyeing him with rage. "Don't you know it's unnatural to sit for so long? This is ridiculous." I'd be celebrating Bolide with my village right now, had they not kidnapped me. Tears line my eyes as a pang of homesickness hits me.

"Would you prefer if I tied you up like a saddle bag instead?" Aramis quirks a brow at me, slightly entertained. "At least I'm giving you the dignity to ride upright. Any other prisoner, I would have made them walk all the way to Shadowvale–"

"I'll take the walking." I almost sit up taller at the option. "Please, I'm dying to move my legs–"

"Unfortunately for you, we're on a tight timeline." Aramis replies, rather indignantly, "you should be grateful for my generosity."

"Grateful?" I reply, my voice raising an octave in mock indignation. "Oh no, I couldn't possibly imagine impeding you with such a preposterous thing like slowing you down by walking to Shadowvale."

Aramis snorts his derision, but I'm too outraged to notice. "I have a better idea, you know."

"What's that?" Aramis says, definitely amused, and I'm ready to elbow him in the gut. "You could just leave me here and go. Trot along back to Shadowvale, right on your merry way."

"Not happening, unicorn," Aramis snaps, amusement gone.

"–Or even better," I bite back, interrupting him. "How about you never took me in the first place." I expect him to snap and chide me, and as I wait, the silence stretches out. Perhaps I pushed him too far this time.

"I thought females were supposed to be more docile. You're nothing but a–"

"A what?" I demand. Goddess, forgive me, but this male has a talent for provoking my temper.

"A pain in my ass," he grumbles, his fists clenching on the reins. Percy tosses his head restlessly into the air.

"Pain in your ass?" I twist around, the movement bringing us mere inches apart. I raise my eyebrows. "That's the best you can come up with?" I laugh aloud with derision.

31

He takes his eyes off the path and meets my stare. "If you want me to list all the reasons I hate your kind, by all means, I'll elaborate." He taunts.

"You're impossible," I huff and turn back to face the path. A pig-headed, good for nothing, spoiled brat of a male.

"And you're wasting my time and energy." He replies, clearly annoyed. "Be a good girl and keep your thoughts and poultices to yourself."

"You don't even know me," I mumble. "How do you hold on to so much anger?" I shake my head, repositioning myself as a numb sensation settles through my legs. My grip slips and I career sideways. Throwing out my bound hands, I grapple for anything to grip, but Percy's silk hair slides through my fingers. I wait for the impact of the solid ground, praying the horses following us would avoid trampling me to death.

Suddenly, a firm grip is around me and I find myself held tight to his chest, Aramis glaring down at me.

"Why must you constantly need to be rescued?" Aramis snarls in my ear. "I thought as a healer you'd have more wit in your head to maintain your balance when riding on a galloping stallion. Do you want to die?" His heated response moves his face closer to mine as his hand grips me tighter.

"No, you fucking idiot," I snap back, with just as much rage. "I am a fucking unicorn! I've never ridden a horse. I don't know how to 'maintain my balance' because I. Don't. Ride. Horses."

Aramis pulls on the reins when the guard in front lets out a shout. Percy slows to a walk as the guards slow to ride more closely to us. A moment later, a whoosh of air brushes past my face followed by a thud beside me. Whipping my head to the side, my eyes widen when I spot an arrow with thick blood red feathers vibrating in the tree trunk next to us.

"Shit," Aramis grunts as he scans the surrounding forest. My heart beats wildly in my chest as I follow his gaze. Fear grips my gut.

Will the oncoming chaos allow me an opportunity to escape? I just need to run far enough and find someone able to remove the enchanted band. Flashes of the shadow chimera come back to me, but I have to take the risk. There is nothing good awaiting me in Shadowvale. They would have sent an envoy otherwise, not a kidnapper. Remembering the promise I made Lemon and myself that I would get out of this mess and that I would study at Nova Ether, I readied myself to flee at the first occasion.

"Nero, take the unicorn and go," Aramis commands, agitation lacing his words.

"But, my prince…" Nero protests, his face contorting in confusion.

Prince?!

The realization of my situation tunnels my vision. Aramis is the prince of Shadowvale. This isn't just some ordinary band of guards sent to capture me. They sent the crown prince himself.

"Do not argue with me. We must ensure her safety and deliver her to the king and queen alive." Aramis frantically yells, pulling Percy's reins to turn him around. "I'll cloak the two of you. Now, go! We will catch up."

I immediately begin to scramble, not caring how I fall off the horse as long as it gets me away from him. How can this male full of hatred be the same who is going to rule an entire kingdom one day? In my frantic fight, Aramis lifts me from the saddle. I kick and try so hard to shift that my nose begins to bleed. Nero eyes me like I'm a rabid raccoon, cautiously grabbing my arms as Aramis places me on his horse. When I'm just about to lash out with my hands, the cool touch of binding magic wraps around me before we take off at breakneck speed.

I scream.

My voice carries through the forests, almost not caring if

our assaulter follows us. Hell, if anything, their presence might be my only chance of escape.

Turning my head around, I watch the rest of the group change formation. Aramis lifts his hands above his head. A pale blue glow emitting from them is all I see before the forest obscures them from view.

Our ride is beyond rough.

Nero was forced to hold a blade at my throat for a good portion of our journey to keep me still, and complained that it would have all been easier if I were knocked out again. Hours pass before we stop at a small stream deep into the forest. My heart gladdens at the glimpse of the rare sky. An orange haze filters between the trees and is cast upon the ground and air. Looking through the trees and up to the hazy sky, I guess it must be close to sunset and almost time for Bolide. My heart clenches, aching to hear the laughter of the children in the village running around, chasing each other with enchanted luminescent moon flowers that cool glowing sparks like tiny fireflies. What wouldn't I give to bite into a fresh hot sweet roll baked with sliced almonds, filled with sweet jam from the harvest.

"Fuck! Where are they? They should be 'ere by now!" Nero shouts with frustration to himself. He stops pacing and slams his fist into a nearby tree, causing bark and leaves to flutter to the ground. It's the first time he's stopped pacing since he started a small fire and offered me a roll of hard bread and dried meat.

"Who cares?" I scoff. The less of these kidnapping bastards, the better.

"I never should have listened and left," he murmurs to himself, ignoring me.

Nero continues to mumble as he drags his hands through

his hair with worry. The riding cloak he took off earlier lay on
the ground by the fire. The ripple of muscles in his shoulders
and back catches my eye in the firelight.

"If we're lucky, maybe they're lost," I comment lightly. At
Nero's glare, I instantly regret my choice of words. I know I
shouldn't speak of the precious prince that way and his look
tells me I should know better. But I don't shy away and give
him a stern look in response. "Oh, come on. Do you think I
really care? Of course, I'm not worried about them. You and
your precious prince stole me from my home!" I aggressively
nibble on the bread, which is so hard it practically bites back.
"There's not even any tea for my bread!" My complaint for
comfort makes my heart happy, even as he scoffs at me.

"Ye know, ye really must be a unicorn. Ye behave like an
animal." He laughs at me as he continues to pace. "Dipping
bread in tea…"

"I heard that." I glare at him. "There were times when I
didn't have much, but I could always make a cup of tea." I
finish that statement on a choke. Mourning a place I may never
see again, my home.

When I turn back to the dirt road, the hair on the back
of my neck stands as if something is out there, watching me.
Something not of this world. I glance at Nero to see if he has
noticed anything out of the ordinary, but he is lost in thought,
worrying about his companions.

The odd sensation fades as quickly as it has come.

What was that?

Nero finally settles as he sits by the fire. After all that
pacing, I release a breath, relaxing with him.

"Aramis wouldn't get lost," he says and looks at me.
"Something must be keeping them." He pulls out a small silver
flask from his pocket and gazes towards the path. The metal
shines golden in the light of the fire, sparkling on its surface.
A dragon mid-flight is sketched into its front, the tail wrapping

around the side. I admire the craftsmanship and the way the figure appears to move as he brings the container up to his lips. A part of me is suddenly angry for appreciating something of theirs. He looks over in my direction once more and catches me staring.

"Is that something you stole from the last shifter you kidnapped?" I accuse, trying to save face.

"Nae." He scoffs. "Look. I can't help what's happened to ye, alright? I serve the prince, and my loyalty is to Aramis. His parents want ye so now we're all here. That's all I can say." The look in his eyes is sincere, but I can't believe there is no further information he can give me.

"Is it true, the rebellion? Are the shifters living in Shadowvale really causing havoc?" I tentatively ask. Only because Aramis had his lips sealed, did not mean Nero would be the same.

"Listen, Sybil. The situation with the shifters in Shadowvale is… complicated. Here, do ye want some? Maybe it'll make ye behave better." He offers the flask in solidarity.

"Absolutely not," I reply on principle alone. Taking a sip will be viewed as an act of consorting with the enemy.

There's a heavy crunch of twigs breaking as he shifts his weight to stand. He takes a few steps towards me before crouching down at my side. I glance up and study the sharp angles of his face. The brown of his eyes take on a golden hew. For a moment, I think I can see golden flames licking around the irises, but I blink and they're gone.

Anatomy lessons with my father come to mind. All healers have to study the physical structure of all known shifters on the continent to ensure the correct procedures are used according to each patient. Growing up, fire draken had always been the ones I was most curious about. One of their most prominent characteristics when bound to their human form were their distinctive irises. Hints of golden sparks that shoot from the pupil over molten gray to bronze smoke, often mistaken at first glance for multihued chocolate brown. Just like Nero had. But had fire-drakes not been missing for hundreds of years? I ponder on this supposition, the wheels in my head start turning frantically and a million questions come flooding in my mind. If he truly is a fire-drake, is he keeping his identity a secret? How can he be loyal to the prince when he so blatantly loathes shifters? How could he stand by all this time as Aramis treated me with such disregard? How would Aramis react if he knew that his right hand man is also one of the creatures he so vehemently hates? But I keep all these thoughts to myself. This is very valuable information I might be able to use if I need to.

I eventually hold out my hand towards the proffered flask. Maybe he wasn't my enemy after all. I concede a glare to Nero. Fine, bring it over here. Nero flashes a wide grin, knowing he's won a small battle. Flask in hand, I take a deep sniff. Whatever it is, it smells inviting… screw it. What's the point of principle when in survival? Before having second thoughts, I down a mouthful, swallowing quickly. I shove the canteen back into his chest and gasp for air as the liquid burns down my throat all the way to the pit of my stomach.

"Whoa there. Take it easy. Sips, lass." Nero grins as he gives my back a firm thump while simultaneously taking another swig.

"What…is…that stuff?!" I gasp out on a cough, grabbing the water flask beside me. I take more gulps as tears well in the corner of my eyes before falling down my cheek. Gone is the chill that has seeped into my skin. The aches in my muscles and bones seem to fade into dull heat.

"In Shadowvale, we call it Dark Starlight," he says.

"And what exactly is Dark Starlight?" I cough once more, raising my hand to my mouth. Nero offers the flask back in my direction.

I shake my head. I don't think I can handle another drop of the liquid. Even though my body is pleasantly relaxed, I need to keep my wits up for Aramis' return, or more shadow beasts. Either way, it would not do me any good to be intoxicated.

"I'm going to gather more wood. Dae not bother trying to escape." He roughly grabs the rope bindings around my wrists and ties it high around the trunk of the nearest tree. Just enough length for me to sit by the fire, but not enough to reach his horse or escape. "It won't be me ye'll have to worry about if ye try to leave through these woods in the dark by yerself."

I huff, dismissing his comment as I turn my back to him. My mind flashes to the ambush as I lay down on the ground.

Who are those people, and why did they attack?

Lemon crawls out from my pocket and curls up in my arms, finishing the last of the dried meat strips before licking the tips of my fingers. Staring at the fire, exhaustion drags my eyelids down and draws me into a fitful, light sleep.

ARAMIS

I briefly watch as Nero and the girl disappear down the forest pass before I return to the fight.

"Gather up!" I yell at my guards, yanking on Percy's reins. Slashing out, I catch one of the attackers with my blade, the metal singing through the air as I parry and counterattack. Sweat beads along my brow, plastering my hair to my scalp as I focus on trying to find the archer. The guard to my left grunts as an arrow pierces his shoulder. I follow the line of trajectory until I see a small glint of metal high up in the trees.

"Got you," I whisper as the corners of my lips curl up. Gathering my powers, I yell, "everyone down!" before blasting a wave of air outward all around me. Two satisfying thuds precede groaning as the two archers fall from their perch. Hopping down from Percy's back, I hold my sword before me as I make my way into the undergrowth.

"Prince Aramis, wait!" Edmund's voice rings out as he quickly catches up to me. He had only been on my guard for a few months before this mission and was as green as a sapling. The closer he stays to my side, the better I can keep an eye on him.

Meeting his eager green eyes, I nod in agreement. I press

39

a finger to my lips, gesturing to my companion to follow me. The thick mist that hangs low around us muffles our footsteps, but the rustling of leaves underfoot echoes in the silence. As we pass the first few trees, dark, shadowy smoke curls around our feet, obscuring our view. I brace myself against a trunk, the rough bark scratching against my palm. My eyes dart around, taking in the depression in the earth where they fell. The archers' bodies should be here, but there are no footprints or other signs of their escape.

Who are these beings? Why did they attack us?

I scan the forest ahead and above me when I hear a guttural scream. Turning swiftly, I spot Edmund trembling with a knife to his neck, another to his groin where the attacker has sliced clear through his skin. Blood runs from the wound, soaking his breeches. My chest constricts as I assess the situation. My eyes slide from the pallor of Edmund's young face to the figure holding him and to the others barely visible behind them. Dressed in shades of black, brown, and green, they blend seamlessly into the surrounding forest. Even their faces coordinate with a similar color palette. The hood that once covered their head has fallen behind, revealing dark black hair plaited down their scalp and delicately pointed ears. One could almost call them beautiful, if it wasn't for the ferocious scowl plastered on their face.

"Who are you?" I call out, advancing towards them. The smell of warm urine rents the air and I watch Edmund's eyes roll into his head as he faints. My fists clench at the possibility of losing one of my men.

"Where did you send the Unicorn?" They reply in unison, tightening their grip on my guard, seemingly unbothered by his dead weight.

"What do you want with her?" I demand. The sound of my pounding pulse fills my ears, but I refuse to back down.

"Not one more step, Prince Aramis." Their voice comes

out as one, soft as silk and ancient. Their lips pull up into a feline smile, sharp canines barely visible in the dim forest.

"Let the boy go." As I take a step towards them, they raise their knife and wave it menacingly beneath his chin. "He's done nothing to you."

"Don't make me repeat myself," they purr, eyes flashing. Was this just a game to them?

"She is gone. Let my guard go and be on your way," I growl under my breath, contemplating how many steps it will take me to reach this creature. I never should have let him come on this mission. He's too young, too untrained. If he gets hurt—or worse…

"What do you want with her?" They ask, a note of curiosity lacing their voice as they cock their head to the side, examining me.

My eyes narrow as I meet their gaze, my thumb absently caressing the smooth leather wrapped around my sword's handle.

"The King and Queen of Shadowvale have requested her presence," I declare formally. As a representative of Shadowvale, I have the authority to state this with pride. I force myself to sound like it matters even though It doesn't…not to me, at least. This entire mission has been a waste of my time.

"I didn't ask what they want with her." Their voice drips with disgust, mimicking the grimace on their face. "I asked what you want with her."

"I want nothing to do with her. My purpose is solely to transport her to the castle." I reach out, slowly gathering the wind around me. If I manage to encircle them, it would be feasible to immobilize them.

"Liar." The uniform voice purrs. Their eyes transition from black to gold, the pupil a dark vertical slit. The surrounding air seems to come alive with a shimmering light. "You're such a pretty little liar."

The forest is quiet around us. Not even the echoing of the insects can be heard. Where are my other guards? They should have surrounded these beings already.

"What do you want from me?" I ask, taking matters in my own hands as I blast my powers out. They're too fast, though. I watch as their bodies dissipate into smoke, unaffected by my wind blowing through them. Edmund drops to the ground with a thud, groaning loudly, and I send a prayer to the Goddess that he will still be alive by the time I get rid of these criminals.

"I want to know the measure of your worth," the voice whispers in my ear from behind me, thin tendrils of black smoke caressing my cheek. I whip around, but nothing is there.

"Come out and fight, you coward!" I yell, brandishing my sword. Anger roils in my gut. How can I fight a creature that can dissipate into thin air?

"How do you judge a man's worth?" The voice echoes through the surrounding forest. I spin around, but all I see is floating wisps of gold and black.

"Stop your riddles. What do you want with the unicorn?" I demand, angrily slicing out with my sword. It cuts clean through the air and mist.

"War is coming, young princeling. I see far and wide, but you—" It pauses and gooseflesh ripples along my skin, my hair standing on edge as its cool, magical touch caresses my arm. "You are an anomaly. You are the tipping point upon which the course of fate may be changed." Its eyes bore into my soul, but I sense its presence lessening.

"You speak nonsense," I retort, my defenses rising. My body quivers with barely controlled rage. I can sense Edmund behind me, his breaths becoming shallower by the second.

"We shall see, Aramis Adrastos." A heavy weight appears in my right pocket. I quickly pull it out and examine the small rose quartz on a delicate silver chain.

"A gift from Alpheaia." The voice is barely audible as it whispers.

Alpheaia? My mind reels as I examine the charm. It seems to glow, pulsing with an unnatural light. I've half a mind to throw it onto the ground to be buried with the mulch, but superstition stills my hand. The sounds of the forest and my men shouting return full force.

"We're over here! Quick, Edmund is injured. We need to stop the bleeding!" I shout, shoving the necklace back into my pocket. I rip the bottom edge off my shirt and tie it in a crude tourniquet around his leg. His eyelid briefly flutters in pain as I tighten the knot and, with the help of another guard, hoist him to his feet.

"Thank you!" I look directly at Alec, my lieutenant. "Is everyone accounted for?"

"Your Highness." He shifts uncomfortably on his feet. "The horses…"

"What about the bloody horses?" I grunt as I move back towards the path. Every moment wasted puts the boy further in danger.

"Half of them took off in the melee." Alec wrings his hands together, casting his eyes at the ground. I turn on my heel with a sigh and clap him on the shoulder. He was newly appointed to the position of lieutenant. I chide myself, a reminder that this is his first real mission outside castle guard duty.

"Don't worry. They are highly trained and will return when they hear the signal." They were trained military horses. There was no reason they should have been spooked by a few forest spirits. Hopefully, they'd return swiftly when they heard the signal before they ran into something far worse.

I pull a cord from around my neck and toss him one of the two whistles before looking at the faces before me, accounting for each person. No one was missing except Nero and Sybil.

"Were there any other casualties?"

"No, sir. A few scrapes and bruises. Jack twisted his ankle, but otherwise we're all intact and hearty." He stands at attention as he wraps his fingers around the whistle.

"Good." I let go a sigh of relief I didn't realize I was holding. "The most important thing is that we're all alive, and together. We need to get Edmund to the clearing so we can get him cleaned up and treated."

He looks down at Edmund's supported body. "He's in no fit state to travel that far, let alone ride astride."

"Then we will have to carry him. Create a stretcher from some of these branches and cloth strips, then bring him to the clearing—just stick to the path and stick together. Blow the signal every five minutes as you travel. The horses will hear it and they will come." I turn and make my way to my stallion's side, running my hand across his soft, velvety snout before rummaging through the saddlebag. Finding an old worn shirt, I toss it to the guard.

"But what about you?" The guard asks hesitantly.

"I'm going after our prisoner," I say as I swing myself up into the saddle, setting my eyes in the direction I had sent my best friend and Sybil. "If you—"

As the guard beside me stops and throws out his arm, I notice a tall stag before us. It's deep in its prime, tail twitching as its nostrils flare, but we are downwind. I reach for my bow from my saddlebag. Taking aim, I let the arrow fly, and it lands with a thud in the creature's side.

I say a silent prayer, nodding my head respectfully towards the creature. Thank the Goddess for small blessings.

"Now you can bring back Edmund, and dinner." I grin at them before turning Percy around and heading down the trail. We were lucky tonight, but Edmund isn't out of the woods yet. My fist clenches the reins tighter and I click my heels, urging Percy onward. If we didn't have to travel half the continent to get one rebel unicorn to Shadowvale, we wouldn't be in this mess. Edmund wouldn't be injured and I wouldn't have had some cryptic conversation with some forest spirit.

Alpheaia.

The tipping point.

What does it all mean?

SYBIL

The snap of branches breaking draws both our attention. My heart thunders in my chest as I scan the dark forest before us. I yearn to shift into my unicorn form, where at least I'd have a chance at defending myself or escaping. Despite my wishes, the enchanted band around my wrist continues to neutralize my power. The wind shifts, and with it comes the unmistakable scent of blood, thick and metallic.

"Someone's approaching," Nero says as he moves with a combination of speed and grace that resembles a sleek beast in motion.

His sword glistens in the light as he lifts it up to block the intruder from entering the clearing. A moment of recognition crosses his face before he sheaths his sword, the sound of metal on leather echoing in the air before offering his assistance.

"Thank goodness you're alive brother. I was dreading having to explain to the King and Queen how I lost ya stupid arse," Nero adds, patting Aramis's shoulder. I can see the relief wash away the worry from his features.

As they move closer to where I crouch in the shadows, I notice dark stains of blood coating Aramis's arms and chest.

Has he been injured? The instinct to heal wars with my desire to flee while they are distracted. As silently as I can muster, I slowly step backwards. A resounding crack of dried wood echoes as my weight snaps a twig in two. Aramis's eyes meet mine where I stand, holding my breath in the shadows.

"Trying to escape, shifter?" He brushes off Nero's attempts to assess him, stalking towards me. My mouth twists into a sarcastic smile—of course he assumes I'm trying to escape, even when I know I've just newly accepted my fate. I wish he would give it a rest. My mouth is dry and the pulse of my heart beats faster in my chest as my eyes roam from his face to the fresh stain on his sleeves. If that's his blood—

"It's not mine," he replies to my silent inquiry. Warmth creeps across my face, and I surprise myself when I silently thank the Gods that it's nothing serious.

"I was just assessing for injuries." I state pertly, meeting his cold stare. Strange awareness settles between us, full of complicated emotions.

"Why would you even bother, shifter? So you can gloat over the fact that one of us was injured?" Aramis sneers and angrily wipes the sweat off his forehead. The expectation that I care only because he suspects I'd use my knowledge over him for gain hurts.

"I wouldn't do that, your Majesty." I retort, attempting to rein in my spite. "I'm a healer and I don't take pleasure in other's pain." It is evident that he lacks knowledge about healers and their mission, as well as the honor and duty I feel compelled to fulfill. Since I was young, my parents instilled in me the belief that healing is an art and a gift from the goddess. Only a select few are born with the ability to master the knowledge of healing and the power to harness it. Although I have not yet taken my healer's oath at Nova Esther, it holds no less significance in my soul.

"What happened? Where are the others?" Nero interrupts.

He grabs Percy's reins and leads him over to the water. His coat is soaked and is frothing at the mouth. How hard did Aramis push him to get to us?

"I–" Aramis sighs deeply, running a hand through his wind disheveled hair. "I'm still not sure. It was an ambush, we barely made it…"

"Who?" Nero's face falls as he stares at Aramis, reading in his expression the words he was struggling to pronounce.

"It's Edmund. They stabbed him."

The sound of shouting fills the air as two guards carrying a makeshift gurney enter the clearing and set it down near the fire. I count as the rest of the guards return, leading the horses who drag a large stag behind them.

"Edmund," Aramis gently coaxes the guard's green eyes open, his brow furrowed. "Edmund, can you hear me?" He snaps his fingers before the guard's face.

"Let me look at him," I say meekly, wiping my sweaty palms on my skirt.

I can do this.

"Why would I let my prisoner lay hands on one of my wounded men?" Aramis glares at me from where he crouches.

Glaring back, I edge around him for a better view, my eyes darting to the injured guard now on the ground. Despite my situation, I'm determined to do what I was born to do and complete it to the highest level of my capabilities.

"He needs care. Please—please give me the freedom to help him." I raise my bound wrists as I look towards my captor. Friend or foe, I will not stand by as this man loses his battle with death. My parents have taught me better than that. "He's in terrible pain, and I have to help."

"Let you go? Why? So I can free you only for your poor attempts at escape? Why would I do that?" Aramis doesn't break my gaze, and the steady reprimand unworthy of my actions makes me want to falter. Had it not been for the guard on the ground, had it not been for this desire to help break me beyond my fear, I stand straighter.

"You're wasting time while your guard writhes in agony, losing blood with the potential to die, when you have a source that's willing and able to do what they can to save him," I scoff, anger leading my words aloud. "I don't see any other able-bodied healers in your company."

"What makes you think I care about a single guard?" Aramis advances towards me, attempting to intimidate me, and my body quivers, on the verge of standing my ground or fleeing. My skin warms with anger–anger at Aramis' doubt and his disbelief that I'm willing to help him. I'm ready to prove the asshole wrong.

"Do you really think I can't see past this farce? You care about your men Aramis, more than you are willing to admit because that would make you vulnerable and goddess forbid, you show some compassion or empathy. Not to mention that you wouldn't have bothered carrying him all this way if you had no hope for his survival?" I keep my gaze steady on Aramis. His jaw clenches and his breathing becomes more laborious, almost as if he is using every ounce of strength he has to stop himself from losing control. I turn and notice that the guards all seem to be on my side too, their gazes desperate to save one of their own. A twist of fear fills me with worry as I meet Aramis's eyes once more and he looks me over.

"You're getting too confident shifter. What happened to only being a half-trained healer?" He retorts, his disbelief hurting more than I care to admit. Heat burns my cheeks, but I hold my ground.

"A half-trained healer is better than none when we're lost in this goddess forsaken forest," I declare boldly. "Plus, if the shadow beasts get a whiff of his blood, don't you think they'll come prowling?" My patience is wearing thin. I am losing precious time arguing when I could be assessing the damage and healing.

I lift my bound hands once again before him, praying he'll do the right thing and let me help him. Silence fills the air between us, the world seeming to slow before he responds.

"Fine." The Prince's resolve settles into me, and I feel nothing but gratitude to tend his wounded. Aramis' hardened gaze glances over me, communicating distrust, despite his allowance. "But flinch the wrong way or harm him and you'll find yourself tied up, gagged and slung like a sack over the back of the horse for the rest of the journey." Before I can reply, he flips out a silver hunting knife from his belt and slices clean through the rope. It falls to the ground with a thud as final as his last words. My relief is past my words. Finally, I can do my job.

Moving around him to the injured guard's side, I allow my instincts to guide me as I do my best to assess the damage done to him without the aid of my magical abilities. His pale complexion contorts in agony, his grip on his right thigh is so tight that his knuckles are white. Someone has tied a crude tourniquet of fabric across what I presume is a deep gash. While created in haste, it is still done well–and has possibly saved the guard's life. I slide my slender fingers across his throat to feel his pulse, watching his chest rise and fall in increasingly labored breaths. A frown tugs at the corners of my mouth. Depending on how much blood the guard has lost this deep in the forest, without my medicine and a suture kit I recognize his chances of survival are small. Providing the wound doesn't become infected; I furrow my brow in assessment.

"We need fresh water, linen, and build up the fire if you want any chance of him surviving." I direct to the guards aloud as I tie my hair back, away from my face. I glance back to make

sure my directions have been heard and nearly double back
with surprise. Aramis glares, pursing his lips at my demands,
but with one look at his fallen comrade, he grudgingly nods in
consent at Nero and the remaining guard.

"Do as she asks, and make haste!" Aramis commands his
men, and an unacceptable swirl whooshes through my gut at
his direction. I hold his gaze a second longer and slightly nod
my head in thanks for trusting my knowledge and abilities, and
he nods back. A silent truce.

"Where are the others?" I continue to peel away the guards'
leather armor, setting it in a pile next to me. A flashback of
helping my father out of his armor as a child crosses my mind.
I shake my head, willing away the memory so I can focus
on the task at hand. As I get to the leg bracers, he takes a
sharp intake of breath as he clenches his teeth in pain before
blissfully losing consciousness.

It'll be easier this way, at least. I won't need a pain tonic to
stitch him back together.

"What does it matter to you?" He replies bitterly. "Tending
to your captors cannot be high on your list of priorities."

"I'm trying to be cordial as I focus on your guard," I reply
slowly through gritted teeth.

"Also," I continue, "my parents always taught me that idle
chatter helps not only to soothe the patient, but also to keep
nerves at bay, and I might be wrong, but it seems that's exactly
what you need." I bite my lower lip to force myself not to
snicker at my own smart-ass remark but I can sense the weight
of his stare on my back. Minutes creep by in silence as I work.
Only the sound of the guard's ragged breaths and the crackling
of the fire filling the air.

"They will be here soon," Aramis replies, focusing on his
own tasks of building up the fire. He continues monotonously:
"After we defeated the bandits, we spotted a herd of deer
on the way back. They split off to hunt. We're almost to the

mountain pass and food will be scarce until we get through it. It will be good to have a full warm meal tonight. We will dry the rest overnight for the journey."

The thought of a warm meal makes my stomach growl in anticipation, but I have a task to complete. "Food always helps with a speedy recovery." I say as I roll back my sleeves that had fallen down.

"Edmund shall have whatever he requires," Aramis says with a sigh. He tosses more logs on the fire, poking at the embers with a stick until the sparks catch on the dry peeling bark, casting an orange glow on his profile. From this angle, I can see how his worry is creased across his face as he glances from the guard to the shadowy depths of the forest they have just come from. My heart clenches as a similar emotion echoes within me. That unsettling fear of losing someone you care about and not knowing if you will be strong enough to survive the grief.

"He will survive," I say softly, and I hold my breath when our eyes meet and for the first time, I can see Aramis without walls of steel guarding his emotions. Fear, confusion, loneliness, all come crashing to the surface for a split second.

Nero and another guard return with a pot of fresh water and a clean white cotton tunic, pulling me from my thoughts. Ripping the shirt in strips, I dip one into the water before untying the tourniquet to assess the damage. The laceration is deep, but it has narrowly missed his femoral artery. The journey ahead will be arduous, but if I can manage to clean and stitch the wound, he might just stand a chance.

"This would be a lot simpler if you let my magic free." I look pleadingly up at Aramis, lifting my wrists up , the iron bracelet a dull orange in the firelight, hoping the life of his guard was worth freeing my power. "Everyone knows unicorn magic is beyond compare when it comes to healing. Ensuring one's life force stays tethered to this world requires an incredible amount of magic, and we can tap into our reserves for longer than any other magic user on the continent. That's why we make such incredible healers." I plead my case, begging him to consider what's at stake if I can't use my magic.

"And risk you taking your true form and escaping into the forest where worse beasts than myself would devour you in a heartbeat?" Aramis' expression is cruel, and I sigh. "I don't think so." He turns his back and walks away from me.

I take a moment to wipe the perspiration from my forehead with my sleeve, then continue my ministrations of cleaning the wound. I sigh, uncertain of the extent of healing I can do without my magical abilities.

A thump next to me interrupts my thoughts as I turn my head. The familiar warm brown leather of my mother's healing satchel lies on the ground beside me. Tears well in my eyes as I lovingly run a hand across the worn soft surface of the bulging pockets. I overstuffed the pack in preparation for Bolide with everything I needed, from burn ointment, antiseptics, to anti-nausea and willow bark tea.

"I—Aramis–" I breathe out barely over a whisper. The words catch in my throat as I look up, my hazel eyes meeting Aramis' icy blues. His jaw clenches, and the stern gaze only highlights the handsome square jawline.

"I don't need your thanks. I just need your skills, however little of them you might possess," Aramis says. Standing above me, his eyes roving my face before he turns on his heel to find Nero at the edge of the clearing. He positions himself to keep me within his sights as they begin a conversation.

My heart clenches as emotions whirl inside my brain. Shaking my head, I turn towards my patient as I pull out an antiseptic wash, healing ointment, and suture kit from their respective pockets. My fate is in the hands of the goddess and I had work to do.

"This might sting," I whisper as I coat a strip in antiseptic wash, hoping my words soothe Edmund even if he's unconscious . I lift my shaking hands and gently dabbing at the wounds. Edmund's face flinches as I make my way to the laceration in his thigh.

"Shhh, everything is fine. I'm just cleaning your wounds so they don't get infected," I whisper in a hushed voice as I continue to clean. With a spare hand, I gently rub at his furrowed brow. The last thing I want is for him to wake up in a fit of pain before I have his wounds stitched close.

Clove oil! I rummage around before I find the small bottle in the bag and pull the stopper. Not only would it provide temporary local analgesia, but it should help with the inflammation and infection. Sweat beads on my brows as I lean over the guard's body, plastering my hair to my face. I lift my hand to clear my face as a gentle breeze brushes against my skin. Glancing up, I see Aramis watching me. He leans against a tree with his arms crossed in front of his chest—a gaze so steady and conflicted. I break eye contact and look around the clearing. With my focus on tending to the guard, I didn't hear the others return to the camp. The fire is brought to life as meat crackles over the fire; the sizzle and pop of the fat dripping into the flames breaking the quiet murmurings. The smell is intoxicating.

I need to focus, no distractions. My stomach growls audibly. Even though they may not believe me, I am determined to prove them wrong, that they are mistaken and I am innocent.

I sterilize the small curved needle before threading it, praying the goddess will give me stable hands. Once done, I tie a clean strip of linen over the fresh stitches and clean my hands in what's left of the water.

"He is steady now," I say to Aramis, who has not stopped studying me since the moment I started tending to Edmund's wound. He must truly care for the boy.

He closes the distance between us and assesses my work. Edmund is still unconscious but has now a peaceful expression on his face, almost as if he is having the best sleep of his life. Aramis exhales deeply, and I can see his shoulders drop. To my surprise, he reaches down and offers me a hand. I hesitate at his gesture, but I am stiff from kneeling, so I warily place my hand in his and let him help me to my feet.

"But he needs to rest," I add, standing so close to him I can see his blue eyes darken like storm clouds on the verge of breaking, my hand still resting in his. "Edmund is in no condition to ride." His body heat radiates off him at our proximity, the smell of bergamot and cedarwood mixed with wood smoke filling my senses. I exhale slowly, unable to break eye contact.

A bark of laughter breaks the moment, and I quickly pull myself away from Aramis's grip. The other guards are passing around a flask of what I presume is more Dark Starlight.

"Fine," he grunts, "we could all need some rest, anyway." He sets off to join the guards eating by the fire. After a couple of steps however, he comes to a stop. His head turns slightly in my direction and I can see his body tense.

"Thank you for saving his life, Sybil," he whispers, without meeting my eyes.

SYBIL

After Edmund consumes some meat and two cups of tea, I finally let him drift off into a fitful sleep. The anesthetic had worn off after a while and the poor boy was starving. He will need to wake up and eat more in a couple of hours, but for now, he manages to keep down what I offer. As I uncurl my legs from underneath me, the tension in my body relaxes, and I watch him slowly take easier breaths, a tinge of color coming back to his skin. The guards have switched twice to keep watch and make sure I don't run off. Standing up, I scoop the two empty bowls from the ground. Although his condition is improving, we aren't out of the woods yet. I stand in a daze, stretching my limbs after sitting for so long.

Delirious from my exhaustion, I find myself laughing at the absolute mess of this situation. If someone had told me a week ago that I would be kidnapped on charges of rebellious activities, dragged halfway to another kingdom, not to mention tending to one of my captor's wounds, I would have said it sounded a lot like one of my adventure books. Maybe I am just dreaming, and this is all a book induced hallucination. I glance down, realizing that I am still holding the empty bowls I intended to clean. Stifling a yawn with my hand, I blink my

dry and gritty eyes; the forest blurring around me. I take a few
hesitant steps, before I tip with exhaustion. The forest floor
flies up to meet me as the bowl falls from my hand. Squeezing
my eyes shut, I brace for the impact of the hard ground.

But the hard impact never comes. A soothing warmth of
air cushions me and propels me up, my back firmly pressed
against the trunk of a tree. The rough bark bites into the
delicate skin of my back as the wind caresses the exposed skin
at my arms, neck, and face. Aramis steps towards me, bracing
his arms on either side of my head.

"Must you always be in need of rescue?" he whispers, a
feverish gleam in his eye.

This close, I can see the muscles of his biceps straining
against the fabric of his sleeves. The slight wave of blond hair
falls in his face as he gazes down at me. Why must he be so
terribly handsome? It would be easier to hate him.

"When I was tasked to obtain a leader of the shifter rebels,
I never imagined you would be so—" He lifts a hand towards
my face before letting it fall clenched to his side.

"What?" I ask, watching him war with constraint. His blue
eyes, as light as the sky, are commanding and tentative at the
same time. With the press of his strong arms caging me into
the tree, I find myself getting lost.

"You." His gaze falls to my lips, causing me to raise my
brow in question. A gentle breeze caresses my cheek, ruffling
the strands of my hair.

"Me?" I raise an eyebrow at him as he slumps to sit at my
feet, leaning against the tree. I tentatively lower myself to the
ground next to him then stifle a yawn.

"You're exhausted," he says with a sign turning his head,
studying me. I have to look a mess; hair disheveled, dark
circles under my eyes. Not exactly your picturesque beauty of
the heroines from my stories. "Go rest before we resume our
journey tomorrow. You've been tending Edmund for hours."

I bristle at his demand. "I cannot rest. My priority at this moment is making sure he's stable."

"How can you care about him so much if you don't even know him," Aramis slurs as he leans closer, his shoulder pressing into mine.

"I am a healer," I say, pausing to brush invisible lint off my skirt. "Or at least I hope to be one day. Saving people's lives is a healer's duty, no matter whose life it is. At this rate, I want to prove to all of you that you have the wrong person." Aramis turns away from me back towards the camp where, through the trees, I can see Edmund's body curled up beside the fire, and choose to move away from those thoughts. "Seems like you know Edmund pretty well…"

Aramis laughs, his gaze is distant recalling a memory from long ago. "I thought I'd never meet someone more obstinate than me, until I met Edmund. When the boy was ten he used to follow me around the capital like a shadow, begging me to teach him how to use a sword. He used to tell everyone he would become the greatest swordsman Shadowvale had ever seen, after me of course." He chuckles and I roll my eyes at the absurdity of his ago but warmth spreads in my core at the sweet memory. "When he turned sixteen, merely four seasons ago, I caved in and agreed on letting him join the King's guard, promising that I would keep him under my wing, and now look at him."

Silence falls between us as we both stare at the male. "How did you and Edmund meet?"

Aramis' body tenses beside me. I whip my head back towards him. What did I say?

"Nero and I were out to one of the cities rumored to have been attacked by shifters, but we arrived too late. The shifters had attacked leaving half the town dead or injured. He was only six, clinging to his dead mothers blouse begging her to wake up. Telling her as tears streamed down her face that he hid like she told him and that the monsters were gone and she could wake up now and stop pretending," he says through gritted teeth.

My heart beats wildly in my chest at the image unfolding in my mind. For a child to lose their parents at such a young age in such a tragic way… An attack like that wasn't an act of rebellion, but pure evil.

"So, I couldn't leave him orphaned to fend for himself in a half-burnt village. I took Edmund back to the capital with me and ensured he had everything he needed growing up. I promised him I would avenge his parents and kill the shifter bastards who did this and make sure no shifter would harm another child in my kingdom."

"Right because we're all bastards in your eyes, I am such a fool…" I move to stand up but Aramis grabs my arm, pulling me. I lose my balance, nearly falling into his lap, our faces mere inches apart. My breath hitches as he drops his gaze to my lips.

"Sybil," he whispers, his voice husky.

A whiff of alcohol on his breath takes me out of my haze, and is a splash of cold water on my face. I lift my hands against his chest and push to my feet.

"Aramis, you are drunk," I scoff, completely unimpressed. "Remember who you're talking to? Your prisoner? I am one of the shifter bastards?" I spit out, hurt filling my voice. "Or did you hit your head and forget?" I cast my eyes to the ground as the complicated emotions of our current position war in my stomach.

"Sybil, look at me." His voice is a rolling wave, powerful and commanding as he stands up and grabs my wrist.

"Let go of me," I whisper vehemently as I tug out of his grasp.

"Sybil, wait…" Aramis' voice is still cold and commanding, but it's softened. He sighs, continuing, "I hate everything about your kind. It's true–or at least it feels like it's true. I even want

59

to hate you. But—" He shakes his head and takes an unsteady step towards me, which I respond by taking a step backwards.

"But why!?" I demand, reliving old frustrations.

Aramis purses his lips, refusing to respond to my commentary. He studies me, like I'm a puzzle he can't solve. And this time my patience ebbs.

"Let me tell you one thing, Prince Aramis of Shadowvale. Your inability to distinguish between some questionable shifters and the whole goddamn shifter population is not my issue. The fact that you are unsure whether you hate me or not, shows that you are not thinking with your own head. Make up your own mind Prince, stop being blinded by the lies they have been feeding you and most importantly, stop being so bloody indecisive!" My voice is escalating to near shouting levels with all my anger. "I'm tired of your hot and cold behavior. You are so out of touch with your emotions you wouldn't be able to recognise happiness even if it stood right in front of you!" I place my hands on my hips, desperate to prevent myself from hitting him and raising his ire.

"I have a duty that must be upheld to my people, my kingdom, and my father. I am the high prince of Shadowvale, and will do what is required of me," he says unconvincingly as he taps a finger at his chest in emphasis. "I am not the bad guy here, Sybil."

"You kidnapped me from my home," I say with a note of finality. "Maybe you are not the bad guy in your story, but you are the villain in mine."

Aramis rolls his eyes at me, and we're back to square one. Any sort of progress we've made has evaporated. "The order to bring you to Shadowvale is not my command, but the King and Queen. I swear to you," he replies, almost on a groan. Aramis runs his fingers through his hair with frustration, takes a few steps towards me then abruptly stops, and stands rigid.

"Then let me go. I have proved to you that I have no ties

to the rebels, they must have made a mistake. Let me go back to my life," I hiss with anger. The fire in my chest quickly simmering to a smoldering hate as I glare at him.

"You know I can't do that," he says with a decisive tone that leaves no room for argument.

My hands tighten into fists and my heart races. "You might not know if you despise me, but I do. I hate you, Aramis. I hate you for stealing me away. I am exhausted. I haven't bathed in days. I miss my bed. I miss my home." These tired truths are slowly killing me.

"Well—you could…" Aramis breaks off his thought, unsure. "What?"

"You could use my sleeping roll. It's the least I can offer after you've saved Edmund's life."

I bark out unexpected laughter—and Aramis glares in my direction like he wishes death upon me. "—I owe you a debt. And it's far better than what you have." He points towards the sleeping form of Edmund laying on my pack and cloak. Frustration flairs in his eyes as he watches me back away from him.

A wild laugh escapes my lips once more, and my eyes roll at the absurdity of sharing the same sleeping space with him. Sitting on a horse all day with him is bad enough.

"You have utterly lost your mind if you think I'm going to share a bedroll with you." I giggle.

"Fine." His mouth sets into a frown as he crosses his arms over his chest.

"Fine!" My heart beats wildly in my chest and I have this overwhelming sensation that I might just leap out of my own skin. I stomp over to the fire and lay down on the hard ground, cradling my head under my arm. I hate him. I repeat the words endlessly in my head but no matter how many times I think them, there's a part of me that refuses to make them sound true.

Rays of sunlight filter through the trees above, mingling with the sounds of breaking camp. Stretching, I slowly rouse to consciousness, the memories of last night causing me to squeeze my thighs together and pull the thick warm cedarwood scented cloak further over my head.

Wait... this isn't my cloak.

I quickly push the heavy cloth off my body and instantly regret the quick movement. I ignore my body's protests as I stretch out my stiff muscles, reaching down to touch my toes before standing up to go check on my patient.

Edmund has survived the remainder of the night. Once I am sure the stitches are secure and the bandages firmly in place without new signs of infection, I put the spare supplies back in the medical bag. The young boy looks warily at me as I bring him a steaming cup of willow bark tea.

"This will help you with your pain," I say, my lips pressing into a thin line.

"Thank you," he says begrudgingly, then grimaces as he takes a sip. "Ugh, this is terrible. Are you trying to poison me?"

"I'm sorry I have nothing sweet to cut down the bitterness, but it should ease your suffering without affecting your ability to ride." I instinctively reach out and check the pulse at his wrist as I watch him drink the bitter brew.

"I don't suppose I could add a dash of Dark Starlight to it? If it has to taste so bitter at least it could have a good kick." He raises his eyebrows in amusement with a chuckle but his cordial affect fades to a stony expression as a shadow drifts over us.

"It looks like you are in good enough spirits to continue on, Edmund?" Aramis moves forward to inspect the boy with a stern face. But it only lasts a second as Aramis immediately kneels next to the boy. "You scared me to death, you little idiot," he says with a relieved grin and tousles Edmund's already unruly hair.

The young guard gasps in pain as the movement causes him to lay his weight on his injured leg, but he is all smiles and duty around Aramis.

"I had to watch your back, Aramis!" Edmund retorts, admiration shining in his eyes. Aramis chuckles but instantly turns serious. "I appreciate that, but you put yourself in danger. You can't become the best swordsman in all of Shadowvale from the grave. No more heroics, you hear me?"

Edmund nods gravely, "Yes, my Prince".

"Now let's get you on a horse so we can deliver the prisoner and get back to those sparring lessons." Aramis adds as he puts one of Edmund's arms around his neck to help him stand up. The young guard is shaky on his feet but he can stand, so he makes his way towards Nero and the other men with a slight limp.

"Oh, back to prisoner again, are we?" I glare defiantly as I stretch my body to its full height, my small frame quivering with determination as I square my shoulders.

"Until I release you into the king and queen's care, you will be whatever I care to call you," Aramis snaps. "Now tell me, is Edmund ready to ride?" He looks over my shoulder at the boy who is now laughing with the rest of the guards.

I move my body to block his view, meeting his eyes again as I put my hands on my hips. "And if I say that he's not safe to ride?" I raise an eyebrow, challenging him.

"If he doesn't leave with us, then he is welcome to stay and face whatever beasties deem him worthy of a snack." Aramis scoffs. "We've already wasted enough precious time. I need to deliver you and return to more important matters."

"Cause you would definitely do that to Edmund. Sure," I declare. "You care about that boy more than you care about yourself."

He grabs my shoulders, pulling me close until our faces are centimeters apart. The heat of his fingers burns into my skin through the fabric of my chemise and a flush creeps into my cheeks at the touch. Goddess, was it only this morning when we were in a similar stance, mere inches apart? Would he have attempted to kiss me had I not scented alcohol on his breath and pushed him away?

"You know nothing about what I care or don't care about," Aramis hisses with anger. Goddess, I can see the hardness of his muscles that bulge from his arms. My heart races as I contemplate my temper and its effect on him.

"If I have ever given you the impression that you are anything more than a low life shifter I have no care for, I deeply apologize. You are a mission for me, prisoner. I will deliver you to the King and Queen and I will never see you again. It's that easy. Now answer my question. Is Edmund safe to ride?" The words taste bitter as Aramis' fingers tighten on my shoulders to the point of pain as he grits his teeth and glowers at me. I fight my desire and stand up for the battle ahead of me.

"You're such an arrogant, selfish bastard—" I start, but the pressure of thick muscular arms pushing us away from each other, abruptly cuts off my words. The sudden interruption takes me by surprise making me lose my balance and I fall onto my rear. Lemon lets out a disgruntled squeak. Quickly covering my mouth with a hand, I hope they did not overhear him in the commotion. That bloody male just gets right under my skin, in the worst and best of ways.

"Now I've heard enough of ye both." Nero looks between the two of us, then up to the meager trail through the forest. "We have a long journey ahead and it does nae anyone good to get into a yelling match. Beyond the facts that we are painting targets on our backs for the beasts, bandits, or anything else." Nero looks steadily at me. "Sybil, is Edmund safe to travel?"

I ignore his proffered hand, pushing myself up from the ground before dusting my body, and pride, off. "If we take it easy and he doesn't try anything wild, then the stitches should hold. He's going to need extra food while his body is healing and replenishing the blood he lost." I nibble on my bottom lip, my eyes casting to the ground as I move a small stone over the toe of my boot.

"That settles it then. Pack up the rest and we will move out." Aramis reaches down and picks up the leather healing satchel and the coat that has kept me warm during the night, then moves to strap them to his stallion's saddle. It was his coat.

"Come Sybil," he says coldly, motioning to me, but I stay rooted to the spot.

"Perhaps Sybil should ride with me for a while," Nero offers.

"No," Aramis growls, taking a possessive step towards me, glaring at his friend. I look up, meeting his gaze. The intensity of his icy blue eyes sends a chill through my body. "If she wants to play with the beast, she will have to deal when it bites."

Aramis grabs my wrists, roughly tugging me towards him. My eyesight fades as he places a dark silky cloth over my eyes. Panic settling in my bones as the knot on the back of my head tightens. My head spins as I begin to hyperventilate from the loss of my vision. I try to steady my breaths, just to settle my rapid heartbeat. I need to keep conscious. I need to know what happens.

"What are you doing to me?" I argue—just one last time while lifting my hands, attempting to push the fabric from my face.

Rough hands grab my wrists and I'm jerked forward, stumbling over my feet. Warm breath caresses my ear as my captor replies.

65

"You are my prisoner, not my companion. You've been granted too much freedom as it is. So don't bother struggling. You won't like where it gets you." Aramis whispers. Icy dread pools in my core at his words. And the dread, perhaps, isn't just from the tone of his whisper, but also the promise it held, should I not obey him.

SYBIL

The next few days pass in relative numbing repetition. They removed the tie blocking my vision, but it was pointless to blindfold me in the first place. I am sure Aramis just wanted to prove, once more, that he is the one in charge, and I roll my eyes at the thought.

I spent the days riding with him, now stiff and quiet since our previous argument. Nero occasionally rides up and makes some small talk before he takes off to scout the forest before us. If we come upon streams, we take brief breaks to water the horses and allow me to tend to Edmund's wound. He is recovering his strength faster than the average human or creature. It is the Goddess' blessing that he fairs so well as we endure this treacherous pass.

"Tell me more about the Elementals," I ask Aramis as I reach out and slowly run my fingers along our stallion's neck. The movement causes my position to shift, my hips pressing into him. His body tenses behind me at the movement. "I have only met two Elementals in my entire life. It was a man and a woman traveling through Bellevue but I never got a chance to pick their brains," I add, hoping to spark a conversation interesting enough to distract me from this torture of a journey.

"Please indulge my curiosity, your Majesty," I jokingly plea, and tentatively ask. "It appears that most of you have some sort of magical affinity, and you heal quickly?"

What else do I really know about my captors, except that Aramis is the prince of Shadowvale and has the power to manipulate the air around us?

Behind me, Aramis clears his throat. "Fine. Most elementals are born with some small spark of magic, while others have magic burning in their veins like liquid gold," he says with pride in his voice. "It's our magic that separates us from one another." The tenor of his voice is filled with as much joy as it is pride, and the change is welcoming. There's a joyful, curious boy in that hardened man, and I find myself begging an audience with the boy as much as the man commands it.

"Ye'll find those born with stronger power are recruited to train in the palace or royal guard," Nero quips in, giving Aramis a friendly clap on the shoulder. "Just look at the company mo charaid here keeps." With a grin, he creates a blue orb of fire in his palm then blows, sending a hundred blue butterflies of living flame dancing around us. I have seen traveling minstrels perform similar illusions with fire but never with such skill as his. I wonder once more if my assumptions about his true nature are correct. The heat of the fire magic pulses in the air until the creatures disappear in a puff of smoke and ash.

"You'll also find that some of us have more important qualities beyond wasting our magic on cheap parlor tricks," Aramis responds through clenched teeth.

"What other magic do elementals possess?" I inquire, turning to face Nero riding beside us.

"We are long-lived, with memories just as lengthy as—" Nero continues, grinning widely at me.

Aramis clears his throat, cutting his friend off, not

entertained by his interruptions. He continues with a lecturing tone, "Most elemental families pass on the same elemental line: earth, wind, water, and fire. However, very rarely is a child born with powers outside their family, or duo wielders. Every person in Shadowvale has a purpose, a role to play to keep the kingdom prosperous."

"Ma mother was a fire elemental, as was her mother an' on and' on as far as our family records indicate," Nero cuts in, stretching his arms behind his head as he leans back on his horse. "The royal family has alway comprised rulers who've been attuned to the air elemental for the last five hundred years. At least the male line has. Aramis's mother–"

"Enough," Aramis orders, this is the second time he interrupts one of his guards at the mention of his mother. His voice is edged with pain in the command. I study him discreetly, learning more about him with that command than he realizes. A swirl of sympathy churns in my stomach, and I begin to suspect that there's a tragedy there. "It's getting dark. Thankfully, we are nearly at the next clearing."

As night falls, we break for camp. This temporary reprieve allows me to analyze my situation as I sneak pieces of meat strips to Lemon. He isn't happy after being confined to my pocket most of the day, but I am worried about what will happen if he is detected. As everyone settles for the night, I place my roll as far from his royal highness as I can, but his eyes burn into my skin long after I've fallen asleep.

The next day, I find myself in front of Aramis again, trotting quickly down the path. My body protests with aching pains as each beat of Percy's hooves takes us closer to Shadowvale. I don't know how I am going to survive two to three more days stuck on a horse with Aramis, but I'm even more terrified of what awaits me when we reach Shadowvale. I turn my attention back to the forest, anything to keep my mind from worrying about my fate. A silver leaf tree I have never seen before appears among the surrounding trees. I sit up straight, whipping my head to see over his shoulder.

"What?" He briefly glances behind us.

"I thought I saw a tree with silver leaves." Turning more to face him, I glance at another two silver trees in the distance as we continue to pick up speed. My eyes widen as a broad smile spreads across my face, causing my cheeks to tingle with excitement. My heart beats faster with joy as I take in the vibrant scene before me. The flash of silver is the most interesting thing I've seen for days. I point ahead where a cluster of trees lines the trail. "There! Up ahead! I've never seen anything like it."

"They are silver apple trees. We call them pomme d'argent. They're native to Shadowvale and only grow north of the Argentsang Forest." His eyes take on a faraway look as he makes a quiet sound of pleasure. "They make the best apple pastries you'll ever taste, sweet caramelized apples, wrapped in warm flakey dough."

"That explains why I've never seen them before." My mouth salivates at the thought of warm, sweet pastries.

"As children, Nero and I got in trouble in the kitchens countless times because we'd steal pomme d'argent pastries off the cooling racks." Aramis confides with a soft chuckle. "There's nothing like them." His friendly and generous conversation is unexpected, and it shocks me to my core.

"Aramis, What ar—"

"I nev—". We both stare at each other sheepishly, as we realize we've spoken at the same time. I bite my lip to stave off my entertainment. Aramis looks grave at the thought of being interrupted.

We fall back into silence, nothing but the distant chirping of birds. I watch, feeling the cool air of the forest around me as the apple trees start multiplying, turning the forest into shades of silver. Do the darker shades show age in the trees? The cascade of silvers is stunning. Light reflects off the petals with a rainbow hue. Percy slows down to a brisk walk as the path narrows.

"What is Shadowvale like? None of my books reached that far on the continent. I've only seen it on maps and heard few stories from passing travelers," I ask with interest. Stretching, I reach forward, letting my fingers run through the horse's tangled mane. It's a matted mess, reminding me that my own hair must look atrocious.

"Shadowvale is more than just the castle, if that's what you're asking." Aramis pauses and I hold my breath, wondering if I've asked the wrong question. He shifts behind me. Putting his weight into the stirrups, he pushes to a stand, reaching up. Aramis wraps his hand around a plump silver apple above us and I watch curiously as he snaps it off the branch and hands it to me once he settles back behind me. The brush of his hand against mine sends unexpected sensations through my body, landing in my core. I roll the apple between my hands, marveling at its matte silver surface, dully catching the light.

"Thank you," I murmur, conflicted by my emotions. The thoughtfulness of his actions surprises me.

"You're welcome," he replies with warmth in his voice.

"Is it sweet?"

"They're saccharine," he remarks. "Try it."

I hesitantly bite into the apple, my eyes closing, and a small moan escapes my lips. My mouth floods with extraordinary sweetness; the combined taste of honey, citrus, and pear.

"This is sensational," I sigh, the lingering taste of the silver apple in my mouth. I lean back in delight, my head landing unexpectedly on his chest. I tense, waiting for a reaction from Aramis that never comes before continuing, relishing in this shared moment. "I love apples—and I think I may have just discovered my new favorite kind."

"They are the pride of Shadowvale," Aramis replies, and I can hear a smile in his voice. "Cook always makes the best pastries in the winter when they ripen."

"My mother and I used to pick lavender together in the fall." A tear pricks at the corner of my eyes as the memory surfaces but the wind soon whisks it away. "We'd hang most of it to dry for infusions and poultices, but she would always save extra for us to make lavender shortbread cookies. She used to teach herbology at Nova Esther before I was born–" my voice catches on the last words. She wanted me to follow in her hoof steps when she saw my interest in herbology as a young colt.

"I love shortbread, but I don't think I've ever had lavender shortbread. What is Nova Esther?" He asks as he reaches forward to pat Percy on the neck. His palm brushes against mine, sending a jolt of sensation up my arm and my breath to catch.

"It's the healer's academy in Kallistar. Healers come from all across Craeweth to study there." Except me. My gut clenches at the thought. No, I will get out of this and I will make my way to finish my studies. "Where are your healers trained if they don't go to Nova Esther, in Shadowvale?"

"Those born with the gift of healing magic, or the will to train in the art of healing, apprentice with senior healers," he replies. "It's one of the things I love about Shadowvale. Everyone has a purpose."

"What else do you love so well about your province?" I ask, encouraged by this engaging conversation. But Aramis sighs, a touch of sadness in his voice.

"What?" I ask, frustrated. "What did I say now?"

"I shouldn't be talking to you... like this, Sybil," he whispers in my ear, careful his men cannot hear us. "You are my prisoner. And I know none of the evidence seems to suggest that you are working with the rebels, but no matter

how much I'd like to know more about you, about your life...
I can't." His tone is softer than usual, but I still bristle at his
words.

"All I want is to have a peaceful conversation to pass the
time," I snarkily reply. "We've been on the road forever. I
haven't slept in a proper bed, taken a hot bath, or eaten a hot
meal at a table since Bolide eve!" Why does this always happen?
I groan internally. We make an inch of progress with little
satisfaction, and then Aramis always recoils from any trust we
build.

Silence meets me.

"If you don't want to hold a conversation with me, perhaps
have me ride with one of the other guards–"

"No," Aramis says, his arms stiffen, pressing my back
further against his chest, setting off a whirl of emotions. "You
will ride with no male except me."

"Do you not trust them?" I inquire.

"I trust them with my life," he replies without hesitation.

"But?" The unspoken words hang between us. He doesn't
trust me. I close my eyes, focusing on the rhythm of the
stallion's hooves rhythmically cantering down the path.

Silence stretches between us before he sighs behind me,
one of his arms releasing the reins to slide in front of me. My
heart and breath speed at the close contact of the gentle weight
of his forearm pressed against my waist.

"You don't trust me." I state flatly, and my heart aches,
more than I'd have ever thought it could, at the words of a
stranger.

"I don't trust any shifters," Aramis says contemptuously,
and before I can respond, he adds with a whisper, "I am sorry."
Taken aback by the sincerity in his voice, I stay silent.

The gravity of my situation crashes on me with
uncomparable might. These last few days had seemed to be the
answer to my prayers for a life full of adventure and purpose.

Like one of the heroes in my books, I stood up to my captors, tried to escape, fought a chimera and showed the grumpy Prince that even a damsel in distress can be a pain in his arse. But there was never going to be a happy ending waiting for me at the end of this journey. No matter how many times I crack Aramis's tough exterior, he is still my captor, and he will deliver me to the king and queen, just like he's been ordered to.

"I get it," I reply softly. "You know Aramis, I might be the one that was kidnapped from her home, but I have a feeling you are a prisoner just as much as I am." He tenses behind me but do not dare turn around to read his expression. "I am not a fool, Prince. I know I have lost all my chances at escape. I will face the King and Queen of Shadowvale and prove to them that I am innocent. Goddess knows that if there's anything the time shared with your lot has taught me, it's that I have to stand up for myself. I am done being shackled by fear." I straighten my back, suddenly more confident as I have spoken those words into existence.

"You are brave, Sybil," he says after a moment, and I notice he has stopped calling me prisoner, or shifter...

I sit in stunned silence, unsure how to respond to his sudden comment. Brave? I scoff internally at myself. If I was brave, I would have packed my bags for Esther Nova years ago and be neck deep in my studies at this point. But, I am not the girl I was five or even ten years ago.

Aramis straightens behind me, his grip loosening on the reins before us. "Queen Tricella is not my favorite person. She married my father shortly after the death of my mother." He pauses, releasing a deep exhale before continuing. "Shortly after she was crowned queen consort, the rebel attacks started to become more violent. Be wary of her. She is power hungry and vicious. The Queen also has a court seer. He is just as bad as she is, don't trust any of them. His visions are supposed to help us catch the shifters before they attack the villages, but every time he gives us directions, we're always too late and innocent people are already dead. Nero and I have been studying the shifter rebel attacks that have happened in Shadowvale for the past 100 years. We have studied their modus operandi, tried to find diplomatic ways to end the bloodshed, but I keep thinking there is something we are missing… something lurking in the shadows that we are yet to discover. According to some indiscretion, there might even be different groups of rebels. Some acting more violently than others. The last towns we were sent to, the destruction felt… different–"

"Why are you telling me this?" Cold fear coils in my gut. How am I supposed to appeal to monarchs of a kingdom who have been attacked repeatedly by shifters for over a century?

Aramis leans forward, his voice barely a whispered caress against my ear, "I have made it evident that I do not love shifters. But I am not a cruel male. I do not delight in the torture of innocents. I might not be able to free you, but I can help you reach the dais in the throne room knowing who you are fighting against."

His sudden change in demeanor shocks my system, but I will take any advantage I can get to plead my case to his kingdom. And maintain this fragile change in our relationship. I whisper, "Tell me more."

SYBIL

We break past the forest's edge and emerge into a field of flowers in shades of blue and purple as far as I can see. As storm clouds gather above us, the sky becomes a living painting with shades of gray and lilac. The heavy smell of petrichor fills my lungs. I always looked forward to the sweet, yet slightly musty, earthy scent that preceded a rainstorm, but this time, so far away from the safety of my cottage, I am dreading it.

"Let's hope these clouds hold off fo' an hour or two longer," Nero says as he reins his stallion closer to our right. He looks up, studying the sky. "It looks like they are getting heavier by the minute, though. That chill in the air suggests we might be in for a bitterly cold and rough ride."

"We should be able to reach Lunaris before nightfall if—" Aramis pauses as a streak of lightning dances across the sky, followed seconds later by the loud rumble of thunder.

My eyes widen in surprise as a raindrop splashes across my face. A half dozen more pepper my arms before I cover myself in with the protection of my cloak.

"Shit." Aramis whistles and gestures to the rest of the group, the water wetting his blonde hair. "We ride on. There is no shelter from here until we get to Lunaris. If we hasten, we may make it there before the rain makes the ground impassable."

My mind goes to Edmund's wounds. Worry creasing my forehead at the thought of a rough ride tearing at his stitches warring with the thought of spending the night in the freezing rain. As if Aramis read my thoughts, he turns his head to the male at our left.

"Edmund?" He questions.

"I'll survive, your majesty," he replies with a nod of his head.

"See that you do." He shifts behind me before leaning forward, snaking one arm tightly around my midsection and directing his horse into a gallop on the open road. "Better hold on tight, Sybil."

I involuntarily shiver as the wind whips in my face as we gain speed while riding through the rain. Aramis seems more at ease around me since opening up about what awaits me in Shadowvale. Almost as if a small weight has been lifted off his chest, although part of me is still in disbelief at his change of heart.

As we ride through the hateful rain, I curse my wool cloak for doubling in weight as it starts soaking up the moisture, making me soon shiver. Praying Lemon stays dry deep within my pocket. I make sure what's left dry of my coat shields it from the rain. Noticing my discomfort, Aramis arches forward and pulls me close to him, trying to cover me as best as he can as we make our way to shelter. A fluttering sensation grips my stomach and I revel in the sensation of his chest against my back. His arms are no longer a cage but a warm embrace around me.

What have I gotten myself into?

A sigh of relief escapes my throat as I lift up my gaze
to see the building towering before me, its windows glowing
a cheery orange. Aramis and Nero make their way inside to
secure us rooms overnight. This tavern is located near the
center of the town. All the shops are closed as the storm
continues to rage on. The alleys are cast in pitch black and
shadows, heightening my imagination of what's hiding in the
dark.

As I sit shivering on his horse, water dripping miserably
off my body, they re-emerge from the tavern, followed by two
stable boys.

"Looks like we're bunking up. They only have three spare
rooms. Come," Aramis commands me, as he lifts me from
the back of his stallion. As I take his hand, I barely manage to
land gracefully on my feet right after dismounting from Percy's
back. After hours of riding horseback in the cold, my are legs
numb. Right now, I'd give almost anything to immerse myself
in a steaming hot bath.

"What about Sybil?" Nero pushes his hair absently out of
his face before nodding in my direction.

"She will be under my guard." Aramis' hand gently pushes
against the small of my back. His rough and stern tone is in
stark contrast to the intimate gesture. As he opens the door,
he looks down at me, studying my reaction to his touch. "Just
in case she gets some last-minute ideas and attempts another
escape." He quirks an eyebrow at me, the corner of his lips
turning up in a smirk. I know he is testing me, so I stay quiet.
Turning back towards Nero, he adds, "make sure the horses
are rubbed down and fed. I've paid for supper and ale for the
evening when you've finished."

Aramis tosses two keyrings at Nero, who catches them
with ease before leading his horse along with the other guards.
Crossing the threshold, we head upstairs. My stomach lets out
an audible grumble as the smell of roasting meat mingling with

fresh bread and mead wafts as we walk up the stairs. Inserting a matching key into the lock of a broad wood door, Aramis unlocks the door, pushing it wide open before dragging me inside.

A warm crackling fire illuminates and heats the small room. The space is sparsely furnished, with only a desk, an empty wooden tub, and a single bed that is barely big enough for two people.

Only one bed? And where exactly does he expect me to sleep? On the floor ,like an animal?

Bustling behind me breaks my spiraling thoughts as servants appear in the doorway carrying steaming buckets of water. They brush past me, pouring their contents into the wooden tub before ducking out the door without a word.

"I hope the accommodations are to your liking, your highness." A willowy pale figure with blue eyes and waist long curly blonde hair appears in the door. Her arms hold a tray laden with soaps and oils. Her tight-fitting bodice leaves little to the imagination as she leans forward, her bosom nearly spilling out to set the tray on the table. "If you need any assistance with your ba—"

Her words stop short as her eyes fall on me, her nose wrinkling in shock and disgust.

"That will be all, Oletta." Aramis replies coolly and invites her to leave the room. He rests his hand on the door and slowly shuts it with a resounding click before turning the lock. The last thing I see is the outrage and humiliation on her face.

He leans his body against the door, gazing at me through hooded eyes. Aramis crosses his arms over his chest and a lock of blond hair falls into his face, obscuring one eye.

"You don't have to lock the door. You know I won't escape," I say as I make my way to the table and examine the variety of soaps.

The heat of his gaze rakes over my body. My pulse

quickens in response.

"Standard procedure, I'm afraid," he says with a shrug.

We've had each other's company for the previous ten days, but this is the first time we're completely alone. I turn towards him and my heart races. How can he make me feel like a trapped animal and more alive than I have ever felt before?

"Bathe, and then we will eat." He adds, pushing away from the door and taking off his cloak before hanging it over a chair next to the fire. He rests his hands on the back of the chair, gripping the wood. My mind strays back to the memory of his hands gripping me the night he told me about Edmund.

"With you here? Watching me?" I reply defiantly, raising an eyebrow.

"We've been on the road for ten days. Trust me when I say you want to look your best when you meet the king and queen." His gaze leisurely travels down my body before meeting my gaze pressed in a sneer. "Lest they find you to be as truly savage as your kind's nature."

"What will it matter? Do you really think they'll care what I look or smell like?" I snap in return, bitter at the constant reminder of my fate. I try to find comfort in my newly found determination in proving myself innocent but tired as I am. My persistence falters and my anxieties rise back to the surface.

"Sybil." His voice holds a note of warning. I look up from his hands as he takes the few steps separating us. I tremble like a doe under the eyes of a predator as he deftly unclips the clasp holding my cloak together. It falls to the floor in a whoosh of wet wool. His rough, calloused fingers grip my chin, forcing my face up to meet his gaze. A flicker of confusion crosses his face, and I fight the urge to pull away. His look is intent, focused on me. I should fight, but just as I have before, countless times across our journey, I fall into that gaze, a familiar tug deep in my core towards him.

What am I doing? Why is it so hard to push him away?

Unless he has an enchanting magic, I am unaware of…

A loud, unexpected knock at the door disrupts the silence, breaking the tension. Aramis releases his grip on my chin and steps away from me.

"Aramis, urgent news." From the other side of the door, Nero's muffled voice calls out. Aramis audibly exhales as he runs his hand through his already disheveled hair.

"I'll be right there," he replies before grabbing one of the soaps from the tray and depositing it in the palm of my hand, closing my fingers around it.

"I expect you to be bathed and changed by the time I return," he lectures. I'm tempted to roll my eyes at him. He points to the cloth bag carefully positioned by the servants on the small table by the bathtub. "I had Oletta bring a change of clothes for you. It's the best I can do at the moment."

Aramis is half-way to the door as he finishes his final instruction. The door slams behind him and the metal scrap of the key turning in the lock echoes. Voices murmur down the hall before I move. A mix of emotions overwhelms me now that I am finally alone, at last. The appreciation I felt for Aramis's kindness turns once again into anger and frustration. But even my rage does not last as it immediately turns to fear and sadness. I fall to my knees, landing on my sodden woolen cloak, tears falling from my eyes.

I bury my face in my hands and weep as exhaustion and the previous day's events sink in. Will I be strong enough for what's about to come?

Lemon peeks his tiny head out of my pocket before crawling up the fabric of my dress to nuzzle at my cheek. A tiny hiccup escapes me as I pull him into a hug.

"Oh Lemon. What are we going to do?" I whisper, holding him in front of me and peering into his dark, beady eyes. He sniffs the air, looking towards the steaming tub of water before looking back at me.

"You're right." I reply, finally standing, then gently placing him on the floor. "It's best not to look a gift horse in the mouth, even if said gift horse comes from an aggravating male."

I step into the water, sighing as I lower my body under its warm embrace. The tub is deep enough that the water comes all the way to my neck. I rarely let myself indulge in such a pleasure at home. Resting my head against the wooden edge of the tub, I let my muscles relax, breathing in the lavender scented water. Another reminder of home. At the thought, I close my eyes, hold my breath and sink under the water.

The cuff around my wrist floats and I wish the slippery water would aid in my plight of getting rid of it. I would not experience half of my aches if I only had my magic. Unable to withstand against the burn in my chest for air, I rise above the surface gulping in large breaths. The rain continues to pelt endlessly at the windows and roof. A loud crack of thunder sends Lemon hissing on the floor at my side as I accidentally splash him with water in my surprise.

I pray the lightning doesn't hit the building and set the roof on fire.

"You can do this, Sybil." I repeat to myself and try to believe it.

I grab the bar of soap and lather it in my hair. The rich scent of rosemary and lavender greets my nose as I massage the soap into my scalp.

"You will survive." I speak into existence, hoping the Gods are listening.

I make quick work scrubbing the rest of my skin until it glows rosy pink from my efforts. Stepping out of the tub, I dry myself off with a soft thick towel warmed by the fire before rummaging in the bag for a clean gown. Expecting to find a low-cut bodice just like the one Oletta was wearing, I am surprised when I pull out a thick cream chemise and drag it over my head, followed by a dark purple wool petticoat and blouse. I hold a matching corset in my hands before shoving it back into the bag, deciding that this was not the time or place for its discomfort.

I begin to pace the room. My bare feet are cold against the smooth wood floors as I try to imagine what I'd say to free myself once we are at the palace. A gentle knock at the door stops me in my steps and I turn to face the door.

Aramis.

"Sybil? I've brought ye some food." Nero's deep voice calls out.

"Come in." I quickly scoop Lemon from where he's fallen asleep on the floor and tuck him in my pocket before I reply. I hear the lock turn a moment before the door swings open and Nero steps into the room carrying a tray laden with a steaming bowl of stew, a pewter tankard, and a small teapot and cup. A smile tugs at the corner of my lips at the comfort foods.

"I remembered ye had a variety of tea cups stacked around yer house and I thought a hot cup of black tea might be the perfect cure to warm yer cold bones." He chuckles to himself as he sets the items on the small desk. Lifting the pot, he pours tea into the small cup before offering it towards me. "But who am I to tell a healer about cures?"

"It's perfect." I reply, my eyes welling at this small gesture of kindness. I walk over and lift the cup to my lips. Closing my eyes, I breathe in the sweet, mellow, and slightly musky scent of fresh black tea. "Thank you." I can't help the tears.

"I must return to our meeting, but there is a guard at your door, lass." Nero says at the door, slightly ajar. "I warn ye, do not try to escape. The castle might only be two days away, but it's a long road, and yer trials will not end at the castle gates." He makes a slight bow towards me before leaving and locks the door behind him.

"As if I can pick a locked door, defeat a guard, and get past the entire tavern without being noticed." I scoff as I consume the food and drink before it gets cold.

I am innocent. At this point, trying to escape would only paint me in a negative view. I will prove to Shadowvale of my innocence and then Lemon and I will go to Nova Esther.

I slowly drag my exhausted body towards the bed. The comforting sensation of the warm sheets envelopes me as I instantly drift off to a dreamless sleep.

ARAMIS

losing the door behind me, I lock it before tucking the key into my pocket. I selected a room on the third floor knowing the windows open to a steep hill and river that runs swiftly behind the building. Sybil would have to be utterly mad to try to escape, although I am starting to think she doesn't even want to escape anymore. Regardless, I chose one of my guards to sleep in the stables, where he can monitor the room's window.

"Tell me the news, Nero," I command as I catch up to him. I cross my arms over my chest, walking side-by-side with my captain of the guard and best friend.

"Ye've received a missive from the kingdom." He pulls a thick folded note from his pocket before handing it to me.

Grabbing the paper from him, I run my finger across the seal stamped into the golden wax. The symbol of a crescent moon with three stars and a sword thrust through it: our family crest. Moving into a private dining room, I sit down in a chair before breaking the seal and running my eyes over the text.

Aramis,
Hasten your return delivering the prisoner. The rebel
shifters will be attacking Larnwick in two days.
You are to leave and deal with the attack when you return.
-Queen Tricella

The paper crumples under my hands as I throw it at the
fire. I slam a fist on the table in frustration. The sound of my
heartbeat fills my ears as I seethe in anger.

"Bad news, yer majesty?" Nero inquires as he lifts an
eyebrow in my direction.

"Don't be facetious, Nero." I push back from the table
and begin pacing the room. "The queen requests we hasten
our return to deliver her prisoner so that we can handle a rebel
group that is going to attack another village close to the capital.
As if she's not the one who sent us on this fool's mission in the
first place."

"Does she think we travel on magical flying horses?" He
snorts with derision. "Why doesn't she send some of her
precious lackey's to do her bidding?"

Nero is interrupted by a knock on the door frame. The
tavern owner's daughter enters the room with a tray laden with
food and two chilled mugs of ale. Just like she did with the tray
of soaps and oils, the woman seductively lowers her chest as
she serves us our dinner, giving both me and Nero quite the
spectacle. I roll my eyes, her constant advances now pushing
on my last nerves. I am the prince of Shadowvale. She is a
mere poor peasant—well beneath me. Beyond the fact that this
is neither the time, nor the place to accept such advances, her
family should be grateful that we frequent their establishment
at all.

Finishing her task, Odetta… Olivia - or whatever her name
is, turns and curls a blonde lock around her finger as she peers
at me through hooded eyes.

"Prince Aramis, if there is anything else I can be of—"

"Leave us." I cut her off. I don't need another female to complicate my life. A sigh leaves my lips at the sight of her fallen features. A prince never regards its subjects as beneath him Aramis. Only because the Gods have chosen a different path for them does not mean they are not your equals. My mother's words come flashing back with a wave of sadness. She taught me better than that. "I'm sorry," I quickly add, and pull a few gold coins from my pocket and hold them out to her. The maiden slips them between her breasts, a hint of a coy smirk curling at the corners of her lips. I may be an asshole sometimes, but that doesn't mean I have to be heartless. I invite her once again to leave the room and say, "Please see that my men get more ale and food."

"Yes, your majesty. You need only call if there is anything else I can do to ease your evening." Her lips press into a thin line while curtseying, hips swaying exaggeratingly on her way out.

Nero lets out a low whistle and leans back in his chair. Taking a deep drag from his chilled mug, he nods toward the open door. "That one is relentless." Nero beams. "It's unfortunate she's nae my type." Setting down his mug, he grabs a chicken leg from his plate and takes a large bite.

"We have more important matters at hand than fraternizing with the serving staff," I reply rather stiffly, sitting back in my chair. I run a hand helplessly through my already disheveled hair. The food wafting up from the plate before me looks delicious, but my stomach churns at the thought of eating. The weight of my duty as crown prince gets progressively heavier the closer we are to Shadowvale. I try to remind myself that I have no control over Sybil's fate, that disclosing information regarding the crown is the best I can do to help her. A voice whispers in my head you should not be wanting to help her, she is shifter scum and part of me can't help but instinctively agree. But then I think about Sybil…

I clear my throat and interrupt my thoughts. "What are we going to do about this rebel group? They're always two steps ahead of us. By the time we reach Larnwick, they'll have moved on."

"Well, if Kieran has seen the rebels attacking Larnwick, we could still potentially reach and set up forces before they attack. His visions are of the future, not the present." He waves the half-eaten leg bone at me in emphasis.

"What's the use of a seer–" I exclaim, releasing my frustration onto the table by slamming my fist on it, "If his bloody visions are always late? Queen Tricella can't even get a decent seer on her court. I'll never understand how my father thought she'd make a fit queen." I pick up my ale and take a sip.

"Who knows what kind of massacre will be awaiting us once we reach Larnwick. The last rebel attack in Walden killed over three hundred brave Elementals. No survivors left. I am so goddamn tired of all this bloodshed. I assure you, the only thing left in Larnwick by the time we get there will be stragglers and children." The silverware clangs as it dances to my fury. The image of Edmund crying over his mother's corpse is still fresh in my mind.

"Mmhh," Nero mutters, lost in his thoughts.

"What now?" I ask, knowing the wheels in his mind are turning by the way he is scratching his chin contemplatively.

"Isn't Larnwick one of the few villages in all of Shadowvale where Shifters and Elementals peacefully coexist? Like… What was the name of that other village, Astrakane? Which was also ransacked about a month ago?"

"Indeed. I can still hear the screams of the few survivors we found at Astrakane. So many dead or missing… both Shifter and Elementals." I pause. Why had the shifters killed their own? I could see a few casualties or accidents from the destruction of the town, but outright killing their own made no sense.

"Have ye ever wondered why the towns are empty like ghost towns, while others are left with death and destruction of both kinds?" Nero asks, tentatively.

"Of course I ask myself that!" I growl in frustration. He always had a knack for reading my mind. "I've been over the situation a hundred times or more. It just doesn't make sense. Unless…"

"What's on yer mind, mate?" he asks.

"What if…" I meet his eyes across the table and speak, a fear festering in my gut. "What if not all shifters support the rebellion?" The thought of Sybil valiantly defending her innocence makes me sick to my stomach for not believing her. All those shifters, women and children alike, I had taken to Shadowvale for questioning, certain they would have information about their own kind. I lower my head and voice words I never thought I would pronounce. "Maybe I've been so blinded by my own vendetta to not see that some shifters are just victims in this story?"

I replay the aftermath of all the villages that had been attacked with this new theory in mind. If the shifters' reason for rebelling is the unfounded accusation that the crown is endangering the Shifter community within Shadowvale, why would they kill their own kind during these raids? Did they maybe consider the casualties supporters of the crown? Deserving of death for not joining the rebellion? The questions keep multiplying in my head, and I wonder how we prove the veracity of this assumption.

Nero studies me before he responds. "Ye know that ye must walk yer own path, Aramis. Ye decide who ye want to be and what ye want to believe in." He leans forward on the table, resting his chin on his hands. His massive frame casts his shadow to creep over the wood of the table from the candle behind him.

"Who are you and what did you do with my goofball guard, Nero?" I grin, helplessly trying to break the tension. I push aside my worry and lean forward to slap him affectionately on the shoulder. Nero smiles in return. He is like a brother to me. The lines between friendship and princely duty blur with him.

"But seriously, when did you grow wise on me, old man?" I grab my tankard of ale and down it swiftly in a few gulps, the cool liquid sliding down my throat. The familiar fruit and hoppy taste of the ale coats my tongue, reminding me of warm summer days.

"I've always been wise. Ye've just been too immature to notice." Nero lets out a hearty laugh and I can't help but shake my head at him. "I, for one, am looking forward to a hot bath and a warm bed with one of Cook's famous apple tarts."

"Oh, you're going to take a sweet tart to your bed?" I wink at him, but at the mention of a warm bath, my thoughts stray back to Sybil upstairs above the tavern room. For the first time, when I think of her, my heart is light in my chest.

"What is on yer mind?" Nero reaches towards my plate, but I swat his hand away.

"If you're still hungry, go try your charm on the kitchen staff," I reply, ignoring his question. "Maybe you'll find yourself some extra food and a warm bed to share."

"What do ye think the queen will dae with Sybil?" Nero asks, his face turning serious and unreadable.

"You know as much as I do," I reply, musing. Turning away from him, I watch the flames crackle in the fireplace, light and shadows dancing on the worn wood floor. Scuff marks mark the surface from years of patronage. With a sigh, I rub at my temples. "We were only tasked to bring the unicorn before my father and the queen for her crimes. I never told you this, but I overheard Kieran telling the Queen about a vision he had in which Sybil was leading a group of rebels," I scoff at the absurdity of it. "She will probably be questioned, just like all the other shifters we retrieved from the raided villages." My head hurts trying to put all the information in order.

"Fuck Kieran's visions. They're shit most of the time anyways," Nero blurts out and I can't help but break into a vigorous laugh at my best friend's honesty.

She is going to prove her innocence; I tell myself. And then me and Nero are going to uncover what is really going on with the rebel group. To hell with Kieran's visions. Indeed, I am going to do this my way from now on.

I finish my meal in silence as we both watch the embers in the fire slowly dim, lost to our thoughts.

My new theory concerning the shifter rebels plagues my thoughts as I make my way upstairs. I gently knock at the door but Sybil does not answer. For a moment in time, I'm aware how unreal the situation is–a shifter is in my room, alone, and I'm worried for her. Fear grips my chest, stemming from a place I can't even remotely understand as I burst into the room expecting her to be gone, only to stop in my tracks. I stand watching from the doorframe. Sybil lays asleep on the far side of the bed, the blanket pulled up to her chin. Her eyes move behind the lids, her face twitching with emotion as she dreams.

Panting, I run a hand through my hair, looking around the room in shock.

This woman is still my prisoner. Yes?

Maybe it's the fortnight I've spent with her. Maybe it's believing, even for a moment, that she might be innocent and I'm about to ruin a life that doesn't deserve it. Thinking hard, I trace back to when that changed–Edmund.

Her continuous protesting and arguing is infuriating. But like a moth to the flame, I am in constant awe of her resilience, courage, and her wide, disbelieving eyes make my heart flutter. How did one female get under my skin so thoroughly that I've begun to question my very beliefs?

She should not be asleep on the bed, but I can't bring myself to disturb her just to make her move to the floor.

Were she any other prisoner, I would have her sleep on a bedroll, and tied her so she can't attempt any escape. I simply can't bring myself to do that to Sybil. Even if she's been accused of treason against Shadowvale by my stepmother, I've seen too many rebels to not believe her story. But she is not just a prisoner, not anymore. So I gently close the door to not disturb her and make my way towards the fireplace. Tossing more wood onto the fire causes sparks to fly, hungrily consuming the offering and warming the room. A draft of air catches my attention and I lift my gaze to the window where the shutters have blown open. The rain continues to drizzle down into the shadows below, the scent of evergreen. I can hear Sybil tossing and turning in the bed. From my pack I pull out a silver flask, stamped with the Aldrostos crest, and take a deep swing of the amber liquid, relishing in its burn. Sleep will be a long time coming for me.

My feet take me to the foot of the bed. I brace myself against the footboard.

"There's enough space for the two of us, you know?" Sybil's sleepy voice catches me by surprise and I turn to face her. The fire is casting a golden glow on her freckles, dusting faintly like constellations across her cheeks and nose against the firelight. A warm tug deep in my core beckons as my eyes trail from the faint star mark on her brow to the dark, long locks of hair framing her face and shoulder.

"Last time I offered you to share my sleep roll, you told me I was utterly insane. So, I thought I'd be more cautious this time and avoid the question altogether," I say and take a sip from my flask. But the liquid does not warm me inside as much as the small smile spreading on Sybil's lips does.

"I remember well. Let's just say I am in much kinder spirit

tonight then," she says and scoots further to the left side of the bed. An invitation.

I slowly get to my feet, unsure whether to follow my instinct or remind myself of my duty. My heart is racing as I make my way towards the front of the bed, Sybil's eyes fixed on me.

"I'll be okay on the flo—"

"Aramis. It's okay," she interrupts me, her eyes shining more than any jewel I have seen in the castle, and moves the covers on my side. I could get lost in those eyes. "It's been a long journey for both of us. You deserve a good rest as much as any."

After removing my boots, I carefully sit on the bed, the mattress sinking under my weight as I stretch my body on top of the covers. I prop my head up on an arm and chance one last glimpse in her direction before fixing my eyes on the window in front of me.

"See, it was not so difficult, was it? I promise, unicorns don't bite, much." She adds, snickering, but I can hear her voice already drifting off.

I force my body to relax, careful not to touch her, but the electricity coursing through my veins at the sole thought of Sybil lying so close to me is driving me insane.

My resistance to look at Sybil crumbles, so I move on my side and face her. Her chest rises and falls under the blankets in a smooth, even rhythm. Her face calms to a peaceful expression. I ease my position slowly, just to fully appreciate her beauty.

"What have you done to me?" I whisper.

Heat radiates off her soft hand mere centimeters away from my own. After a few breaths, I turn and lay on my back, crossing my arms over my chest, careful not to wake or disturb her. I stare at the canopy above us and pray for morning to never come.

SYBIL

Sunlight streams through the cracks in the shutters, waking me like petals blooming at daybreak. I yawn and stretch, delighting in the embrace of the blankets cocooning my body. My house's familiar scents of lavender and herbs permeate the room.

What a strange and terrible dream. Kidnapped and held prisoner as they take me to an entirely foreign kingdom. Yawning, I push myself up into a sitting position, rubbing the sleep from my eyes and looking around for Lemon when I spot the unfamiliar furniture around me.

Where am I?

The memories of the last few days come flooding back. Not a night terror, but reality, and with it comes the dread that today we would journey closer to Shadowvale. Frantically, I look around the room for Aramis, but there is no sign except an indentation of his body on the bed next to me. Running my hands over the fabric, remanents of heat cling to the sheets. Warmth floods my cheeks as I remember the way he stood at the foot of the bed, drinking me in. The door abruptly opens and the female from the night before comes bustling in the room, breaking my flow of thoughts. She stands in a sheer chemise that hardly leaves much to the imagination, carrying a tray laden with fruits, cheese, honey, and ale. She stops and looks at me, still laying in bed; an angry blush coloring her pale cheeks.

"Where is Prince Aramis?" She asks, her voice sickly sweet. Her eyes sweep over the bed, seeing the remains of his imprint on the cover. I can see the tick in her jaw as she grinds her teeth the more she stares at me in bed.

"How would I know?" I reply, pushing myself up to sit, drawing the covers up to my chin. I comb my fingers through my hair, attempting to detangle some of the knots. "I haven't seen him. I just woke up." And based on her expression, I'm pretty sure she hasn't seen him either. She couldn't possibly think there was something going on between the Prince and I, could she?

"Well." She purses her lips and looks around the room one last time, her eyes catching his cloak drying over the chair. She shifts the tray in her arms and glances back at me. "Do you know when he will be back?"

"I come and go as I please, Oletta." Aramis's tall form stands behind the blonde, his eyes watching my fingers confront a rather hateful knot. "Good, I'm glad to see that you're up. And it appears we have breakfast."

Aramis grabs the tray out of Oletta's arms, who storms out of the room, slamming the door with unneeded force, and places it on the bed next to me. Leaning forward, his hand sinking into the mattress, he grabs a raspberry, popping it into his mouth, all the while never breaking his gaze from mine. "Eat, Sybil. We leave within the hour." Our eyes lock on each other, never parting. A whisper of wind greets me as it curls around my cheek—almost friendly and sweet. My breath falters, unsure of how to interpret the gaze and greeting.

"I, uh, an hour?" I stutter as I nervously bite at my bottom lip, heat rushing to my cheeks at his obstinate studying.

95

"Yes, Sybil," he drawls softly in a deep baritone. His eyes darken as they lower, focusing on my lips. My breath hitches at the sight of his tongue darting out to eat another berry deliberately slow as he meets my gaze. I am losing my mind. "Or do you have a problem with that?" A twist of wind brushes through my hair and caresses down my neck, causing my toes to curl. Contrasting feelings battle within my heart and brain to the point that I no longer know how to address the man in front of me. Is your captor still your captor when he is rooting for your survival? When he tells you his court's secrets to prepare you to stand trial? Or when he looks at you like you are the one good thing left on this continent?

"No. Yes. Uhm." I blurt out and I am unsure whether I answered Aramis's question or the ones afflicting my mind. I scoot back and shake my head to clear it. Reaching forward, I grab a piece of cheese from the tray; better take advantage of the good food before we get back on the road.

I'll need everything I can get when preparing to face the king and queen.

"How many days will it take to reach Shadowvale from here?" I ask casually, trying to restore some normalcy between us. Whatever this is, I have much bigger problems awaiting me. I cannot risk getting distracted.

"Not more than two days if we stay on track. I have urgent matters to take care of. My people need me." The message Nero delivered yesterday must have contained important information. Before I wonder if it involves the rebels, he meets my gaze and continues, "A shifter attack has been foreseen directed at Larnwick, I need to make sure no innocent blood is lost." I nod understandingly, and this information reminds me that for the people of Shadowvale, I represent the enemy. I cast my eyes down and quickly cross my arms over my chest. My movements have caused the blankets to fall away, revealing my thin chemise.

"Sybil." The way he says my name…

"Aramis!" Nero's voice barks from the hallway.

I scramble to pull the covers back up, my eyes darting to the gown I'd lain out at the foot of the bed the night before. I meet his gaze, holding my breath.

"We're not finished," he says huskily, before he briskly turns and walks out the door.

I have no idea what's changing in him, but I also don't want to stop it.

The next two days creep by in silence. We are all restless from the journey it has taken, but my apprehension grows with each stride closer to the Shadowvale castle. I can now see the fortress stands tall and imposing, its shadow cast upon the rocky terrain surrounding it. The mountain range towers above the castle, its jagged peaks piercing the sky, radiating a sense of foreboding, as though something ominous is lurking within the imposing structure. I shiver as the cold wind whips through my hair, blowing the scent of pine trees and fresh snow towards me. I hear the sound of a wolf howling, a chill washing under my skin that mixes terribly with the cold. Was it only a few days ago that I was sitting in the pouring rain at the entrance to the tavern? The past fortnight feels like a blur as my jumbled thoughts turn to focus on what my future holds.

Let alone all the considerations with the prince.

"Aramis," I start, words forming in my head. We have hardly spoken a word since we left Lunaris, both unsure on how to process the moments we shared now that our little bubble is about to burst. Not that I wanted to speak with him, but the alternative was letting my thoughts consume me, eating away any barrier I have erected to prepare for the coming days.

"Sybil, you must address me as Prince Aramis from here forth." His body tenses behind me, his tone is cold and clipped.

My heart clenches at how cruel he sounds. "Oh? Back to formalities, your royal highness?" My reply drips with sarcasm and a hint of attitude, but I am careful to mask any hint of the sadness that has taken over me. He has never made it a secret that he lives for his duty as crown prince. It was foolish of me to think I might have changed his mind on my kind and made a friend. With an exasperated sigh, he loosens his grip on the reins.

"I'm sorry. There is a lot on my mind." His tone is sullen, lacking the heat from our usual banter. "What do you need?"

"What assurance do I have that they will not harm me upon reaching Shadowvale?" I blurt out, my insecurities winning over logic. As his silence stretches out, my heart rate increases. The only sound is the rhythmic beating of hooves against the ground.

"Sybil, you are—" He starts.

"I'm afraid." The honesty of my words hangs heavily between us. I clench my fists in my lap, trying to stop my hands from shaking and I have to remind myself to take deep breaths. A panic attack will do me no good in this situation. Aramis sighs behind me and gently takes one of my hands in his, absentmindedly drawing circles on the back of it to calm me down.

"You could help me. Vouch for me in front of the king and queen. Tell them about these last few days." My voice breaks as I plead once again my case to the Prince of Shadowvale.

"It's not that simple, Sybil. I cannot get involved because I… I can no longer be objective about you." His hand squeezes mine for a fraction of a second, and I wonder if I have imagined it. "I have a duty to uphold to protect my kingdom at all costs," Aramis continues. "Absolving you from your crimes without a fair trial would not be just. Believe me when I tell you that I have already helped you more than I have ever helped any shifter." He sighs heavily behind me. "Being afraid is part of being alive."

The sound of hooves echoes across the drawbridge as we cross onto a stone cobbled courtyard. Aramis slides off before removing me from the horse's back. My legs quiver beneath me, threatening to give out. A firm grip at my elbow steadies me, and I look up at Aramis.

"Promise me," I whisper as I stare from the massive door to his endless blue eyes. Eyes that only a few days before couldn't waver from me. Eyes that laughed as we shared a saccharine sweet silver apple. "Promise me they'll be fair. Promise me I'll be okay."

"My father will know the truth I have seen." He tears his gaze away. "My father is a just and honorable male and will see the truth. His word is law, even above the Queen's." Aramis sounds weary and resigned.

"Aramis," I plead. Pages rush out and take the horses, leading them away. My heart aches as I watch them, hoping they'll get the rest and care they deserve after the journey we've had. "I can't do this. They think I'm actually leading a rebel army. How am I supposed to prove I'm not involved with no proof except my own testament?"

"Yes, you can, Sybil. Believe in your truth. You saved me from a chimera, remember? You're braver than you think." Aramis refuses to meet my eyes as he whispers words of encouragement. His grip around my elbow holds onto me tightly, and the lithe and graceful stance I've come to expect from Aramis is all rigid stone.

"I don't belong here," I whisper. Panic settles into my bones like an electric current and I fall back into my old habits, scared to stand up for myself and wanting to hide from the world. I buck against his grip, my breath increasing. "Aramis— you know I don't belong here. "

"Come." His face twists into a scowl as he drags me towards the front door. "What will they think of your actions if you run away in fear? How will you prove your innocence, then?"

"Let me go," I seethe through clenched teeth. The iron cuff bites into my wrist as I pull away, digging my feet into the ground. I am not going down without a fight.

"Stop fighting. Please. Hurting yourself will not do anyone any good." His face is a mask of apathy, his features cold and distant.

Why is he acting like this?

"Sybil lass. We can nae just let ye go. Be strong." Nero steps up to my other side.

"I don't want to be delivered like some prized mare." Aramis wants to capture a wild pony. I'll fight him like one. I lift my leg, kicking him in the shin. The grip on my wrists loosens and I don't hesitate, pulling from his grasp before turning and sprinting towards the drawbridge.

Abruptly, I stumble and crash to the ground, my skin scuffing against the coarse stones. Strong, rough hands seize me, pinning my arms to my sides and my face against the cool ground. A bolt of panic has me pulling at my restrained arms.

"Sybil," Aramis grunts, and a soothing wind cascades over my skin. "I didn't want it to go down like this."

How dare he use his winds against me like this! I reach desperately for my magic. Aramis' grip on my arm is like an iron vice as he drags me upright and towards the carved stone staircase and the massive wood doors—my fate looming.

"How else is it supposed to go down? You're delivering me to my doom," I seethe through clenched teeth. "Who will believe me?"

I was such a fool to believe this would work. Of course, it won't! It felt so realistic when I saw the change in Aramis, but now I have to convince a king.

Another wind brushes against my cheek and temple, and I soften. Why didn't I fight harder? Why didn't I try harder to escape earlier? He did this to me. Aramis lured me into trusting him! I should have never stopped hating him.

Frantically looking around, I open my mouth to scream for help, but the rush of air leaves my lungs. I fall to my knees, black clouding the edge of my vision. A soft buzzing sounds in my ears as I take in the night sky, stars sparkling in its black void.

My body trembles involuntarily as he stands towering over me. "I'm sorry." His words are barely a whisper over the roaring in my ears.

"Then promise me you'll speak to your father and the queen about my innocence—" I beg at the last moment. "Promise me you'll fight for me. That the man I met isn't a lie. You speak of duty, then protect me, one of the people you owe by title alone."

I look at Aramis—waiting for a fraction of the male I was beginning to know. But he offers me nothing, and I drift away into oblivion as my heart breaks.

SYBIL

The distant sound of voices breeches my consciousness. Blinking, I find myself splayed on a cold marble floor. My hands and wrists are bound by heavy gold chains, in addition to the iron cuff still coiled around my wrist. The warm glow of sunlight filters through the intricate stained glass windows high above me, casting a rainbow of colors onto the stone floor. The vibrant hues depict a valiant knight locked in battle with a fierce dragon, their swords colliding in a fiery clash of steel. As my vision clears, I attempt to move to one side to get a better view of my surroundings. The room is eerily quiet. The flickering candles cast shadows on the faces of the nobles gathered around, their expressions varying from curiosity to apprehension. The air is thick with the scent of burning wax and incense, mixing with the subtle fragrance of perfumes and colognes worn by the courtiers.

"Leave now," an icy voice commands and draws my attention to the far end of the room. On an elaborate marble dais, the king and queen of Shadowvale lounge on their tall thrones. Aramis stands in front of them, his posture rigid, and Nero stoically by his side. "Attend to the task I have given you," the queen adds as she moves to rise. Her beauty is hard to look at. She has porcelain skin, white as fresh cream, her golden hair is cascading down to her waist in perfect soft curls. Emotionless gray eyes scan the handmaiden beside her, ushering her forward with a curt wave of her hand.

My eyes rove to the king, who sits still as a statue. He would look kind if it was not for the empty stare observing the whole proceeding. It's as if a prisoner being chained on his throne room floor was nothing more than a regular afternoon activity. His hair is the same sandy blonde as Aramis', but his eyes are a vibrant green of spring meadows.

"But, your highnesses," Aramis protests with a bow. "I have more to report."

"Did I ask for your report?" She replies sharply. "You're dismissed."

"I will speak to my father, the king." Aramis interjects, moving towards the dais.

"You have urgent matters that need your attention. You are dismissed." She flicks her wrist towards the door.

"Tricella—" he glowers, lips pressing into a thin line. He sinks down to one knee facing the king. "Father—"

"Enough! Boy, need I remind you again?" The queen walks down the steps before him. "Your father may be king of this castle, but until you take his throne, I am your queen and you will address me with respect." She turns and a slap echoes across the room, causing the room to fall to silence. Kneeling on the floor beside Aramis, Nero's cheek burns red. Aramis's jaw clenches and I see his friend meet his eyes in a silent plea not to push her. Nero lowers his head and chances a quick glance my way, giving me a grim look.

"Next time you defy me, your guard will have more to contend with than wounded pride." She pushes past them and heads towards me.

Aramis's hand tightens into a fist at his side, the knuckles turning white as he pivots to face the queen. A bead of sweat trickles down his temple as he locks eyes with her, a pulse beating in his throat.

"Your majesty, I have information for my father that simply cannot wait." I watch as he puts his body between the queen and where I lie on the ground, unable to move. "Father, I insist on your counsel."

"Boy, you are testing my patience and good will," Tricella seethes. She snaps her fingers and Nero begins to choke, his face turning an ugly shade of purple as he claws at the invisible binding around his neck. "Now, I suggest you take your guards and leave me. Have I made myself clear?" She flicks out her wrist and Nero is thrown to the floor, gasping for air.

"Yes," Aramis replies flatly, heat creeping up his neck, and moves to help his best friend from the ground. He casts one last look at me before departing the throne room.

The door closes with a deafening boom. I cringe at the sound and close my eyes, praying to the goddess to take pity and free me, or my magic. But my only answer is silence.

"All of you, out!" The queen's sharp gaze sweeps across the courtiers, who scramble to gather their composure and exit the grand hall. The rustling of their silk garments echoes against the marble floors, and the clacking of their polished shoes reverberates throughout the room. The queen's regal presence seems to fill the space, leaving a palpable sense of authority and power in her wake.

I fight against my chains and try to sit up, ready to defend myself from whichever accusation the crown holds against me. Anger rises within me at the way I've been treated so far. How can they consider this fair? Knocked unconscious, chained and sprawled on the floor at their mercy like an animal.

"Now, what do we have here?" Magic buzzes around me, biting at my skin like hornets stinging, before the chains magically lift my body. My hands are above my head, feet dangling inches above the ground, my head starts pounding and my fingers go numb. The queen slowly paces around me.

"What do you want from me?" My voice barely comes out as a whisper, cracking on the words as anger leaves way to panic. Standing so close to me, I can now see how her beauty is actually that of a woman that has already witnessed many seasons pass. Under layers of powder, wrinkles adorn her eyes and the sides of her mouth. The illusion of plump cheeks is given by the rose-colored blush that sits heavily on her features. The shine of her hair is the result of golden threads which have been masterfully attached to her natural roots, much duller in color from this distance.

"It looks like my stepson finally did something right for once and caught me a unicorn. Alive." Tricella's lips curl into a malicious smile as she lets out a low murmur of satisfaction. A shiver courses through my body at her words. I strain against the invisible force that keeps me suspended in mid-air. The iron chains that bind me dig into my flesh, leaving a trail of hot, burning pain and I can hear the clanking of metal against metal. The air is now thick with the acrid scent of magic, a potent aroma that stings my nostrils. Sweat trickles down my skin, mingling with the blood seeping from my wrist wounds. Every breath I take is labored, as if the very air around is conspiring to suffocate me.

Caught a unicorn alive?

"I have committed no crimes against Shadowvale," I cry out.

"Oh darling," she laughs, and fear like I have never felt before takes over me. "I know you are not a criminal," she announces offhandedly as she continues to examine me like a prize mare.

"But Aramis…" My heart is racing and the pounding in my head increases. "Why did you have Aramis capture and drag me here under the guise of committing treason against the crown if you knew of my innocence?" I retort, glaring at her.

She throws her head back in laughter, hand flying to her chest. "You honestly think my dear sweet stepson, with his righteous, do-good attitude, looking out for the good of the kingdom, would travel halfway across the continent to bring me back a prized specimen for my own pleasure? No. Only a threat against his kingdom would give him enough drive to do that."

I glance pleadingly to the king, but he stares in the distance with a faraway look on his face. The sudden realization that I have been dragged to Shadowvale for much, much darker reasons dawns on me and leaves me unable to speak. There is no innocence to prove, no trust to win.

"He's too wrapped up in his war against the rebel shifters," she continues, and her lips pull up into a smirk. "I have to say, I thought he'd be harder to manipulate. But he's so insistent on playing the white knight, come to save the day. He's blind to what's right in front of him."

"You won't get away with this!" I yell until a tight grip clamps down on my windpipe. Crushing pain radiates around my neck, my vision flickering before it releases.

"Alice, my knife." At her words, I buck and panic as I frantically look around the room, but it is empty save for a few guards who evade my pleading glances. A firm grip on my hair wrenches my head back and causes me to arch backwards. The queen's cool gaze assesses my face as she delicately runs a finger over the star on my brow. My skin burns at her touch and I glare defiantly. She twirls a loose strand of my hair around her finger. "What pretty hair you have. We can't have you trying to woo your way out of here. Males can be so... sentimental when it comes to a beautiful female." She glances towards the king on the throne, her face a mask of emotions. What did she do to him?

"Let me go!" I croak out, my throat raw.

"Oh, I don't think so, little unicorn. I've waited a long time for you." Another sharp tug on my scalp brings a glimpse of silver in my vision before the blade saws through my long, waist-length dark hair. The sound of the blade echoes in my ears and the weight of my hair falls to the ground. When her grip releases, the edges of my now shorn hair tickle my jawline but she is not done yet. Blade still in hand, she proceeds to slice through my layers of clothing until I'm left in nothing but a sheer chemise. Heat floods into my cheeks as I stare at the piles of scraps and hair below me on the ground.

"Why?" I meet her icy gaze.

"Why?" She tosses her head back, her laughing echoing in the room.

"I am no one. Just let me go back home." A note of desperation enters my voice.

"Oh, you are so much more than you know. I've waited a long time for you and now that I have you, I won't be letting you go. That's all you need to know." A wicked smile plays across her lips as she runs the flat of the blade across my side, scratching at the thin fabric separating the cold steel from my skin. She raises a hand and the same biting sensation of magic runs along my skin before I'm lowered to the ground on my hands and knees.

What magic is this? I've felt nothing like it before.

I open my mouth to retort, but feel it snap shut, the skin of my face reverberating with her magic. She walks around me in a circle, appraising me. Stopping, she runs a finger across the mark on my brow again, then frowns. Her eyes catch on the iron bracelet around my wrist.

"Ah, I wondered how he contained you." My arm jerks into the air, the familiar bracelet falling off into the queen's hands. As soon as the cuff leaves my wrist, the warmth of my magic floods my body and I bare my teeth.

Now we'll see who has me.

I reach deep into the core of my magic, willing it to shed

my mortal form. Heat radiates from my star mark as my skin radiates a luminescent glow. Greed flashes in the queen's eyes as she watches me before pressing her hand once more to my forehead. A shiver runs through my body, like my veins are filling with ice, before the draw of my magical energy leaks away. I buck trying to pull away, but I'm held firm by her magic as I watch in horror the glow of my powers dance along her skin. Instantly, the small creases at the corner of her eyes and mouth smooth out, her hair takes on a golden shine. She looks as though she's turned back the clock of time. Releasing her hand from me, I fall to the ground, her powers no longer holding me in place. I am hollow, save for a small spark of magic at my core. I call to it, but it only flutters weakly inside me.

"Oh yes, you are exactly what I was looking for." She looks over to her handmaiden, Alice, standing at her side. The girl has a glassy faraway look, but she turns her face towards the queen. "It appears that looks can deceive. Have her taken to the tower, bathed and fed. I need her alive. And clean up this mess." She kicks at the pile of rags and hair around me.

Lemon!

My heart races, terror for him squeezing my gut. My limbs are heavy as if weighed down with lead, and I can't seem to lift my body up. A guard I do not recognize scoops me up and follows the little maid as we head towards the great doors, leaving the hall.

SYBIL

By the time we reach the door that opens to a small room, I've lost count of the steps we've climbed. The guard deposits me onto the floor of a small chamber and I am surprised I have not been thrown into a cell in the dungeons. My entire body is hurting and my spirit falters at the thought of what is going to become of me. The room is small and round, no larger than twenty feet from wall to wall. Thick burgundy velvet drapes obstructing the view of what I assume is a window. The material looks plush and luxurious to the touch, the color a deep shade of red that catches the eye. A small fire burns in a fireplace to the opposite wall illuminating the scarce furniture in the room; a small writing desk, a chair, a double bed, and an empty shelf.

A small wooden tub nestled against the far wall, barely spacious enough to accommodate a seated person. The memory of Aramis towering over me in the tavern chamber surfaces and makes my eyes swell with tears. The aged wood is smooth, with a faint scent of earthiness emanating from its pores. Despite its diminutive size, the tub's presence adds a cozy and rustic vibe, contrasting the cold barrenness of the room. Alice swiftly walks over and pulls on a chain hanging from the ceiling. A hollowed wooden beam folds out from the wall, and with the tug of a second chain, steaming water pours into the tub. Despite everything that has transpired, my mind fixates on the intricate and fascinating design. How can a place filled with such evil also contain such wonder?

"How does it work?" I ask Alice, my voice breaking over the words. I push my body into a sitting position while waiting for her reply. My wrists and ankles are raw from the heavy gold chains, but I'm otherwise intact, aside from my pride.

Alice stares at me with her glassy, blank expression. Her eyes remind me of a glass doll, void of emotion. She then pulls a bar of soap from her apron pocket and a wooden comb.

"The queen has ordered you bathed and changed," she replies in a monotone voice, standing still as a statue.

"Your queen seems to think a lot of herself. She is not my sovereign, and I don't appreciate being bossed around." I push to my feet, my head spinning as the room partially spins. Stumbling, I catch myself on the footboard of the double bed. The air is thick with silence, and the only sound that fills my ears is the sound of my own breathing. Disoriented and confused, my head pounds with a dull ache.

"It would not do well to displease her." Her lips press into a thin line of annoyance, the only sign of emotion that I've seen from her yet. I wonder if she's always been this way, or if she is under some spell.

I lift my gaze, taking in the sight of Alice as she approaches me, silent on her feet. She grabs my elbow and guides me towards the tub. I wrench out of her grasp and take a few steps back, but she only stares at me with her absent glossy eyes, the same ones as the king's. Another wave of insufferable pounding hits my forehead, right above my star mark, as I remember the feeling of my magic being drained from my very soul against my will. I have never felt more violated... or weak, in the face of the queen's powers.

Sighing, I glance down at the bruises forming along my pale skin. The bath at the tavern feels ages ago. Dirt covers my calves and forearms from my struggle to get away from Aramis. I do not want harm to fall on this girl because of my defiance. If I want any chance of escape, I need to be at my full strength.

"Alright, hand me the soap and I'll bathe. Is there at least a gown I can change into when I'm done?" I hold my hand out towards her.

"Yes. When you finish, pull this chain to drain the water." She drops the soap and comb into my hand then gives me a small curtsy before laying a thin cream chemise and gray overskirt on the bed from another pocket. Turning, she leaves the room without another word. The metallic click of a lock echoes in her wake. Embedded in the door is a window with thick metal bars.

I'm not in a room. I'm in a cell.

After I finish bathing and changing, I pull the chair in front of the fire and begin combing what little remains of my hair. I'm not particularly attached to the locks, but the absence of its weight is a heavy reminder of the previous evening's events. I try to reach for the soothing warmth of my magic, but all I discern is the small flicker. Is it gone for good? Is this spark all I have left?

There has to be a way for me to get my power back.

Despair coils like a snake writhing in my stomach. How could I have been so naïve? I have often felt loneliness in my life, especially after my parents' death. Our family cottage suddenly felt too big for one person, so I learned to fill my days with activities, enough to keep the terrible thoughts at bay. I tried to find my place in the little community in my village, surround myself with people and Lemon's existence filled some of that void too. But I have never felt loneliness as strongly as I do now, in the face of true danger, knowing there is no one left in this world who is coming to save me. My eyes sting from the bright flames in front of me and I let the comb fall into my lap as my shoulders curve in under the weight of my desperation.

You are brave, Sybil.

Aramis's words come back to me like a lifeline. I quickly wipe away the tears that are now cascading along my cheeks. I am brave and I refuse to let this be the end for me. Thoughts of Lemon fill my head, and I feel renewed determination. What happened to him after I left the throne room? He is clever and I pray he finds a way to escape. Just as I need to escape, rescue him, and return home. Or make a new home. As a citizen of Kallistar, I could request shelter and protection from my own king and queen. Now that the kingdom of Shadowvale has outwardly kidnapped and imprisoned me, they have a duty to protect me. I just need to make it out of here alive.

I search the room for anything that I can potentially use to defend myself but only find a silver gilded hand mirror in the small drawer of the desk. I catch my reflection and gently prod at a bruise forming on my cheekbone where I hit the ground. My hazel eyes stare back at me, dark circles blooming under them. Not entirely recognizing the woman staring back at me, I place the mirror back where I found it, noting that I could break it and obtain shards sharp enough to cause some damage. Pulling apart the thick drapes reveals a small glass window, too small to fit my body through. I push the glass and it swings open on small hinges. My cell floods with a cool breeze and the scent of the night blooming jasmine. Stars pepper the sky before me. Below me, I can see the dark shadows of the forest and mountains.

Less time has passed than I thought, considering all that has transpired. I close the window, and turn away, lying down on the bed, pulling the coverlet to my shoulders.

Who knows what trials tomorrow will bring me?

A knock on the door awakens me from a dreamless

slumber and I sit up, my body tensing in defense. The door
quickly opens and a tray scrapes across the stone floor before
it shuts again. Sunlight is now streaming through the window.
The fire has burned down to embers overnight, and I do
not see any logs in the room to feed it. The temperature has
dropped, the cold stone biting into my feet as I walk carefully
over to the food.

At least they aren't starving me.

Picking up the tray, I carry it over to the table. Slices of
bread, a broth, and a small plate of cheese with fruit are strewn
across the tray. There is a stoppered pitcher which I remove the
cork and sniff the contents. The sweet smell of wine reaches
my senses, followed by the sickly sharp undertone of valerian.

But it seems they're trying to poison me into submission.

Used in small doses, valerian root helps with treating
insomnia. In larger doses, it can render the victim into a
comatose state, or worse. Turning to the rest of the food, I
notice all of it has been dusted with a fine powder that I do not
recognise. I push the plate away and rub my temples, wishing I
had learned more than the basic herb lore.

Resentment pushes me away from the table. I try the door,
hoping whoever brought my poisoned meal left it unlocked,
but the thick wooden door doesn't budge. Standing on my toes,
I grab the iron bars and peer out. A winding staircase spirals
down into shadows.

"Hello? Is anyone there?" I call to the dark, my voice, raspy
and dry, echoes off the stone before it's met with silence. My
tongue is dry as sandpaper, my stomach growling in protest.
When was the last time I ate? A person could last for some
time without food and water, the body turning to its stores for

energy. Gazing down towards my slender body, I gently prod my bony hips that protrude through the thin fabric of my dress. After two weeks of lean rations on the road, I had little reserve left.

The wooden tub catches my attention in the corner of my periphery, and a smile tugs at the corner of my lips. Without food, a person could fast and live for a couple of weeks. Without hydration, a person could only survive up to a few days. Luckily for me, they unwittingly left me with my greatest necessity untempered.

Repeating Alice's motions, I pull the wooden beam down, then pull on the chains. I let out a small whoop of victory before cupping my hands and bringing the water to my lips. I greedily gulp at the liquid, filling my aching belly and thirst. A tug at the chain stops the flow and I discreetly push the wood back into place. My body craved more, but I knew if I drank too much too quickly, I would only make myself sick.

I don't want to know what the punishment is, should I not appear to look like I was adding nourishment to my body, so I push the food carefully around my plate and dump the liquid down the tub's drain.

Hours pass as I watch the trail of the sun move across the floor. I wish I had more than an ounce of my magic. Not that it would do me any good. Just as I am powerless in this mortal body, I would be just as powerless in my mystical equine form, trapped in this locked tower. If only I could turn myself into a bird, then I could fly far away from this nightmare.

The sound of the lock turning whips my head to the door, but it is only Alice and the guard from last night. His tall frame blocks my exit, his eyes watching my every move as I push myself up from the bed. Alice sets a tray with roasted meat, potatoes, vegetables, and dark brown bread on the table along with another corked jug. She frowns at the still full plate from this morning.

"Unicorn, you must eat more," Alice states matter-of-factly, then frowns taking in my thin form. "You are too thin and you need your strength."

"I need to leave and return home," I reply, meeting her glossy stare. My stomach twists with hunger as the scent reaches my nose. I dare not throw the accusation of poison around. They don't need to know the extent of my knowledge.

She turns away from me and grabs a stack of wood from the guard's arms, carefully arranging them in the fireplace. With a snap of her fingers, there is a buzz of magic in the air before a blazing fire roars to life.

"The queen will be displeased."

"She cannot keep me here forever," I protest, bunching the fabric of my skirts in my hands. "I'm a healer, I have a life duty to fulfill."

"The queen has plans for you. Your duty is now to serve her. Eat. You will need your strength." At her words, she grabs the old tray and heads out the door, the guard locking it behind her.

"Wait!" I jump and run to the door, banging against the bars with my fists. "Please."

They ignore my pleas, continuing down the steps into the darkness. I slump against the wood. Hot tears spill down my cheeks as the silence once again creeps in.

ARAMIS

ero and I ride side-by-side in silence as we canter towards Larnwick. A group of soldiers follow behind us with wagons for prisoners and arms to defend the town. According to the guards, the King has sent a troupe to Larnwick already during my absence to inform the people of the incoming danger and protect them. I am only glad Edmund stayed in Shadowvale this time around. He needs to regain his strength and allow his wounds to fully heal. A familiar pressure constricts my chest as I prepare myself for what I will find once we reach our destination.

Thanks to Kieran's vision, we have a time advantage of two days. Once we reach the town by nightfall, we will set up our defenses and prepare a trap for the rebels, but our plan can only work if the seer's prediction is accurate. Worst-case scenario, we will reach Larnwick and be welcomed once again by death and destruction. Not as the saviors we should be, but merely there to help with the consequences of the attack.

Memories of the ambush that destroyed Astrakane still haunt me. The seer had foretold of an impending attack that would result in our citizens being ambushed. To prevent this, we decided to arrive a week early. It was only a three-day ride southwest of Shadowvale, so we made the necessary arrangements. However, when we finally arrived in the city, a pungent smell of smoke and burning debris filled the air. The sight that awaited us was nothing short of heart-wrenching. Half of the buildings had been reduced to smoldering ruins, all valuables had been taken, and half of the town's population, including shifters and elementals alike, had been slaughtered. As we watched the chaos unfold before our eyes, a feeling of hopelessness and despair overwhelmed us. It was as if the gods were playing a cruel trick on us.

What sort of evil creature would kill their own kind and take off with the spoils?

Bile burns in the back of my throat at the memory of loading the surviving shifters into wagons to be questioned. Memories of tears streaming down their faces burn in my mind. It's not the most desirable outcome, but it is necessary. Ever since the first attacks, Shadowvale's security council has deemed it safer to capture all the remaining shifters found at the towns and villages ransacked by the rebels and take them to the capital. There, everyone undergoes a trial to uncover potential rebel sympathizers and spies, but blinded by my own hatred for the shifters, I never stopped to consider just how many prisoners were eventually deemed guilty by the royal court. But how could the shifters be both the attackers and the attacked? My theory of the possible existence of two rebel groups comes back to me.

"Aramis." Nero takes me out of my thoughts. His eyebrows are furrowed and his lips are pressed together. "Ye have nae said a single word since we left," he says, and I am forced to contend with the guilt of making my best friend worry about me when I should be the one concerned about his state. The way Tricella treated him inflames my rage and I curse myself for not stepping in.

Glancing sideways, I look once more at my friend's profile

in the rising sunlight. "Don't worry about me. I just have a lot to think about," I say, sounding less convincing than I hoped I would.

"You did what you could." Nero looks at me, and I sadly realize there are not many people left in this world that truly see me, like my friend does. I nod, unsure what to say and focus on the path in front of us.

I wouldn't be alive today if it wasn't for Nero. Not a week goes by that I don't recall the day he burst through my bedroom doors and rushed me to see a healer after a vagabond group of shifters sliced their blade against my collarbone. Raising a hand, I rub the scar under my vest.

Only eight summers had been known to me when my world shattered.

The raised flesh makes my expression deadpan, the wound occurring only moments after my mother–the true queen–had been brutally murdered by shifter assassins. And hell, I would have been next If I didn't have wind magic to throw them over the balcony's edge, to which Nero would have walked in to see my corpse.

All for a shifter's war.

The very people that Sybil belongs to.

Taking a deep breath, I sit up straight, trying to keep my emotions at bay. I used to rush to these missions with such ferocity, ready to inflict my vengeance upon any shifter I could find. Why do I feel like I am the villain now and no longer the savior? Sybil is an anomaly, not the rule.

The cold winter winds pick up as we make our way out of the woods. I adjust my cloak to the best of my abilities and think about Sybil's warm body nestled in front of me during our journey. She is probably undergoing her trial right now, and I have to stop myself from turning around and running back to the castle as fast as I can. Sighing, I grasp Percy's reins with more force. Our paths intertwined for a moment, but were never meant to stay together. If the Gods are willing, I will see her one last time, just once.

Thick plumes of smoke rise high into the sky, casting a dark shadow over us. The acrid stench of burning material fills our nostrils, making us cough and squint our eyes. The crackling sound of flames can be heard from a distance, the heat so intense its as though we are standing too close to a raging fire. I glance at Nero beside me as we slow the horses to a walk. He nods his head, confirming my suspicion that we've once again arrived too late.

Fucking Kieran.

"Let's split up. I'll look for signs of the rebels at the north of town while you head south." Urging my horse, I make my way through the buildings. The only sounds I hear are the cries of ravens circling above. Deep claw marks scrape the sides of buildings, leaving dark gouges. Multiple houses stand in ruin, their roofs collapsed and charred. Smoke lingers in the air, obscuring the view of the surrounding area, gray flakes of ash floating around me. The smoldering fires cast an eerie orange glow, illuminating the destruction. The scene is a haunting reminder of the devastation the rebels can bring.

"Is anyone out there? Come out and show yourself," I call out while looking for signs of life. Where are the guards my father had promised he'd send to protect the towns? There is no sign of any creature, living or dead.

A loud crack resounds in the air and I whip my head around, my horse whinnying beneath me. I watch as flames burst out the window of a building across the street and the roof slumps inside, defeated. A large wooden sign hangs from one corner. The painted words "Margerie's Bookshop" are barely legible from the smoke stains. A pang of regret clenches at my chest as I imagine all the tomes inside. The dry thin pages being mercilessly consumed by the flaming beast. Instinct urges me to run into the building and rescue any remaining books, but duty compels me to turn my horse and continue on our path.

"Aramis, ma lord!" Nero calls out from in front of me, leading his horse by the reins. He must have made it full circle around the town already. I spot something in his hands as I slide out of the saddle and approach him. There is a crunch under my boot as I take a step forward. A rag doll lay squashed under my foot. I scoop up the discarded toy and regard its simple brown hair, brown eyes, and olive tone skin before I notice two fluffy ears atop her head. Frowning, I let the doll fall to the ground where it sends up a small cloud of dust and ash. Where is the shifter child it belonged to?

"I found naething except this." Nero hands me a large, monstrous claw. "Nae sign of anyone, elemental or shifter."

I scowl at the large jet black claw in my hand. It is nearly the length of my forearm with a wickedly sharp point.

"What shifter has a claw this size?" I ask as I hand the monstrosity back to him.

"None that I am aware of. It makes me wonder…" Nero trails off as he runs a finger along the edge of the claw, his brow furrowing in concentration.

"That the shifters have grown considerably larger in the last couple of decades?" I laugh, but the joke rings hollow to my ears.

"Nae. I wonder if we aren't dealing with rebel shifters, but another creature entirely." Nero looks up and meets my gaze and I cross my arms over my chest in defense. The list of certainties I have lived by for most of my life are crumbling one by one. First the possibility that not all shifters are involved with the rebels, and now the existence of a new enemy entirely. If the claw does not belong to a shifter, then maybe it belongs to one of the monsters that roam Craeweth? But everyone knows those creatures live far within the woods. Why would a monster this size venture so far out of its habitat and kill all the inhabitants of a town of this size?

"Nonsense. Here I thought I was the one with my head full of tales. Have you found a fondness for reading after all these years, Nero?" I try to diffuse the situation. It would do no one any good to panic now.

He punches me lightly in the arm. "If ye spent more time in the training yard and less with yer secret pastime, perhaps I wouldn't kick yer arse so easily when we spar. But Aramis, I truly feel like there is more to this attack. Look around ye. We've never seen destruction of this caliber in the past."

"Each attack in the last year has become more gruesome, Nero. They're getting desperate. They've even killed their own…" My thoughts return to the discarded doll. What is the point of destroying a peaceful village where elementals and shifters lived together? How did this attack help their cause? Doubt lingers at the back of my mind as I cast my eyes across the burning remains. Something is not adding up, but I am not ready to contemplate the depth of all that seems wrong.

"This does not look like an attack of desperation. This looks like malice." Nero tucks the claw into his bag.

Pulling myself back up into the saddle, I turn back towards the palace. "There is nothing to report here. We might as well head back to the castle."

Something is very wrong about all of this.

SYBIL

I lay on the bed with a cool wet cloth ripped from the sheets that rests across my throbbing forehead. It pulses to the rhythm of my heartbeat and although I haven't moved, the room spins as though it's dancing around me. Taking steady, deep breaths, I assess my aching body. My injuries have healed, but fatigue wears at me from fasting for three days with nothing but water. At the thought of food, my stomach lets out a loud grumble and cramps painfully, causing me to curl into a ball on my side. Last night, the aroma of the warm beef and vegetable stew filled the air, making my mouth water in anticipation. The sight of the hearty chunks of meat and colorful vegetables in the bowl was tempting, but the dimmed visage of a sprinkling of dust on the vegetables reminded me to take caution. My logical side fought and eventually won against my basic animal needs. As I walked away from the table, the warmth of the stew radiates towards me, taunting me to come back for just one bite. This food is poisoned and I must remain strong.

Nimble footsteps make their way up the stairs and I close my eyes tighter. I am in no shape to argue with Alice this morning. The door slowly opens and I am ready to tell her to

122

let me free or leave me be, but I stare in confusion as the tall figure in front of me is not Alice, but two tall guards wearing the royal crest on their chest.

A foreign sigil, one that shouldn't even command me.

"Shifter, you are to come with us," one males states flatly.

"Where am I going?" My voice is raspy from disuse. I heave my body up into a sitting position, the thudding of my heartbeat echoing in my ears. The room spins around me, the walls and furniture blurring into indistinguishable shapes. Black spots swarm my vision, obscuring any clear sight. A faint scent of stale air and sweat lingers in my nostrils as I struggle to keep myself upright.

"The Queen has demanded your presence," the other guard replies, grabbing my elbow and forcing me to my feet.

"No!" I try to pull out of his grip but my strength fails me and I nearly fall to my knees. I cry out in pain as the guard wretches my arm upward, causing my shoulder to burn. The other guard supports me on the other side and together they frog-march me down the winding steps. I lose my sense of direction as we turn away from the large hall that leads to the courtroom. Out of the corner of my eye, I spot a flash of white and cream scurrying down the hall and my heart clenches in my chest.

Lemon!

I struggle against the guards' tight grip, but they hold firm as we pass through another door and descend down a flight of winding stairs. The musty scent of damp air fills my nostrils, and the sound of our footsteps echoes off the stone walls. Only sporadic torches cast a flickering glow on the passage. They illuminate our path as we continue downward, reflecting ominous shadows on the stone walls. My heart pounds in my chest, and my palms grow slick with sweat as we descend deeper into the unknown depths of the dungeon.

At the bottom, we stop in front of a carved wooden

door that appears centuries old. The door creaks as they push it open, revealing a vast room with stone walls and a low set ceiling. In the center of the room, a large stone slab sits, its rough texture visible even from a distance. The air is cool and damp, making my skin prickle with goosebumps. My eyes catch on the straps around the table and the dark stains in the stone.

"Bring her to me." Her sweet melodic voice echoes through the room and I turn my head to see the queen reclined on a plush couch. Her golden curls hang loose, draping across her breasts like a golden waterfall. She shifts her position to better observe me, her sheer cream gown flowing around her. The fabric hugs her curves, leaving little to the imagination. From our proximity, the scent of her perfume wafts through the room, a nauseatingly strong blend of floral and musk. Her beauty is the kind that inspires poetry and art. But I know better. Underneath her seemingly gentle exterior lies a serpent waiting to strike. The guards release me before her, and it takes all my will to keep my balance as my body shakes with fatigue.

"Welcome to my little sanctuary, unicorn." I watch as she sips from the silver goblet in her hand, then runs the tip of her tongue delicately across her lips.

"I have a name." I grind out between clenched teeth.

"Oh, that's right. Sybil isn't it?" She hums in disapproval before slowly dragging her gaze from my head to my feet.

"What is it that I can do for you, your highness?" I lay heavy sarcasm in the question and ball my hands into fists.

The queen raises her delicate brows at my tone, her lips curving into a knowing smile.

Goddess, help me, what have I just done?

I dare a glance at the guards behind me. They are the only thing standing between me and my freedom, but in my weakened state I doubt I'd be able to physically out maneuver them. The taste of bitterness fills my mouth as I bite down hard, trying to suppress the frustration that's been building up since she stole my magic. "What is it that you want?"

She laughs, setting the goblet on a table beside her before pushing to stand. "Men always think that power is only a step away from them. Kill a king and take his place. Start a war and kill your enemies. Marry the daughter of a rich Lord and you'll be her master. Sacrifice the unthinkable to a God and he will grant you gifts." She curls a strand of her hair with a finger, her gaze so unfaltering it makes me want to hide. "What they fail to realize, however, is that there is no point in gaining power if you don't have the time to fully use it to your advantage." Her plush lips curl upwards, revealing a wicked smile that sends chills down my spine. The sharp glint in her eyes glimmers with hunger, making me feel like prey. The room is silent, except for the faint sound of our breathing and the rustle of fabric as she moves closer.

"I searched for hundreds of years for a unicorn shifter. I wanted your parents, really." I gasp at the mention of my mother and father and remember Aramis mentioning that Shadowvale believed my parents aided the rebellion. But with the recent discovery that the Queen does not act with the intention of stopping the attacks, I fear her need for my parents had a darker motivation. "Two unicorns would have meant not only double the power at my disposal but also the potential to breed an unlimited supply of magic to help me turn the clock on time over and over again." She swipes her hand angrily across a nearby table, knocking glass and metal to shatter on the stone floor. The heat of her gaze burns as she turns back towards me and growls. "But no, they had to go all noble to the end, sacrificing themselves in order to protect you from my sights."

My breath catches in my throat and an old pain I had carefully managed to suppress deep within my heart comes rushing back. My body begins to shake, and I desperately look around for something to steady myself on. This cannot be real.

She is the person responsible for ambushing and murdering my parents? And they sacrificed themselves to protect me?

The shock must be evident on my face because she laughs and grabs a hold of my chin. I lift my arms to fend her off, but the crawling sensation of her magic pins them back against my sides and seals my lips closed.

"Not so fast. You are mine now, pet. Thanks to you, I will witness kings and queens die, kingdoms crumble, and I will take it all. I don't care if I have to drain every single shifter on this continent to do so. Starting with you." I try to scream but my windpipes constrict even further." Lifting her hand to my forehead, I feel the tug against my power, but nothing happens. I watch as her face contorts with concentration and I scrape of her magic grapple inside but fail once more. Only the flicker of my magic dances like a silver flame in my core, evading her.

"Something wrong, your majesty?" The corners of my lips curl up in satisfaction as I hold on tight to the tiny flame of magic inside of me. The resulting slap stinging my cheek, no doubt leaving a red welt, is absolutely worth the defiance.

"Where is your magic? Why has it not replenished?" She seethes, the knuckles of her hands turning bone white as she grips the front of my dress. Small creases form at the corner of her eyes before an unfamiliar voice has me peering over her shoulder behind her.

"Perhaps she cannot recover as quickly, locked up so far away from the elements. She is a mere creature, after all. They thrive on the earth and in the sunshine." The man's voice has a soothing quality, and I am pulled by its rhythmic deep lilt. He moves with the grace of a dancer to my side and runs a finger down my ribs, visible through the thin fabric. The touch instantly clears my senses and I struggle against the magical hold on my body.

"Perhaps you're right, Kieran." The seer. Laying down on the lodge chair, she sighs and drapes her forearm across her eyes. "Give her what she requires to regain her strength. I want her at her full potential the next time she's brought to me. Now, leave me."

"As you wish, your highness." He bows low at the waist in her direction, short dark hair falling into his face. I observe in fascination as he gradually rises to his feet, the luxurious silk of his mage's robes pulled tight against his muscular back. The rustle of the fabric echoes softly in the stillness of the room, and the subtle scent of sandalwood wafts through the air. As he stands, his movements are graceful, yet purposeful, as if he is summoning some great power within himself. The air around him seems to hum with energy, crackling with a palpable electricity. Are all mages built like immortal warriors? For surely this male is a scholar, not a guard.

"And Kieran? Make sure that insolent stepson of mine is out of the way, then have the guards bring in some of the shifter prisoners from the dungeon. He's starting to get too nosy, and…go find me a refreshment. I need one, now." Queen Tricella sits up and turns towards us. She lifts her hands and the constriction around me releases. I wobble unsteadily on my feet as black spots dance in my vision. I want to run and flee, but my trembling weak muscles refuse to take that first step.

Firm hands grab my forearms, turning me back towards the door. I attempt to wrestle out of their grips as the two guards escort me back upstairs, but my strength is no match in my current weakened state.

Keep Aramis from knowing she's taking shifter prisoners for their power? Does he not know what his stepmother does?

My mind reels with hundreds of questions as I play his words from the road over in my head. He thought I was involved in a rebellion to bring down his kingdom, but the queen is using shifters to gain more power for herself. He must be told the truth.

Sunlight blinds me as we pass through a large stone

archway. I lift my arm, shielding my eyes from the stinging pain, waiting for them to adjust. Chancing a peek through my fingers, the first thing I take in are the rows upon rows of rose bushes in hundreds of colors. Goosebumps pepper the skin of my bare arms as a chill breeze wraps around me. Then I smell the scent of honeysuckle, chrysanthemum, and aster flowers. How does a land on the northern edge of the continent have such bountiful growth and blooms on the cusp of winter?

"There is a magical field placed over the gardens to keep them in a perpetual healthy growing state. We have many talented earth, wind, and water mages who reside in the castle." Kieran's melodic voice speaks softly behind me, as if reading my thoughts. Turning, I quickly back away from him, glancing frantically from side to side, looking for a route to escape. His laughter chimes like deep bells, as he leans against the rough brick wall of the castle exterior behind him, not moving in my direction.

"Why have you brought me here?" I ask. The guards who escorted me out of the queen's sanctuary are nowhere to be seen, if Kieran is the only person I have to get rid of, I might have a chance at escaping.

"For the sunshine and flowers?" He lifts his hands towards the sky.

"I do not belong here. Please… please, let me go." I beg. It has to be approaching midday based on where the sun is in the sky. "She's already stolen my family. I've given her enough."

"Walk with me." Lifting a hand in my direction, he walks towards me before he pauses, his eyes taking on a milk white color, completely blocking out the iris and pupil for a split second.

"Who are you?" I ask once his eyes go back to their normal deep grey color. I stand still, refusing to go anywhere with this male.

"My name is Kieran," he says, giving me a half grin and

mock bow. "High seer to queen Tricella. You can choose to act as you wish unicorn, but I recommend that you and I become friends rather than enemies. It's in your best interest."

"And what makes you think I should trust you?" What an arrogant asshole. Is this what a kingdom is like? Everyone believing they are above the rest of us? That my life–my family–is expendable?

"I see you, Sybil Vandeleur." He draws out the syllables of my name, his eyes taking on a faraway look. "How much do you know about seers?"

His question throws me off, and I nibble on my bottom lip as I contemplate. I didn't know much about seers except for the fact that they are rare. They could be born to any race, regardless of family lineage. "I know that seers are blessed by the Goddess with the sight, just like healers are blessed with the power to heal."

"Yes," he says with a sigh, rubbing his forehead before pushing off from the wall and pacing before me. "We are gifted with glimpses of the future, and sometimes the past. But looking into the future is not as easy as everyone thinks because that time has not been written yet. It is fluid, ever changing." He lifts his hands and an orb of water floats from a small pond beside us, its surface reflecting the light. "To every event, there is a tipping point. When key players make changes, it changes the course of the future path they are on."

"We are vessels of our own free will, as the goddess allows," I say. "But we cannot control the future any more than we can control the seasons."

"Ah, but that is where you are wrong." He smiles and inside the orb replays the night Aramis broke into my house and captured me. The vision fades and flickers and images start playing faster and faster until they become a blur. "Each small event, each change in the pathway, can change the future. Just as water wears against stone. You just have to move the right pieces."

"As much as I appreciate the lesson, what is the point of dragging me out here, giving me a taste of freedom only to lock me back in the tower? I'd rather waste away than be some pawn in assisting the queen."

"You are more than just a mere pawn, Sybil." The orb slows to an image of the queen standing before the people of Shadovale, Kieran at her side and me kneeling at her feet. As soon as it appears, the vision changes to one of me astride a dappled stallion riding across a field filled with wounded, charging towards a castle.

This castle.

My eyes flick up at the stone walls, breathing in the damp scent. This place? I'm meant to attack this castle?

In my peripheral, I see the vision change. Spellbound to the possibilities, I tilt my head downwards, mesmerized by what unfolds before my eyes. To my astonishment, I see myself on a ladder, situated in a vast and magnificent library. The next moment, the scene changes, and I see a vision of myself kneeling before the king and queen of Kallistar. However, this image quickly fades away, replaced by a new one. Now, I am wandering through an endless snowy forest. The visions continue to whirl around the orb, growing faster and faster, granting me only fleeting, fragmented glimpses of possible futures.

If that is my possible future, I must escape this place. Somehow. My heart clenches and I can't tear my eyes away. I need to know more, but the images return to a spinning orb of crystalline water.

"Your future is rich with possibilities, but one thing is consistent throughout all the visions the Goddess has granted me: your destiny is tied to that of my queen. You will be the reason for her success or her demise. " He lets the orb float mid-air to gently brush the dark circles that have now become a permanent feature of my face with the soft pad of his thumb.

"Get. Your. Hands. Off. Me." I shiver and recoil from his cold touch. "I might not be a pawn in this plan but you certainly are. You are a tool to her. How can you live with yourself knowing you're aiding her in this madness?" I spat, anger rising. His fingers move from my cheek to my chin and lift my face up in his direction.

Even if the visions took my breath away, I also can't just trust the right hand of the queen.

"Talking to me like that isn't very friend-like now, is it Sybil?" His eyes darken, and I wonder if I have once again underestimated my opponent. "A word of advice. I am nothing but the queen's loyal servant. Her success is all that matters to me, so you do not want to be an obstacle in our plans. It would be such a shame to have all of… this," he says as his gaze leisurely roams down my body, "go to waste." I swallow uncomfortably as he lets his hand fall to his side and takes a step back. Crossing my arms, I keep my gaze fixed on him in defiance. "Now, love, why are you not eating?" Kieran asks nonchalantly, as if he hasn't just threatened to kill me if I do not cooperate.

"Why would I eat poisoned food? I can recognize the scent of valerian." Watching the muscles in his jaw tighten, I smirk. I am not a fool.

"You are not what I expected," the seer says, letting the orb of water drop to the ground with a snap of his fingers, splashing our feet.

"I never expected to be abducted from my cottage and stolen away to be used as a pawn either!" I shout, losing my temper.

These people in this castle are asinine. I'm supposed to just believe them because of a vision? For all I know, he's not even a real seer. How am I supposed to know what qualifies him as one? How am I supposed to gauge anything?

"I have been looking for you for a long time, Sybil."
Kieran's head tilts to one side, studying me with curiosity.
"Countless days I wasted, waiting for visions of potential
shifters in Shadowvale that could grant the queen the amount
of magic she needs. We tried everything from wolves, tigers,
and bears to rare exotic shifters. Sometimes even entire
families of a specific kind of shifter!" He shakes his head in
disappointment. "All of them useless, merely able to turn the
clock a couple of months back, and they would never last more
than two or three uses. We knew, of course, that we needed
a unicorn. The only known shifter able to tap into the well
of magic deep and long enough to truly grant the queen the
gift of time. Were it not that your kind is so hard to come by
these days, I would have found you as a young colt if it weren't
for your parents." I stop frozen, unwilling to process what I
just heard. My stomach cramps up, bile rising in my throat.
Countless shifters lost their lives. Entire families are dead for
this madness. Just like my family…

"What do you mean, if it weren't for my parents?" My
hands clench and I bare my teeth at him.

"I saw them, in a vision, traveling home from delivering the
Queen's baby. We meant to intercept them before they reached
Kallistar and prevent the heirs' birth. I had foreseen its demise
as a stillborn, but your blasted mother arrived early." A muscle
ticks in his jaw.

I remember that week. The babe wasn't due for another
month, but my mother said she felt an intuition from the
goddess and convinced my father to leave for the capital
a month early. Her last letter to me was that the queen of
Kallistar went into labor a month early and, had she not been
there, they both would have died in child labor. Tears prick at
the corner of my eyes, threatening to spill over.

"You were supposed to be with them," Kieran says.

"What?" I break out of my memories and face him once

again.

"In my vision, the three of you were to travel to Kallistar. After the birth, your parents planned to finish your enrollment in Nova Esther."

"Why didn't they take me?" I grab the front of his robes, demanding he tell me. I have to know.

"That, I do not know. Mother's intuition? Luck?" He pulls out of my desperate grasp and runs his hands down the front of his scholar's robes, straightening them. "All I know is that upon her death, your mother prayed for the Goddess' protection and you were blinded from my sight until one day, shortly after your twenty-fifth birthday, you were suddenly there. My vision revealed a young unicorn shifter wasting her life and talents in a poor village. You have the power to change Craeweth as we know it, love."

My knees buckle, hitting the hard stone floor as hard as his revelation of my parents' sacrifice to protect me. This kingdom, these people, they are all sick and twisted. How can I change anything when I can't even help myself? I stand numb, reeling in his revelations, and before I can say anything, his eyes take on a milky white hue again that eclipses the iris and pupil. He immediately shakes his head, his eyes returning to their regular piercing gray, and sighs, running a hand through his tidy, short, dark hair. "Unfortunately, I have to cut our first encounter short, I'm afraid. There is a matter I need to attend to. I promise, I will make sure your next meal is not contaminated."

Moments after the queen's seer returns me to my room, Alice appears laden with a tray of food and a hot pot of black tea. As promised, the food contains no trace of valerian, poppy, or any other discernible substances. I cautiously pick at the food, debating if there is some trick to my senses, but hunger wins. Pacing myself, lest I lose the contents of my stomach after fasting for days, I pick up a chicken breast, taking

133

small deliberate bites before washing it down with a cup of hot tea.

After finishing my meal, leaving only bones and dregs, I lay on the bed, exhausted but full, staring at the dust motes dancing in the air above me. Tears stream silently from my eyes as I reflect on the countless shifters who have tragically lost their lives within this castle. The weight of their losses leaves me feeling hollow, but something else is slowly warming up my chest. Next to the little spark of magic I have left, a new sensation takes form.

The need for revenge.

SYBIL

The sound of scratching awakens me from my fitful sleep full of nightmares. Pushing myself into a sitting position, I glance around the room, but nothing is amiss. No light filters from behind the thick curtains, and last night's fire has burned down to embers. It is too early for Alice to be bringing me breakfast. Running my fingers through my hair, I try to detangle the knots from my tossing and turning.

My heart clenches, tears lining my eyes, as an unexpected memory of my mother surfaces—a vision of her combing my hair as she tells me about her upcoming trip to the palace to aid the queen's delivery. "It will only be a couple of days, my little healer," she said to me as she hugged me goodbye. I begged her to stay but the last thing she said to me the day that everything changed was "The Goddess will watch over you," and I saw them leave for the last time. I brush the tears angrily from my face and slide out of bed, the cold of the stone floor biting into my bare feet. Making my way over to the window, I move the curtains, push open the glass, and lean my arms against the sill.

White flakes land and melt against my face as a gust of wind whistles through the small opening. The first official sign

135

of winter. I have given up counting the days they have kept me locked in this room, devising a way out, while dreading being summoned again by the queen. It has been days since the last time I have been taken out of this room, since that brief moment in the garden where I felt the sun and breeze dancing along my skin. I have not seen a single soul save for Alice and I thank the Goddess for this mercy. My power slowly grows inside me, but my body feels weak. I was lonely in my village, but nothing compares to the endless cycles of days in this tower.

And the stupid prince… I don't know if I care about that anymore. Everything is too chaotic for me to remotely consider Aramis in any capacity.

Scratch. Scratch. Scratch.

I turn and face the door, but the hallway beyond through the small window is cast in darkness. "Hello? Is someone there?" I hate the pang of hope that rises in my chest.

Who would come and rescue me?

"Great. It's probably rats," I mumble to myself, shivering involuntarily. Rats brought nothing but disease and trouble. Letting out a deep sigh, I turn back to the frosty window and extend my hand outward. The scent of pine and winter air wafts in, filling my nostrils. I watch as the delicate snowflakes softly brush against my skin, creating a cold, tingly sensation and hear the muffled sounds of laughter and chatter coming from outside down in the courtyard.

I peer out at the land, slowly becoming blanketed in a soft white. Servants quickly race across the grounds like tiny ants from where I watch in the tower. A few guards exchange blows in the practice yard. Even if I could escape through the window, I'd never be able to climb down the side of the tower.

Again, I hear a scratching noise, followed by a metallic thump. I walk cautiously to the door, drawing on my power. My forehead tingles as my horn manifests. I have yet to regain enough power for a full transformation, but if they come for me, I am not going down without a fight. Pressing my body against the smooth wood of the door, I push up on my toes and peer through the barred window, but I am met with only the darkness of the stairwell.

"Great. It's rats, or I am losing my sanity." I lean my cheek against the door, inhaling the stale scent, when something cold and metallic shoves against my foot.

"Ow!" I step back and glance down at the antique brass key that has slid under my door. "This can't be…"

I kneel on the cold stone as I slide the key towards me. The metal is cold as frost bites into my delicate skin, but I clutch it to my chest before peering under the door. Two familiar beady eyes stare back at me through the crack.

"Lemon! You sneaky rascal!" I quickly slide the key into my side of the door and turn the lock. I don't realize I am holding my breath until I hear the click of the metal and the door swings open with a deep groan. I lean forward and scoop my ferret up in my arms, crushing him against my chest. Kissing his soft head, tears flow silently down my cheeks.

"I thought I'd lost you forever. Where have you been hiding?" I hold him before me and look into his eyes. He cocks his head to the side, his only response. Glancing around the room, I realize that if I want to escape, I need to go now before Alice comes with breakfast. The sky is already turning shades of purple and pink.

Lemon pushes his cold nose against the palm of my hand, then looks down towards the door. He still wears the small leather pouch around his body with my family's crest ring. I pull it out then slide it over the index finger of my left hand, marveling as the metal slowly reshapes to fit perfectly snug.

"Well, that's unexpected. Thanks boy," I whisper to Lemon. I drop a kiss on his nose in thanks. "What would I do without you?" Lemon licks my cheek in response, and I laugh as I

deposit him in my skirt pocket. Glancing one last time at my
prison, I quickly pull on the soft slippers at the foot of my bed.
An idea dawns on me and I stuff the pillows under my blanket
to make it appear I am asleep.

Goosebumps raise along my arms as I slowly creep down
the stone stairwell. I rub my arms, willing warmth into them
as I try to envision the hallway that leads to the back gardens.
My teeth chatter as I move further away from the warmth of
my fireplace. If the Goddess looks favorably on me, perhaps I
will find a pair of boots and a cloak before venturing outside. I
shudder, imagining the early winter's chill this time of year, but
enduring the cold is a challenge I am willing to take if it means
leaving this demonic place behind.

My lungs burn by the time I reach the bottom of the stairs.
I am more out of shape than I realized. The chattering of
voices from down the hall has me pressing back against the
wall. My heart beats furiously in my chest as I hold my breath,
listening as the voices fade as they turn into another hallway. I
wipe my sweaty palms against my skirt. That was close. Lemon
pokes his head out of my pocket and squeaks at me.

"Sorry, boy." I gently stroke his head before daring to
lean out the archway. The girls' voices have gone to the left,
presumably to the kitchen or servants' hallway. While I do not
think many of the servants would recognize me, I don't want
to risk running into Alice.

I step into the hallway and turn right. There is no one
in sight. Keeping my head bowed low, I hurry through the
passageway, retracing the same steps I had taken when Kieran
had led me back from the gardens. If I can make it outside,
there is a chance I can escape into the forest and improvise
from there. My magic has been slowly returning, there is a
chance I could shift. Picking up my pace, I continue down the
hallways; left, right, and left again.

"The Queen grows restless. She's been taking out her

frustration on—" A male's voice speaks from the hallway I have just turned out of.

"Be quiet, lest one of her spies overhears, and she takes it out on you." Another male replies. My heart races as the icy grip of fear coils in my gut, leaving me frozen in place. I am no better than a deer in the forest with a hunter's eyes burning holes into my back. As quietly as I can, I force my feet to keep moving on, but as I round another corner, I slam face first into a warm and familiar chest.

As I stumble back a step, my heart races with fear, and I lose my balance. His arm lunges out, and a rush of air envelopes me as his hand catches me around the waist. The sound of my gasp fills the air as he pulls me close. I can smell the faint scent of him as the warmth of his grip burns into my skin through the thin fabric of my gown. I tilt my head up and meet Aramis's familiar icy blue gaze.

"Sybil?" Concern and surprise spark across his face. A moment later, his expression turns back to a stony coldness.

"Aramis. I—" My mouth is agape as I stand there, at a loss for words. The silence is deafening, only broken by the faint sound of our breathing. I find myself unable to break my gaze from his.

"What are you doing here?" he says as he looks from the hallway beyond me to Nero beside him.

"N-nothing," I stutter, trying to pull out of his grip.

I'm too confused, too lonely to sift through my heart. Not after everything I've learned. Whatever draw I have to him must just be because he's the prince, which means I need to pull myself together. He doesn't say a word, but his fingers tighten around my waist as he takes in the look of my bruised body after weeks of malnourishment and abuse. Even if my soul knows better, there's something in the touch that beckons me. A brush of wind moves my hair away so he can assess the sharp lines of my face and neck, the action swiftly pulling down my walls, even if I don't want it to. My lips part at the familiarity. Aramis' gaze widens slightly at the severity of change over my physique.

"Who did this to you?" Aramis questions, his tone stern, but edged with concern. "You're nothing but skin and bones. Where–"

"Ah, your highness. I'm so glad you apprehended her. I was about to alert the guards that the rabid shifter escaped the tower." Kieran's smooth diplomatic voice comes from behind me. His icy fingers settle along the back of my neck, causing the hair along my scalp to prickle. My limbs suddenly feel heavy as lead, my eyelids drooping as a sensation of calm passes over me.

Aramis glances up at Kieran and a muscle ticks in his jaw. "We are just returning from our mission. Unfortunately, we got there too late. Again." Anger lacing his words directed towards Kieran. He is talking about Larnwick. Should I do it? Tell him about the Queen? What if Aramis already knows and I look like a fool once more?

Then again, I owe the shifters of Shadowvale. If their prince truly doesn't know, then surely I need to find a way to tell them about the attacks and Triscilla's plans.

"Well, isn't that a shame? What will your mother think, coming back empty-handed?" Kieran's hand moves and clasps around my elbow. Panic fills my veins.

"She's not my mother." Aramis's fingers do not loosen their grip on me. "Where are you taking Sybil? Surely her trial should have concluded days ago. Why is she still here?" His voice filled with wrath.

I gather all the courage I have left and try to pull out of Kieran's grip. "Aramis you need to know the tru—" I shout, but my words are cut short as another wave of extreme calm washes over me, so strong this time that I start slipping into a trance, completely conscious but with no control over my own body.

"Mother—stepmother." Kieran shrugs, ignoring me. "It matters little. She is our queen and thus mother to the whole kingdom and to answer your question, we are still assessing the case of this particular prisoner. In the meantime, the queen ordered me to move her to the dungeon with the other shifters." The seer pulls on my elbow with more force, but Aramis refuses to relinquish his grip.

"Why?" He asks through gritted teeth, his body tense like a predator ready to jump on his prey. Nero shuffles restlessly behind him, the sound of his boots scraping against the ground echoing through the quiet hall as he lays his hand along the hilt of his sword at his waist.

"Are you questioning a direct order from the queen? You know she has a tendency to punish the people you care about when you do not cooperate, Prince Aramis." My mind swims like I'm stuck in a fog from the magic binding me, barely registering the scowl on Keiran's face as everything blurs in and out of focus.

"Your highness, if I may," the seer continues. I stare at the stone floor, breathing heavily as I try my best to focus. "I'd suggest you do not worry yourself with political matters such as this. This woman is just another criminal, and your focus is better spent on finally eradicating the rebellious threat from these lands." Aramis's hold tightens around my waist. "After all, as crowned prince, the safety of the kingdom of Shadowvale should be your only priority," Kieran says with a courteous smile that does not reach his eyes and bows his head. Aramis's nostrils flare at the disrespect neatly masked under false politeness, and I know he is using every ounce of self control he possesses to not to rip the seer's head off his body. "And please, your grace, do not forget to take your guard dog with you. It would do no good to scare the help at such early hours of the morning," Kieran spits in Nero's direction, disgust written all over his face, but the guard simply smirks, unruffled by the insult.

Aramis takes a step forward, my body so close to his now that my nose gently brushes his leathers, the scent inviting through my stupor. He towers over me and leans towards Kieran, his eyes narrowing. "Do not think for a second that you hold any real power within these walls simply because Tricella has a soft spot for your useless visions. I would have thrown you into the gutters years ago. The royal guard will no longer act in accordance with whatever it is that you see." Each word is measured and deliberate, laced with a chilling calmness that sends shivers down my spine.

"As you wish, your grace," is Kieran's only response, and if Aramis's threat has affected him in any way, he does not show it. Aramis hesitates one more second before he reluctantly lets go, and with one final curtsey, Kieran forces me to turn away. My steps are unsteady as we march down a set of stairs to our left, my hand gliding against the cold stone walls for balance.

Even though my mind may be altered, I swear his icy blue eyes burn holes into my back as we descend.

SYBIL

The cell door slams in my face, the sharp clang of the cold metal bars echoing through the dimly lit room and his power over me instantly washes away. Leaning forward, I grip the bars tightly, the rough texture scraping against my skin.

"Why are you helping her?" I stare vehemently at Kieran standing before me, most of my cognizance returning now that we're alone. Red-hot anger bubbles and churns inside my stomach, like a boiling cauldron, making me clench my teeth tightly together. I raise my fist, and with a sudden burst of fury, I slam it hard against the bars. The impact sends a sharp pain through my hand and a jolt through my arm. "How can you condone her actions?" I can smell the metallic tang of blood on my fist and the salty tang of tears as they well up in my eyes.

I had only been two turns away from freedom.

My fury dissipates into an icy, bitter feeling in my stomach and I wonder why the Goddess hindered my escape. Do I deserve this ending? This punishment? Meeting Aramis in those halls had felt like salvation, but the moment he let his arm fall from around my waist and watched as Kieran dragged me away, I felt my heart shatter.

"Oh, love." Kieran laughs coldly before reaching through the bars like a viper, gripping my chin in an iron grip and pulling me towards him. I flinch as the metal scrapes against my cheeks. "This tendency of yours, to always hope to find something good in people will get you killed one day. I am the seer to Queen Tricella. Her greatest confidante. I have seen the world she will create and it is glorious." He has lost his usual composure, his eyes now wild and unsettling. "Power like you cannot even fathom will be ours, and there is nothing I am not willing to sacrifice to ensure her vision becomes reality, so why would I let the most precious thing she's sought for over 100 years escape?"

My fists ball and I pull back my arm, preparing to slam into his most sensitive parts but he uses his magic once more to force me into submission. My muscles relax of their own accord and it's all I can do to keep upright.

"But the garden," I whisper as I stare over his face, trying to gleam any semblance of goodness in him. "You ordered the poison to be left out of my food and drink. You helped me."

"You were starving yourself!" He shouts in my face. His thumb lifts to trace my bottom lip, and I recoil from his touch. "You were withering away to nothing and your power was not manifesting. You're no good to us if you're dead or unhappy." He lifts his free hand to my shorn hair which has grown back just past my shoulders and grips it tightly. Through the bars, he leans in close so that our faces are just inches apart. The warmth of his breath envelopes my face with the sour stretch of ale laced with the hazy, powdery floral undertone of opium poppy. I lift my brows in surprise.

"You expect me to be your prisoner? Drain my powers over and over again but you also want me to be happy? Unicorns are meant to be free to canter in the fields under the stars. I do not belong locked up in a dungeon in a kingdom hundreds of miles away from my home." I sneer, my nose

144

wrinkling up as I reach out and weakly grip the front of his mage robes. "From the scent on your breath, I know you are unhappy yourself or in great pain to be self medicating with opium."

"You know nothing. You are nothing but a poor half-trained peasant from Kallistar. Your only use is the power and happiness you provide my queen. Until your usefulness wears out." He scoffs and roughly lets go of my chin. I lose balance and careen towards the dirty stone floor littered with moldy straw. My head hits the stone with a resounding crack. Lights flash in my periphery as I stare up at him, smiling at my prostrate form. He takes a shuddering breath, raking a hand through his tidy, swept back hair before straightening his robe.

"You will be the means to get what I have always yearned for. I have foreseen it." With these last parting words, he turns and walks away from my cell, his long silk robes whispering against the floor. I descend into unconsciousness with one final thought.

I'm going to die.

My head is pounding as I'm awakened by the sounds of a child crying and a warm tongue licking my cheek. I can hear water droplets fall one by one in the distance, echoing through the silence. I squint, trying to adapt my vision to the low light. The dampness in the air is palpable, the musty odor of the surrounding area penetrating my nostrils. A chill dances across my skin, perhaps due to the coldness of the atmosphere or the eerie stillness of the surroundings.

Where am I?

I raise a hand to the back of my head and wince at the pain. My fingers gingerly brush across my tangled hair, matted with the familiar sticky viscosity of drying blood. I palpate the tender flesh, nausea roiling in my stomach from the pain, but I don't feel the crepitus crackles that would indicate I had fractured my skull. Small blessings, but I had likely sustained a concussion. Pushing myself slowly into a sitting position and drawing my knees up to my chest, I wipe my dirty fingers on the hem of my skirt. Lemon scampers up the fabric and nestles his body between my chest and legs.

"It's okay, boy. We tried and we can try again." The singular light source is the flickering orange hue from a small torch down the hall. The pungent aroma of neglected flesh and stagnant bodily fluids mingled with the musty scent of decaying hay assaults my every breath. Muffled sounds of groans and moans echo off the walls, creating an eerie cacophony of despair.

"We don't need a prince on a white horse to save us. It's up to us to be the hero in our own story." I whisper into his furry head with a kiss.

Voices whisper from the cell across from mine. The tones are quiet but shrill, as though their owners can't be more than children. Rising to my feet, I move towards the bars and peer into the darkness. Two pairs of glowing eyes stare back at me, only broken by their occasional blinking.

"Hello?" I whisper hesitantly, as my brain conjures images of different monstrous creatures they have locked down in the dungeons with me. A shudder runs down my spine as I think of the countless beasts known for luring their victims with an innocent voice or the promise of riches and sweets. The eyes disappear into the darkness behind the other cell's bars. The whispering stops and only silence responds.

"Who is in there? My name is Sybil. I will not hurt you." My body slides down to the ground as a wave of exhaustion and dizziness hits me. Leaning the side of my face against the cool bars, I close my eyes and take a deep breath.

What I want is my mother, and to ask her what to do.

But thanks to the queen, my parents are long departed

from this world.

Licking my lips, I decide to recant a story my mother once told me. I won't let their deaths be in vain, and for that, I need a distraction. "Once upon a time, there was a maiden who was kidnapped and trapped in a tall tower…" My eyes roll at the similarities to my current situation. "Locked in the tower with only books and birds for company, she would spend all day reading. She yearned to be free and go on adventures outside of the ones in her books, find a handsome beau, and spend her days free in the sunshine. Days passed, turning into weeks, but her captors underestimated her heart and determination. The maiden grew strong in will and mind as she bid her time, waiting for her chance. It didn't take long as she made a ladder from rags and twine, then climbed down to freedom. As she walked through the forest, she met a young man."

My heart clenches at the thought of Aramis. How would our story have ended if he had not started out as my kidnapper but just as a man crossing my path in the forest in Bellevue? Taking a deep breath, I shake my head to banish thoughts of him before continuing the story. He did nothing to stop Kieran.

"Together they talked, laughed and learned about the world they wanted to create. The maiden's mind and heart, he quickly earned." I scoff at myself. If only people were so easily swayed.

"But he wasn't just an ordinary man, but the prince of the land. She wasn't just a pretty face; her intelligence, inspirations and love he couldn't replace. He knew he'd found his match, his equal in mind, spirit, and heart. They fell in love, and it was true. The prince loved the maiden, through and through. They lived happily ever after." I finish the story and peek open an eye to see two identical faces watching me with glazed, far away expressions. Dark brown hair frames their dark orange and brown complexion. Two furry ears poke between the matted strands, twitching restlessly as faint striped tails whip behind them. Shifter children who have not gained full control of their power often settle in an in-between state of humanoid features and their creature aspects. They are the shifters Tricella has captured from the nearby villages to drain their powers.

"Well, hello there, little ones." I paint a gentle expression on my face as I peer at them. Their noses quiver and I watch their bodies tense as if readying to scamper back into the dark. Lemon pokes his face between the bars and cocks his head at them, whiskers twitching. They giggle, then look at each other before turning back to us. More noses, ears and tails are poking out of the cell doors as if they too are listening to my story.

"How long have you been here?" I ask quietly. I am afraid the wrong question might send them scurrying away.

"I don't know. There were monsters, and so much smoke, yelling, and fires." One cub pipes up in a squeaky little voice, her twin nodding in agreement.

The scrape of boots and muffled voices down the hall drags my attention away from the children.

"The queen wants the most recent group brought up to her for inspection." A deep, gruff voice says.

"The women and children?" Another voice responds.

"Yeah, from the recent raids. You should have seen the look on Aramis's face when he had to report that the town was vacated. He has no idea the games his stepmother plays with him." A deep grunt, as though one was jabbed in the side, then the footsteps continue.

"Hush. The queen will have your tongue. She has eyes and ears everywhere. Do you reme–" Two guards I do not recognize walk down the hall, the polished handles of their broadswords gleaming in the torchlight. They pull up to my cell and leer down at me. Between their legs, I see the two tiger shifter cubs have disappeared back into the corner of their cell.

"Well, what do we have here?" One of them whistles in a low cat call. Chills creep up my spine as I stare up at their smearing faces. I bare my teeth at them as one cups his groin through his pants and winks at me. I shudder at the thought of his calloused hands touching me. The sound of their crude laughter echoes around the dingy room.

"I'd like to have my turn with this one before we send the next lot to the mines."

"Isn't she the one the Queen has been looking for? Look at her forehead. Kieran would nail our hides to the wall." He glances warily down either side of the hall as if speaking his name would draw his presence.

"Send who to what mines?" I ask as I push myself to a standing position. A wave of nausea and dizziness hits me and I throw out an arm towards the stone wall to brace myself. My hand squelches as it hits a thick gelatinous slime dribbling down the walls causing the guards to laugh loudly. Between the noise, the smell of the dungeon, and the sensation as my fingers envelope in the cold slip; I lose my battle with my nausea and vomit directly on the guard through the bars.

"You fucking bitch! You vomited on my uniform!" He bellows as he moves to slide his sword from his belt. The sound of a door slamming shut has his companion laying a hand on his arm. I don't take my eyes off the guards as I brace my body for a fight, wiping the slime on my skirt. I didn't know what it was, or how long it had been growing down here.

"Leave the dirty shifter alone for Kieran and the queen to deal with. It's not worth losing your head or job over." He grimaces as he glances down at his friend's ruined tunic and shrugs sheepishly before glancing between me and the sound of the slammed door.

"You'll get what you deserve, whore." The guard with brown hair stands before me, his face twists in disgust. With a loud and repulsive sound, he spits a thick glob of saliva on the ground, right by my feet.

"I am no male's whore. When I get free, you'll see exactly

who I am. I will serve the vengeance my people deserve." I laugh bitterly as I wipe my mouth with the back of my clean hand. The crackling flames of my fiery determination grow stronger. The flickering light dances on the faces of the innocent children across from me, casting long shadows on the grimy walls of their prison. The sound of their quiet sobs and muffled cries echoes in the damp, musty air. My heart races with a mix of anger and sorrow as I vow to protect these children and any others who have been wrongly imprisoned. I will find the camps they spoke of and free them, then take down this entire kingdom if I have to. I stand still, my eyes fixated on the guards' retreating backs as they disappear around the corner. The sound of their footsteps echo through the cold stone dungeon, making the hair on my arms stand on end. I clench my fists, relishing in the rough texture of the wall against my fingertips, as I let my anger fester.

Tricella thought she had caught a tame unicorn to siphon.

She will find there are reasons unicorns are both revered and feared.

ARAMIS

The clack of my boots reverberates off the cold, damp stones as I descend down to the dungeons. I can't get Sybil out of my thoughts since apprehending her yesterday. Her usual scent of tea, lavender and vanilla was completely marred by the smell of damp stone and sweat. If fear had a smell, there's no doubt it would coat her pale skin.

Seeing her so frail and scared, with her hair roughly cut and eyes empty of their usual light, had nearly driven me insane. I had promised her a fair trial and found her a shell of the woman I had retrieved from that cottage. Something is very wrong and I hate myself for not knowing what to do. Why am I so willing to sacrifice everything I have and everything I am to save her?

After presenting my report to both my father and Tricella the night before, I was determined to clear my mind of her. I tossed my shirt into the fire and submerged myself in the steaming water, but despite scrubbing my skin until it was raw and red, I could still feel and smell her. Even though she has been a prisoner for some time, I swear her lavender scent still lingers, as if my imagination can't release her. Never have I experienced fury such as when Kieran laid his filthy hands on her and I was ready to see the light leave his eyes for that one small gesture. Goddess knows I only stopped myself because Tricella would have undoubtedly claimed a life for a life and killed Nero or Edmund to punish me. In a desperate attempt to dull my senses, I drank a few drams of dark starlight before finally succumbing to a deep, fitful sleep. Visions of her hair caressing her cheek as she tilts her head in thought, her soft rosebud lips, and those damnable soft hands still plague my dreams. Shaking my head, I rake my fingers through my hair.

The unicorn must have cast a spell on me once Tricella unleashed her powers, it's the only way I can explain this obsession, this urge to make sure she is safe. Shifters are abominable creatures, only with animal instincts to fuck, kill, and conquer, I tell myself. My words ring false, even in my head, and I wonder why I keep trying to tell myself this, when I know Sybil has proven to be the only exception, demanding that I change my mind—that I do better.

"Why was she even free in the castle?" I question aloud as I turn the corner and proceed through another door, slamming it behind me. My movements are guided by an instinctive need to see her.

Another flight of stairs and over the reek of the dungeon. I smell the faint hint of her scent. My heart is pounding in my chest as I sprint toward the ominous entrance of her cell, but my steps grow heavy as I get a first glimpse at what lies behind the bars. Curled up in the muck, shivering from the cold and covered in dried blood, Sybil seems to be asleep. I slowly take a step forward, careful not to wake her. My breath comes out in ragged gasps, each exhale a silent prayer for her well-being. A low growling sound emanates from deep within me, reverberating through my chest as my eyes lay on her tear-streaked face in the dim light of the dungeon and time seems to freeze. A magnetic pull tugs at my gut, urging me to move closer. Every detail of her presence is magnified, as if the world around us has faded away and we are the only two beings left. In that moment, the air cracks and my heart, already racing with fear, now pulses with new found intensity.

This can't be. No. She is a shifter. She is nothing to me.

My knuckles turn white as I grip the bars of her cell, watching her. I can't seem to look away from the heartbreaking sight in front of me. Her thin gown is stained and ripped. My breath catches in my throat as shock and recognition wash over me.

Save her. Free her. Mate. My Mate—

The tug inside me demands. I recoil from the cell and quickly step back, cursing under my breath as my boot splashes in a puddle of fluid.

No. She can't be. But I feel the relentless insistence down to my very core. Mate.

Her eyes flash open, their hazel depths peering into my soul.

"Aramis," she says venomously. Her eyes are full of malice as she continues to stare.

"Sybil," I reply. My practiced speech and witty remarks fail me; a deadweight on my tongue.

She pushes herself up to a sitting position, a wince briefly flashing over her face. "Come to gloat, Prince of Shadowvale? You've managed to capture a scary group of—" she pauses, her breaths coming out in labored grunts as she pushes herself to stand unsteadily on her feet. She gestures towards the cell behind me. "Scared, defenseless men, women and children."

"They are rebel shifters and spies—" I begin weakly, before I spot a dark substance on the ground behind her. I can't tear my gaze away from the thick, sticky puddle of blood slowly drying on the floor of her cell. The crimson liquid seems to have seeped into the cracks and crevices, staining the stone a deep, rusted red. My gut boils with rage as I imagine the pain she must have endured, and that strange sensation tugs me towards her once again.

"Yes, yes, so you've told me. Rebel spies to sow dissent among your people and tear your kingdom down from the inside." Sybil spits her vitriol at me, reciting words I've said to her, over and over again. It's pure hatred, and I'm astonished at the rage coming from her. Did I sound like this when I said these words aloud? "Evil creatures bent on destruction and chaos. Look around you, your highness! Do these prisoners look like evil creatures bent on the destruction of your kingdom?" My title drips with sarcasm, and I'm forced to look at her.

The demand of her questions pulls on me, and I look at the shifters surrounding her. The hatred in her voice is forcing me to put my prejudices aside and truly look at the prisoners. Not as shifters, but children and women forced to survive in these dungeons in putrid conditions under the false pretense of a fair trial. Once again, Sybil makes me wonder if I've ever been the savior in this story, or only another villain.

But they are shifters. These people killed my mother—they have been organizing rebellion to tear down my family's legacy; our very kingdom. Sybil might be a victim, a wrongly accused suspect, but the shifters in these dungeons have reasons to be here. She cannot tell me that my life's mission is built on a lie.

"I have seen the destruction they have caused with my own eyes, Sybil. They are here because they have been found guilty of treason, of conspiring with the rebellion," I argue. Soulful eyes inquire mine, and I have to shut mine to stop the questioning.

"Do you even hear yourself? Look around you!" Sybil demands, and the pull to answer her, to fulfill her needs, overcomes me. I return her gaze. "Aramis, these people are not rebels. They are your people. Your citizens. Haven't you been wondering where the shifters disappear to after the raids you're endlessly trying to tidy up?"

154

How does she know this? "What business do you know–"

"Your queen is sending her lackeys off to kidnap the shifters! Kieran's visions are not focused on predicting rebel attacks. They scout for powerful shifters in nearby towns," Sybil cuts me off. "The Queen destroys their homes and drains them of their power, and when they're rendered useless, she disposes of them as she pleases!" Tears swell in her eyes. The desperation in her tone is like a slap to my face.

"You always arrive late at the attacks because they are not real. They send you to these towns once they are done with their destruction because they want to fuel the hatred this bloody kingdom has for shifters. There is no rebellion, Aramis. Just lies and a selfish bitch who wants to use shifter magic for herself."

Every word hits me like a brick. Doubts surface again in my mind. No, it can't be true... Stealing another's magic requires dark magic—forbidden magic that we have outlawed from Shadowvale. Tricella would never... or would she?

I exhale slowly, my head pounding under the weight of all these revelations. It's too much to endure–this can't be true. But the bond between us–the one I'm attempting to refuse, binds me to the truth of them. It's the honesty of Sybil's anger that I'm currently trying to defend against. She and I–we hold the same rage in our bodies, for entirely different reasons. I step back in denial at the power of those thoughts.

"This must be a falsehood—" I stammer. What is this hold she has on me? The impatient, demanding part of me that screams Sybil is using her magic against me–to entice me, fights the truth of her words. "This is just part of the deception you're weaving to escape." I lash out in anger. My hands clench at my sides. The words burst out, but they ring false, even to my own ears. This stupid, idiotic pull–the call of the mating bond crashes around me.

Fuck this. Sybil isn't my mate—she can't be. This isn't

happening. And if she's right, everything I've ever known has been a lie. My entire purpose to end the rebellion and to save my people is all a fucking lie. Thoughts of my mother's assassination hit me. What of this hatred that has been weaved into my entire reason and purpose? Goddess help me—I don't know what to do. My chest clenches as panic rises inside, warring between denial and need.

"Why would I lie? I'm trapped in a cell," Sybil speaks, not missing a beat. She looks around her and gestures to the people she's imprisoned with. "Your stepmother continues to drain my power to fill hers and preserve her youth and beauty. Hasn't she looked particularly glowing since you brought me to your castle?" She turns away, facing the wall, her back straight and head held high. A queen in her own right. "In the brief time I've known you, I have always hoped there was more to you. Something hidden behind this cruel facade you put up and at times, I thought I had managed to crack it and see the real you. Do you remember when you gave me the pomme d'argent? That moment stays with me, all the time. But I was wrong. You are so blinded by the lies you keep telling yourself. I don't think you even know who you are."

That moment stays with me, all the time. I stiffen at the mention of those sweet moments we shared. "You know nothing of me," I reply coldly, bottling down the urge to use my powers to rip the iron door out of the wall and carry her out. "And I was just doing my duty. There was and is nothing between us. " I step closer to the iron doors and abruptly halt. Don't be an idiot. I chastise myself. Walk away. Now.

Our gazes lock. The air is an electrical storm around us. I can't help but wonder if she too has felt that tug I am desperately trying to ignore.

I turn, heading straight to the training grounds. This was a mistake. I shouldn't have come. The answers I sought have only turned into more questions.

"Taking it out pretty hard on that dummy, aren't ye?" Nero leans against the outer stone wall of the castle. Flurries of snow flutter around on a breeze, the chill cutting into my cheeks like razors. My muscles ache with an intense heat, as if each fiber is engulfed in flames.

"Go. Away. Nero." I pant as I continue to slam my fists into the straw filled body hanging from the post. My knuckles are swollen, pulsing with a throbbing pain that echoes through my entire hand. Blood oozes from the wounds, dripping slowly onto the ground with a sickening sound as I move forward, throwing punch after punch. The stench of sweat and exertion fills my nostrils, but it's not enough to overpower the lingering scent of her.

"If ye need to take yer frustration out over what happened the other night, maybe ye should pick on someone more yer own skill and size." His feet scrape across the dirt floor of the training ground. We've been sparring in this small training ring outside the east side of the castle since we were boys.

Turning my body, I catch the sword he tosses before it slams into the back of my head.

"Do nae tell me yer getting old and slow on me now?" Nero jests as he performs a flashy flourish, twirling his sword in the air before striking towards me.

"Old?" I question as I fall into a defensive fighting stance. I can see the glint of my sword as it clashes with the other, the sunlight bouncing off the metal and creating a dazzling display. The clash of steel sends a resounding whistle through the air, echoing off the walls and sending shivers down my spine. The smell of sweat and metal fills my nostrils as I focus on the rhythm of our movements, the dance of battle. "If I recall, it was you who was complaining about your aching backside and needing to soak your weary bones when we returned to the castle."

He lunges at me, his eyes locked onto mine. I raise my sword just in time to parry his attack, the clash of metal ringing in my ears. The force of his strike sends shockwaves down my arm, the weight of his attack almost too much to bear.

"Ah, but I already had two lovely lasses fighting over who would get to scrub my back. What male would turn that down?" He retorts as he advances on me with a slash to my weak side. I parry as I swivel on my left foot, kicking my right in an attempt to trip him. He nimbly jumps out of the way, a wicked grin plastered across his face.

"No retort, Aramis?" He stabs and narrowly misses as the edge of my sword deflects his. "Jealous?"

"Jealous? What would I have to be jealous of?" A surge of excitement well within me as I lunge towards him with a swift motion. The sound of our boots scraping against the ground echoes in my ears. A broad grin appears on my face as I push him back, feeling the resistance in his body. The energy of the moment courses through me, and I relish in the thrill of the fight.

"That I left yer poor ass alone for prettier company," he replies. He deftly parries every attack I throw his way with ease, sidestepping my every move with eloquence.

"Who taught you to dance like a girl with a sword?" I pant as he lunges towards me, the tip of his sword slicing through the fabric of my sleeve.

Fueled by his near hit, I take advantage, feigning to his left and slash while simultaneously sending a powerful push of my air magic against him. He grunts as he barely blocks my attack, his balance thrown off by the force of the gale. His eyes light up with a sparkle of flame, his teeth flashing as those same flames start dancing along the fingertips of his free hand.

"Oh, you want to play with magic? Two can play that game." He dances around, swinging his sword with another flourish. He shakes his head, sweat trickling down his tanned forearms. Heat fills the air between us. My lungs are burning from the exertion of our duel, but my lips curl up at his taunting invitation.

"I win, and you scrub my chambers for a week." I call the wind to me, swirling around my left forearm into an invisible shield.

"An' if I win?" Nero lifts an eyebrow.

"As if you will beat me. What do you want if you win, old man?" We exchange a few more blows and parries.

"If I win, ye tell me what is on yer mind. Ye haven't been yourself lately. I can't recall the last time ye've drunk yourself to sleep." Concern laces his voice as he quickly counterattacks my parry. The cold stone castle wall hits my back, and the tip of his sword pierces the front of my shirt. His deep brown eyes pierce mine and I am forced to look away, knocking his sword to the side. The rough stone scratches through my shirt as I slide down the wall to the ground. A cloud of dust wafts up as he sits beside me.

"It's nothing." I close my eyes, evading him.

"It's nae nothing. I've keen you for over a hundred years, Aramis." His eyes bore into me.

"It's Sybil." I sigh and stare at the blue sky above us filled with dark gray clouds, heavy with the promise of snow.

"What of Sybil?" He tenses up, his breath becoming shallow and rapid.

I pause and glance at my friend. His furrowed brow and down-turned mouth betray his concern. We have known each other since we were boys and I trust him with my life. But I am not sure if I even trust my own feelings.

"I'm not quite sure where to begin." I rub at my temples. I can still feel that tug deep inside. "I can't stop thinking about her, smelling her, seeing her in my dreams. I vowed the night my mother died at the shifter's hands that I would not forgive them for trying to take down my kingdom." I rub at my chest, willing the sensation to go away. Not even drinking myself stupid has been enough to stop this growing pull. "I don't know if she's cast some sort of spell on me, but I just can't stop. They have her locked up in the East dungeon with the other shifters." The image of her lying unconscious on the stone, her hair plastered to her head with drying blood, fills my mind. I lift a hand and rub at my forehead.

"Wait. They have Sybil in the East dungeon?" He quickly rises to his feet, his dark brows furrowing. "I apologize, my lord. But I forgot I have an urgent matter to attend to." With that, he swiftly turns and walks away, leaving me puzzled over my emotions and his strange behavior.

SYBIL

stare at the tray pushed through the small slot of my cell door hours ago. Calling the contents in the small weathered bowl food would be considered criminal. The dubious, thick, gelatinous gray sludge quivers slightly, as if it were alive. I shiver, imagining how it might come for me in my nightmares. A putrid smell emanates from it, like the stench of a decaying animal. Beside it lies a hard roll covered in a mold that reminds me of sickly green fur. The overall scene is terribly repulsive and makes me nauseous just being in its presence. I close my eyes, haunted by the images and sounds of the cubs greedily slurping at the meal, nipping, and growling at each other for the last scrape.

They don't deserve this. I don't deserve this. What is to come of us?

After Aramis departed, I scoped out my cell, looking for any weaknesses. They placed spells on the iron bars, repelling any magical attempts I made, trying to coax them open. But all that came from that pitiful attempt was an aching head.

Goddess help us.

I kick the bars, letting out a string of profanity. I'm so fucking tired of not being able to accomplish anything of worth.

The sound of a door gently opening and closing makes me pause my pacing. My mind wanders back to Aramis. It seems like days have passed since I last saw him, his expression full of shock and hatred as he observed the state I was in. He probably thought I got what I deserved, what any shifter deserves. A part of me can't help but hope my words have fuelled the few doubts he already had about the Queen's intentions, if not for my sake then for that of all the other shifters suffering in these cells. Maybe he will re-evaluate his certainties.

I strain to listen as quiet, deliberate steps make their way down the hall.

What if it's Kieran, back to bring me to the queen for another 'session'?

My body temperature suddenly rises at the thought, leaving my skin hot and clammy. Unsteady on my feet, tremors run from my fingertips down to my toes and my heart seems to pound fast and hard. I take a deep breath and attempt to calm myself, but my chest tightens, and my breathing is quick and shallow. The world around me seems to shrink, my vision turning hazy; stars blinking on the periphery.

You're dying, the voice in my head says. This is what death feels like, and you're going to die alone.

"No!" I throw my arms out, grabbing the iron bars of my cage. The surrounding walls are closing in, inch by inch, from all directions. It's getting harder to breathe as the space around me continues to shrink. Each breath takes more effort than the last, as if the air itself is being squeezed out of my lungs. Panic sets in as I realize there's nowhere to go, no escape from this suffocating space. The walls continue to press in, unrelenting.

I will not go out like this!

Tears stream down my face as I clench my eyes tightly together. I force myself to take deep breaths, imagining my mother as she talks to one of her patients through a panic attack. I'd never had a panic attack before, but this must be what one feels like.

"Sybil." A rich male's voice breaks through my spiraling thoughts and memories.

"Sybil, get up. We have to go. Now." The urgency in his voice confuses me. It reminds me of my father, but he died over ten years ago. I slowly open my eyes, blinking away the tears as I peer through the bars.

"Come Sybil." The deep tenor resonates in me, and I recognize the tone. "We need to go. Now." He commands.

I know this voice.

"Nero?" I question from the ground, my tear filled vision clearing. He glances in both directions, then back at me. Taking a key ring from his pocket, he slides it into the lock. The door opens with a click, groaning slightly as he pulls it open. "What's going on? What are you doing down here?"

I remain stunned on the ground looking between him, the open cell door, and down the hall. He reaches out a hand.

This must be a hallucination or a trap. It must be, because why would he want to help me?

"We have nae time for questions. I'll explain everything later." Nero gently grips my forearm, but my body is too out of sync to make the progress to stand. Nero pulls me to my feet, steadying me. "We have nae time to linger, do ye understand? Come!" He throws a dark, thick cloak around my shoulders, quickly buttoning it around my throat and pulling the hood over my head.

"But. What—" I quickly register what is happening and glance at the cell behind him. Two pairs of eyes blink at me from the darkness.

"Do ye want to escape, or stay here as Queen Tricella's personal power reserve?" He hisses, tugging roughly at my hands in the opposite direction of the hall that he came from.

"You knew?" I glare directly in Nero's eyes, pulling out of his grasp. "What about the other shifters? Did you know about them?" I cross my arms over my chest, resolute in my stance. I am not going anywhere until I have more answers.

"Sybil, this is nae the time to be stubborn! Of course, I know about them but we cannot help them at the moment. Ye are my priority right now."

I raise my brows at him in disbelief. "Really!?" What a callous, son of a—

"I am working with the rebels to free them," Nero replies gently. Uncertainty crosses over his face as he watches my utter disregard and disbelief.

"The rebels don't exist. The Queen made it all up. I don't trust you, you are lying to me," I say, frustration lacing my every word. How is it possible that every person in this kingdom is corrupt?

I take a step away from him, weighing my options. There is no way I'm trusting my life with him–no matter how friendly we've been with each other. His kindness to me could just lead me to a trap. I'm light on my feet and he doesn't possess wind magic like Aramis does. If I get a head start, there is a chance I can outrun him. I have to try.

"Ugh. Stubborn females." Nero grumbles under his breath. "That's what ye are–ye keen that, right?" He roughly pushes back his hood. "Fine. Ye want to know why ye ken trust me? Take a look at this." His eyes take on a glow of living flame, iridescent blue and purple scales manifesting up his neck and the skin of his face.

A fire drake.

A gasp leaves my lips. The sound of my breath echoes through the quiet room, the only noise breaking the silence. The sharpness of the moment is palpable, like a knife cutting through the stillness.

I knew it.

"You're a—" I gasp, leaning in to touch his forearm. "Nero—you're—"

"I ken what I am," Nero grabs my wrist to guide me out of the dungeons. "Let's go. Be quiet. We can nae afford questions now. If we run into anyone, act docile. If they ask questions, I'm escorting ye to the queen's private chambers." Nero grabs a torch from his belt and lights it from the sconce on the wall before heading down the dark hallway.

As we make our way through multiple halls and stairways, each one guiding us deeper into the depths of the castle, we come across a chilling sight. The cells we pass by are completely empty, except for the presence of iron chains hanging from the walls and the floors covered in decaying bones. Continuing down another hall, we encounter wide metal doors, devoid of any adornments except for a small window near the floor, just large enough to slide a tray under. This raises an intriguing question: What kind of creatures could possibly necessitate the use of such formidable iron doors, reinforced with powerful spells to keep them securely locked inside?

We cross through another set of doors when Nero sweeps his arm out across my chest. The stone wall collides with my back, sending a jolt of pain through my body that knocks me breathless as he pins me. The flame of his torch extinguishes, leaving us in darkness. He pushes his warm body up against mine, covering us both with his cloak, and lifts a finger to my lips in warning. I hear the faint sounds of voices talking up the path ahead. Trembling, I force myself to take small, even breaths.

I can't be caught again.

There is a tingle of magic in the air. My jaw drops as I slowly watch his body and my hands take on a translucent appearance. Panic grips my gut and I push towards his solid chest, a reassurance that he is still there. His steady heart beats under my palms, as real as my own.

What is this magic?

I'm torn between fascination and fear as I listen to the approaching guards. The light of their torches dances along the walls as they get closer, then turns down walking straight towards us and my eyes widen as I watch them approach.

Nero presses his body tighter against me, as if willing us both to melt into the wall. How is this even possible? I am in awe and incredibly scared of the magic I have witnessed since leaving my home. There is so much I've yet to discover, so much to live for. Before me, Nero shifts, raising his hand as I watch the guards' torches flicker and dim, casting us further in darkness.

"Fuck Roy! What was that?" One of the guards shouts with a glance at his torch.

"I don't know, but being down here near the catacombs always gives me the creeps," Roy replies, visibly shivering. "I heard a rumor that the ghosts of the kings and queens of the past haunt these halls. I can't wait until we aren't on this shitty new recruit duty anymore. Let's go." They quicken their pace, passing by us without a second glance. Once they are out of earshot, Nero steps away. I exhale and rub my arms, attempting to vanquish the coldness that's seeping into my skin.

"What was that?" I ask.

"I just made us invisible." Nero answers as if it's the most normal thing in the world, a quirk turning his lips into a smile. He relights the torch with a snap and continues down the path.

"What happened to, 'I'm going to pretend you're a prisoner being delivered to the queen'?" My tone is full of doubt, but I hurry, nevertheless, to keep up with his long strides. Pulling my cloak tighter around my body, I'm grateful for its thick warmth as the temperature has dropped several degrees in our descent.

"Plans change," he says curtly. "Here, hold this." Handing me the torch, he pulls out another set of keys as we reach an enormous rusty iron door. Based on the number of cobwebs and dust coating it, I doubt anyone has opened it in years.

"What other tricks and secrets do you have up your sleeves?" I raise a brow in question.

He peers over his shoulder, his teeth gleaming mischievously in the light of the fire. "How do ye feel about corpses?"

The air is cool and still as we step into the darkness. Nero firmly pushes the wooden door closed, creating a loud thud that reverberates through the abandoned room. The sound of our breathing punctuates the silence that follows the noise, amplified by the emptiness of the room. The sudden movement disturbs dust, filling the air with the scent of stale, musty earth. As the particles settle, the feeling of unease settles in as the darkness envelops us, illuminated only by the faint light seeping in through the cracks in the door. My senses heightened by the eerie atmosphere. I wave my arm, clearing the air before me. Three domed archways shape the large room, with one directly in front of us and two on our sides.

"Welcome to the crypt, lass," Nero says with a flourish of his hand.

"A crypt," I repeat flatly, turning to face him. "Why would you bring us to a crypt? There is nothing here except dead ends and dead people."

"Aye, well, that is where ye are wrong, Sybil." He taps me on the nose and winks. "Luckily for ye, I happen to ken this particular crypt has a secret exit. When Aramis and I were little lads—'"

I shove my hands into his chest, my blood boiling with rage. Goddess, grant me the patience I need to deal with this bullshit.

"I don't want to hear some story about when you and his

royal highness were children. If you knew about the exit, why haven't you freed my people? Our people?" I narrow my eyes at him as I shove him once more.

"Sybil–" Nero protests. "Come on. It's just a—"

"How about we begin with why you have been assisting the arresting, and locking up our people in these dungeons in the first place?" I let my fueled anger lace every word. He grips my forearm in argument and I buck out of his grasp. The audacity of this asshole is incredible. My horn materializes on my forehead, my vision slowly sharpening using the little magic I am able to conjure. My heart beats faster as adrenaline rushes through my veins, causing my hands to shake slightly as I continue to back away. But a wide smile spreads across my face, a mixture of shock and glee filling me as I revel in the comfort of my demi-form. It has been too long since I was in anything but my human shape, powerless and weak.

"Nae, Sybil, wait." Nero lifts his hands into the air. Scales form along his arms and up his neck, a living armor. "This is incredibly complicated, and this takes more than just a moment of conversation. I need ye to work with me here. Please? Just listen for a moment, and if I don't answer yer protests to yer satisfaction, ye can gouge me with that horn. I swear!"

Stepping back, I warily watch him. I still need him. I could get lost for hours or days if I tried to find the exit down here myself.

"Fine," I say, each word enunciated. "Explain yourself. And make it quick. You don't have a lot of time." I stamp my foot, tossing my hair over my shoulder.

"Aramis doesn't ken–" he pauses, his hands clenching at his sides "–yet."

"What do you mean he doesn't know yet?"

"I didn't ken I was half fire-drake until I was well into my maturity." Nero pauses, making sure I'm still listening. I arch my brows in doubt. Well? "Ma mother was a fire mage, a well-respected lady in the court," Nero continues. "My da was a traveling merchant and a draken. From what she says, it was love at first sight."

I tap my toe impatiently on the floor. I loved stories, but I had my people to free. Not to mention escaping.

"He begged her to go away with him, see the world, but she told him she had a role to play here in Shadowvale and to return to her to settle down. He died at sea during his final voyage. My mother did not even have a chance to tell him she was pregnant with me." Nero patiently explains. I furrow my brow in concentration. Where is this going?

"Aramis' mother was killed nearly a decade later, leaving us both without a parent, and essentially pushing us closer together. Rumors spread about a group of rebel shifters responsible for the assassination of the Queen, wanting to overthrow the long line of Elemental rulers in Shadowvale and have a seat at the royal table. But as always, rumors come and go. Until, to the shock of the court, the King announced his engagement to Tricella, and coincidentally, wild accusations of shifters attacking villages started resurfacing, igniting the tension between elemental and shifters. When I began showing signs of my fire ability, everyone chalked it up to inheriting my mother's powerful fire mage skills, but then I started exhibiting other odd abilities. My mother, in her attempt to protect me, told me everything about my father's real identity and made me swear to keep it a secret. As you can imagine, halflings don't have it easy in either community. By that time, Aramis and I were the best of friends. I was not only his deepest confidant, but sworn in to be his right hand."

I nod my head in acceptance, prompting him to continue with his story.

"Aramis doesn't ken my truth. For years, I was scared to tell him. How could I?" Nero laughs, clearly frustrated. He runs his fingers through his hair and sighs. "The rebel group exists,

Sybil, but it is not what Aramis believes it to be. It was created after Tricella became queen to protect the shifters from her attacks, from her demonic monsters. As a lady of the court, my mother, Evangeline, was among the firsts to uncover Tricella's machinations to stir chaos within the kingdom. She risked her life, her reputation, to warn the shifter community of Tricella's use of dark magic. My mother was an extraordinary woman, Sybil." A subtle, tender smile plays on Nero's lips, each word spoken with a gentle cadence, and I can feel his pain echo within my own heart.

"I've been working with the rebel group since my mother died twenty years ago, taking her place on their counsel. Despite being an Elemental, she had been deeply in love with a shifter and she had a halfling son, so she did everything she could to ensure I could live in a world where I would nae be persecuted for the natural color of my skin, or my race." His final words are accompanied by a ripple of magic as his skin takes on a deep purple blue, glittering with scales. There is a delicate sadness in his eyes but also determination radiating like an unyielding flame.

"I ken ye believe Aramis is just like his father and stepmother, but I swear to ye Sybil, he is nothing like them. His father was a great king until that witch Tricella came into the picture. All this mess. It's her fault. She corrupted his mind, convinced him the shifters killed his wife and attempted to kill his son just so she could take his throne. Aramis has had nothing but Tricella's poisonous words in his ears since he was a lad." Nero gently takes my hand and intently looks into my eyes. "But I see him, Sybil. I see the pain in his eyes every time we are sent to capture those innocent people. I just don't know how to help him see past the years of lies and deceit."

I know Nero is telling the truth, but changing Aramis's mind is no longer my responsibility. Goddess knows, I have allowed him to break my trust too many times. Within my heart, I know he will accept the truth that is right in front of him, if he only allows himself to be his authentic self , for once. Not the Aramis tormented by his duty, but the loving man that helped an orphaned kid and took him under his wing. The Aramis that gently laid next to me with worshiping eyes and solemnly told me I was brave, at a time when I only felt weak and pathetic. But I can no longer sit and wait. My responsibility now lies with all those children, men and women, unjustly tortured in the dungeons. My people. All my life I have been looking for a purpose and for the first time, I know what to do and I am not scared.

"Help me escape. Take me to the rebels."

SYBIL

Walking along the dimly lit corridor, my fingertips brush against the rough, icy surface of the stone wall. A cloud of dust fills the air, tickling my nose and causing me to sneeze. The sound echoes down the empty hallway, bouncing off the walls and fading into silence. The musty smell of old stone and dampness permeates the air, making me feel as though I have stepped into a forgotten place. Despite the chill in the air, the wall is oddly comforting beneath my fingers, as if it holds secrets waiting to be discovered. Each room contains a single, large, white marble coffin. The air seems to twirl with an otherworldly energy.

Do the dead still haunt these passageways?

"How much further?" I ask, watching Nero guide our passage through the catacombs. The echo of our footsteps as we rush from room to room, our only companion.

"We're almost there." Nero glances back at me. He pauses before the entrance of the room, narrowing his eyes in concentration, ready to confront any possible trouble that could be waiting for us. As soon as the room passes his inspection, he steps in, waving me to follow him.

I instantly notice how unique it is compared to the rest.

I pause, my gaze dragging from the meticulously clean floor, up the walls to the dark blue ceiling dotted with hundreds of painted constellations. Walking into the room gives the sensation of being transported into the night sky itself. I approach the white marble tomb and the coolness of the stone as I run my fingers over its smooth surface, pristine and gleaming in the torchlight is a stark contrast to the warmth of my hand. The magic here has a distinct energy that I have never felt anywhere else, and I can't help but wonder who was laid here to rest.

Who is buried here?

As my fingers run along the edge, I notice that the lid of the tomb sits askew. Nibbling at my bottom lip, I lay my palm against its flat surface. Kings and queens of old do not just wake up and climb out of their forever resting places. Shaking my head as my folly, I cast my eyes across the room. Intricately woven tapestries depicting lush forests and vibrant fields decorate the wall.

The designs are a feast for the eyes, with shades of green, brown, and blue blending together seamlessly to create a serene and peaceful atmosphere. I can almost hear the gentle rustling of leaves and the distant chirping of birds, transporting me to a tranquil, natural haven. A faint scent of freshly cut grass and blooming flowers lingers in the air, bringing a sense of freshness and vitality. Hand-stitched creatures seem to crawl across the weaving, giving it a sense of movement and life. My eyes settle on a small herd of what are unmistakably unicorns, their coats in different shades of white, brown, gray and black. I blink repeatedly in shock.

Why are my ancestors depicted in this tomb?

I lean forward to examine the artistry closer, and the faint scent of jasmine fills the air. My eyes close, my body swaying involuntarily. The scent is revitalizing after the tumultuous series of events settle on my shoulders. A lavish bed fit for royalty now lies before me where a cold and lifeless stone coffin once rested. The plush mattress is covered in midnight blue satin sheets, glimmering in the dim light of the room. The lush pillows are thick and overstuffed with down feathers, offering a soft and comfortable resting place for a weary head. The air is still and quiet, where no sound will disturb the peaceful atmosphere. As I approach the bed, I can't resist from running my fingers over the smooth fabric of the sheets, reveling in the luxurious texture. The stark contrast of the soft plush bed to the rough and unyielding stone that was there moments before eases my weary soul. My eyelids droop with the weight of exhaustion, as if they are being pulled down by a heavy blanket. My body is heavy and sluggish, as if I am moving through molasses. I sigh with content, knowing that I can finally rest.

"Welcome, child of Alpheaia," a woman's gentle voice says, which reminds me of my mother's soft lilt as she would start one of my healing lessons. The memory is a shock deep enough to flutter my eyelids open. "I have waited a long time for you. Come, rest for a moment. There is much I have to tell you, but I don't have much time."

Who is Alpheaia? Where is Mother?

A faint brush of wind runs over my hair, and I settle into the comforting gesture. I rub at the heavy ache in my chest as the recollection of my mother leaves. Taking a brief break can't hurt. I deserve it after all I've been through.

"Who are you?" I ask, stifling a yawn. I see nothing in the room but the luxurious bed and decorated walls. Where does that voice come from? I must be so tired that I'm hallucinating, or I have hit my head harder than I thought. I ignore a nagging sensation that I need to continue on.

"Sweet Sybil." The warm, familiar tones of the voice soothe me, amusement dancing in her voice. "I have gone by many names, but that is not important. You may call me Rose.

There is something important you need to know."

"Sybil!" The sound of Nero's voice is faint with worry. But it's coming from a distance, and I ignore him, turning back to Rose's voice. I feel safe sharing the burden with her.

"I am alone, hunted, and only half-trained." I yawn. "I've been taken away from all that I love and that's comforting. I don't offer much to anyone, so what could you possibly have been waiting for me for?" I mumble as I climb on top of the massive bed. A contented sigh escapes my lips, and I gently lay my head down on a plush pillow, the satin caressing my cheek. I can't remember the last time I felt so relaxed and comfortable.

"Child, now is not the time to sleep," Rose whispers urgently. "Sybil! Pay attention!"

"Huh?"

"Your journey has only begun. A great wrongness has been done to my kingdom. It needs to be healed." Rose continues whispering, deeply troubled. "You are the healer we have been waiting for. You must seek your training with the white witches in the forgotten library of Harpalyke."

Why is she tempting me with dreams I've long cherished?

"Sybil!" Nero's voice is louder, urgent. Why is he yelling? Doesn't he understand how weary I am? He's half the reason I'm in this place. The least he could do is let me languish for a few moments.

"Leave me be, Nero." Yawning, I curl onto my side.

"Wake, Sybil. You must not linger here," Rose urges as a gust of wind brushes my face. A warm fuzzy body moves along my side before tugging at my hair.

"Stop Lemon. I'm too tired to play. You need to hide before someone spots you." I move to push him away, but he nips my finger with concern. A rough arm shakes my shoulders and cold liquid splashes over my head. I sit up abruptly, blinking at Nero who is standing before me with a flask in his hand. I blink faster, my vision doubling as my sudden movement. Water is dripping down from my wet hair and my eyes widen as I take in the room once again. Gone are the rich tapestries. Shredded, moth-eaten strips of weaving hang in their place. The floor is thick with dirt, disturbed by our footballs, the ceiling faded and cracked, the paint peeling along the edges. My stomach drops and I squeeze my eyes closed, refusing to move.

"Nero." I pause, inhaling deeply before meeting his gaze. "Why am I sitting on top of the coffin, and what happened to the room?" Chills run down my spine as I push myself off the edge, my feet sending up clouds of dust.

"I was just about to ask ye the same thing." Nero replies, eyebrows raised in question. "We were moving through the room and one minute I was telling ye that the exit was a tunnel away and the next, I turned, and ye weren't behind me. When I found ye, ye had climbed on top of the tomb and the room started to glow and I could swear I smelled jasmine and the ocean."

"Jasmine? But wh–"

"Ye were just laying there, barely moving or breathing. What did ye expect me to do?" Nero crosses his arms over his chest. "I'm trying to help ye escape the castle, not fall under some spell meant to trap robbers. Ye left me no choice." He waves his arms in exaggeration at the tomb behind me.

"That can't be possible." I laugh with disbelief and shock. "How could it have been a spell to stop robbers? I don't think you understand. I heard this voice, a woman's voice." My head whips wildly around for any signs of proof of what I have just experienced. She was just here. I swear–she was. She had to be; it had felt real.

"There is no one here but ye, me, that thing." Nero points towards my pocket. "Ye wouldn't awaken no matter how much I or yer creature tried. I had no choice, don't ye understand? I had to douse ye in the water." He shrugs sheepishly, holding up the empty flask.

"My creature?" I scoff with annoyance. I glance down at Lemon who looks up at me from my overskirt pocket. Lemon nods his head in agreement, chittering his fears at me. He nuzzles his head into my palm and rests under my hand. "He's not a thing. He's a ferret." I frown down at his innocent face, whiskers twitching. A very long lived, too smart, for his own good ferret. Wait. Did he just—

"How did yo–" I narrow my eyes at Nero, studying him carefully.

"How did I ken ye stowed away a pet the whole journey to Shadowvale?" Nero laughs openly at me. "Ye weren't stowing meat strips away in yer pockets for yerself. Plus, that little beast snores terribly at night. I'm surprised ye sleep at all with him around." He lifts an eyebrow at me, like the thought of a drowsy ferret companion isn't a problem.

Heat creeps along my face. I push past him towards the doorway. "Let's get out of here. Whose tomb is this anyways?" I shiver, the linger of the magic tingling along my skin.

"This is where Aramis's mother, Queen Rosalind, goddess bless her soul, was laid to rest." His head dips toward the crypt before returning to meet my gaze. "We've come here to pay our respects for almost a hundred years, yet I've never seen a flicker of her magic here before."

"Rosalind." Rose. The name echoes in my head. "What do you mean, her power?" I turn around and face him in the doorway.

"Queen Rosalind was a wind elemental, but that wasn't her true power. Known for two great things, she possessed a loving nature and a magical art. Through her paintings, she captured the essence of both the past and the future, depicting prophecies of the time that was and the time that will be."

I stare at the stagnant coffin that had just given me so

much warmth and life.

What in all of Craeweth is going on?

SYBIL

Stars glitter like diamonds in a velvet sky, greeting me as Nero shoves open the heavy iron door at the top of the stairs. He turns around and gives me a hand, pulling me out of the crypt and closing the door with a resounding thud behind me. We stand on a crest outside of the castle walls. The bitter winter air burns my lungs, the sensation imprinted on me as the taste of freedom. . From our distance, I can hardly discern the twinkling lights through the castle windows. Have we really come this far underground in such a short time?

"This is where I must leave ye." Nero unclasps the cloak from around his neck, then removes my healing satchel from his back. "Head north and then east. The rebels have a safe house about fifteen miles into the woods. I sent them word that I'd be freeing ye and sending ye their way. I need to return before I rouse suspicion on myself, but I will be in touch."

I stand still as I look out into the depths of the trees, searching for secrets and answers hidden within the foliage. After all the pain and sorrow I have endured, it is difficult to let the doubts stop clawing at my determination to let go and jump into the action. Am I truly free or will this last act lead me to my ultimate death? A gentle breeze caresses my cheek like the touch of a lover. Closing my eyes, I send a silent prayer to the Goddess, begging her to give me the strength to survive this.

"I know our first encounter wasn't on the best of terms, but I am yer ally, Sybil. Ye can do this. Together, we can stop this madness," Nero murmurs quietly, as if he understands my doubt and turmoil.

I watch his face, his short, dark hair blown back by the wind, but it remains solemn; honest as an open book. "Northwest? That's not very specific," I say. My lips pull down into a frown.

"Just look for the thorns." He hands me the empty flask. Just as I take it, the male is already moving away as his silhouette fades into the blackness of night. Without so much as a farewell, he heads back towards the looming castle.

Taking that first step, all alone in the woods, feels like the beginning of a new life.

The faces of the children locked in their cell, fighting over gruel, resurface in my mind. The icy winter chill can't cool the fire that is building inside me. I can't let Tricella take any more of my people.

With renewed determination, I glance up at the night sky. Noting Nordfeu, the northern star, I tuck the flask into my satchel and ensure I safely tuck Lemon into my overskirt pocket as I quicken my pace ready to join the rebels.

Leaning wearily against the rough bark of a pine tree, I inhale deeply. Cicada chirps fill the air with a melodic hum contrasting the stillness of the night. Hours have passed since I left Nero at the edge of the forest. My stomach lets out an audible rumble. It has been even longer since my last meal.

I stare up at the night sky, trying to orient my direction by the stars. The tips of my fingers and toes have long gone numb from the frosty air but I have to keep going and put as much distance between me and the castle as I can. Teeth chattering, I blow air on my fingers before rubbing my palms together. How much longer until I reach the rebel's camp?

"Hopefully they'll have hot food available," I say, and the thought of food makes my stomach twist into painful knots. I lick my lips, dry and cracking from the icy wind.

Why did that fool waste the entire flask of water to wake me? Clearly, he didn't think about the possibility of me dying without food or water.

"I'd even be happy with a loaf of soft bread and cheese," I mutter to Lemon. Exhaling, my breath materializes in misty puffs; a visible reminder of the winter's grasp. I yearn for a hot cup of tea to warm my hands. Oh, how happy I would be with just these simple pleasures.

Lemon shivers in my pocket, despite his thick fur coat. He licks the tip of my fingers as I stroke the top of his head, letting out a mixture of content noises. I pull him out and gently kiss the tip of his nose. Cocking his head to the side, he wriggles in my grasp, swinging his head from side to side as he stares at the trees around us.

"Oh, how I wish you could talk some days. I could use–"

A great splinting rents the air as I step onto a large fallen log. The wood disintegrates below me and I lose my balance, stumbling through the snow and crashing hard into a giant tree. As my body collides into the hard, frozen bark, I step on something uneven, my ankle rolling with a crack as my knee gives out to take the weight off. Landing ungracefully, I collapse into an awkward heap on the ground.

"Fuck!" Black dots swarm in my vision, making it difficult to see. Every inch of my body aches and throbs with pain. I push myself into a sitting position, wincing as the gravel and ice bite into the bare palms of my hand.

"Lemon!" I cry out. My heart races with adrenaline and

pain, holding my leg up as a sigh of relief leaves me when I
see him poke his sweet head out of the snow pile he landed in.
He scampers over to my side and I scoop him up, my hands
shaking. "You're okay," I mumble as tears sting my eyes. My
jaw trembles from the agony as I bury my face into his fur.

For a brief moment, pure terror grips my heart as I openly
cry, the tears leaving icy streaks on my face. I'm alone and lost
in the woods. Settling him in my lap, I perceive the devastation
of my ankle before even looking at it Groaning; I try to set
my leg down on the ground to rest it while wiping at my nose,
doing everything I can to slow the tears. To my shock, I seem
to have more stability than I thought.

I summon the strength to rise, leaning on the rough bark
and taking care not to let my foot touch the snow until I'm
ready. Lemon clings to my shoulders as I wince, trying to gauge
how much weight I can put on it. My ankle throbs but there's
people waiting on me, and I dig deep into that motivation to
think this one through.

"Okay. Okay, I can put some weight on it. Maybe… maybe
I can make a swift splint." Lemon climbs down my arm and
nudges at my family's crest ring on my hand. Not a single
scratch marks its surface from my fall.

"It's a miracle I haven't lost it." Sniffling, I wipe my running
nose on the edge of my cloak but he keeps nudging my hand
persistently.

"I don't know what you want, boy. I don't have any
food. I'm sorry." Sighing, I lift my gaze to the sky to pray for
guidance. Even if I can make a splint, walking in this snow is
clearly not reliable. I can't see if there's anything underneath,
and even if I can put weight on my ankle, it's not sturdy–my
eyes widen as I notice a small etching in the bark. At first
glance, it looks as though it's part of the wood grain, but as I
hobble closer, the image becomes more discernible.

A small vine with delicate thorns.

"Thorns!" I glance from trunk to trunk, now seeing what I hadn't before.

A sky of thorns surrounds me, etched high on the trees.

This is it. I have to keep going.

I take a deep breath and tentatively reach into the well of my magic. The weight of exhaustion pulls at my limbs. My muscles scream in protest with each movement, and my head throbs with a dull ache that seems to permeate my entire being. But despite it all, I press on, driven by a fierce determination that refuses to let me give up. This has to work. I need this to work. Images of the queen's hands on my body, draining me of my magic, flash in front of my eyes and ignite my anger. The tingly sensation of magic dances along my fingertips. It is so close I can taste it. Breathe, Sybil. I try to relax my throbbing muscles and embrace my power.

"Alright, maybe instead of a splint, I can try shifting."

Heat envelops my body as it twists and transforms. Hooves replacing hands and feet. A spiraled pearl horn elongating from my forelock. I toss my head, my long white hair whipping at the motion. My eyesight clarifies as my ears twitch, ready to detect sound. My mother's satchel transforms to fit my equestrian form comfortably, without adjustment. Leaning down, I gingerly touch my horn to my injured foot, feeling the magic securely wrap around as the bone knits back together. I forgot how much stronger my magic is in this form, and how quickly mending breaks deplete it. I won't be able to maintain this form for long.

Casting my eyes to the etched thorns, I mark my path before lowering my head to the ground. Lemon quickly scampers up my neck and tucks himself in one of the satchel's empty pockets. I've never felt more grateful for my mother's wit for having it spelled to change form to accommodate our shifting. I take off on a slow walk. The pain in my left rear hoof recedes to a dull ache. Unsure of how long I'll be able to hold my remaining magic to keep this form, I push on.

The sky is painted in a rich shade of purple, reminiscent of a bruised plum, indicating that the first light of dawn is on the horizon. Faint chirping of birds rises as they prepare for a new day. The forest no longer feels like an enemy out to catch me but has rather embraced me in this new form. With each powerful stride, the ancient trees blur into a backdrop as I gallop through, the cool and crisp air carrying the promise of hope. I am on the right path, but how much further do I have to go?

The snap of a twig behind me sets me on edge, ears twitching and scenting the air full of winter berries.

What was that?

I proceed with cautious steps, the rustling of leaves and the crunch of snow under my hooves echoes through the trees. As I scan the area, the wind shifts, carrying a pungent odor of musky fur that permeates my nostrils. I pause, my heart pounding in my chest, and my eyes dart around, searching for the source of the smell.

A beast.

I take off at a gallop, pushing myself as hard as I can go, ignoring the throbbing pain in my back half with each step. The sound of paws pounding the ground behind me fuels my determination to get away. Weaving in between trees, I no longer care what direction I am going. My magic is waning as fast as my energy, but I am not about to let a monster devour me just as I have escaped from another one.

I realize too late that the trees are thinning and I see a drop off approaching. I dig my hooves into the ground but lose my footing in the forest mulch hidden beneath the snow. Sliding to the edge, the control of my magic slips and I shift back into my human form, plummeting off the edge. As I'm hurled down the steep muddy slope I curl into a ball and land on my back at the bottom of the ravine, my satchel cushions my fall with a splash and crunch of glass.

Above me, on the edge of the ravine, stands the largest wolf I have ever seen.

ARAMIS

A knocking resounds on the thick wood door.

"Come in," I bark gruffly. Nero and I stand opposite each other over the large table in the middle of the library, poring over a map of Shadowvale and the surrounding territories. I desperately try to focus on the territories and borders of my kingdom but its as if someone has taken a piece of my being and run miles from me. The Queen's seer has been down for the past two nights with a migraine, unable to see where the rebels plan to attack next. He should be thankful a headache is all he is recovering from. Fingers tap impatiently on the polished surface of my desk, a futile attempt to distract myself from the restless thoughts swirling within. Winter is coming and we can't afford to lose any more crops or livestock, lest my people starve. You always arrive late at the attacks because they are not real, Sybil's words come back to me and I close my eyes, willing her voice to disappear.

"Your majesty?" A voice trembles out behind me. Slamming my fist against the table, I open my eyes and turn around.

"This better be important—" The words die on my tongue

as I see the small messenger boy standing in the doorway. His entire body quivers, his eyes wide. Shit. I didn't mean to scare the poor boy. I soften my stance and gaze before taking a deep breath. "I'm sorry. We just have important matters to discuss in this meeting. What do you need?" I raise my eyebrow in query, and the young boy visibly shakes as he takes a deep breath, ready to share.

"The Q-Q-Queen requests your presence immediately, sire." He stammers before dropping his gaze to his feet.

"Of course. Let her know we will be down momentarily." As he swiftly leaves, I run my hands through my hair and collapse into the nearest chair.

"Aramis." Nero draws up a chair next to me. His gaze is laser focus with intent, and it's clear he'd like to discuss something with me. We just don't have time for this now.

"Not now, Nero. I just... need a moment," I mutter, pressing fingertips against my brow. The moment I close my eyes, all I can see is the vision of her hazel eyes peering at me with hatred, like I was the most vile creature in the world. Why can't she see that I am only trying to defend and protect my people.

"Aramis," he says urgently.

I stand, ready to take action. "The longer we stall, the more she will take it out on you or that poor boy. Or one of her many other servants."

"There is something I need to talk to ye about." He begins again, stepping into my path.

"It has to wait." Walking around him, I grab my cloak from a peg on the wall and sling it over my shoulder. "Let's go see what she wants so we can get back to defending this kingdom."

Nero lowers his gaze and nods in acceptance.

"Yes, yer majesty." He replies quietly, falling behind me. I briefly glance back at him. His face is a mask of calm except for the furrow of his brows and the frown that tugs at his lips.

187

A hint of guilt pains my chest as I wonder if I am as good a friend to Nero as he is to me. I make a silent promise to talk to him and find out what is causing him to worry so much. We only have each other left in this world.

As we enter the throne room, I reluctantly bow before the King and Queen. "Father, Tricella. You summoned me?" I raise my head and look at my father's face. He gazes at the empty corridor with a glassy, faraway look, lost into the distance where dust motes float in a beam of sunlight shining through the colored glass window panes. The last years have not been kind to him, deep lines now crease his face. Long gone is the man that taught me how to ride a horse, laughing uncontrollably as I struggled to balance, whilst mother painted in the garden, her loving eyes following us with apprehension. I've watched him slowly disintegrate, pulling further into himself, his grief forever clawing at him, intensifying like ever-growing weeds in a garden of despair as I simply stood there, powerless.

The tapping of fingernails on the marble throne draws my attention back to my stepmother. Her lips pinch in displeasure.

"I have another task for you," she commands coldly.

Great goddess, what could she possibly want now? I study her face; her smooth, porcelain skin, and the way her long hair shines as it curls around her face and body. Even as my father looks beyond his age, Tricella is more youthful, more delicate in physique. Hasn't she looked particularly glowing since you brought me to your castle? Sybil's words echo in my mind once again, and I shake my head. My jaw clenches in a silent struggle against the tumultuous emotions threatening to unravel my carefully constructed world.

"How can I be of service?" I rise from where I kneel on the floor. I allow a hint of smugness to tug the corner of my lips, knowing it will infuriate the woman standing in front of me. There was a time, when I was just a boy desperate to fill the void his mother had left, where I desperately tried to win Tricella's affection, hoping she could replace what I had lost. I soon realized, however, that she was just like one of those monsters I used to read about, but dressed in the finest silks and with the face of an angel, and you never trust a monster.

"A certain important prisoner of mine has escaped." Tricella says. Lifting a hand, lazily inspecting her nails. She flicks an imaginary dust mote to then glances at Kieran. He kneels before her, head bowed on the hard marble floor beside her like a dog on a leash, utterly pathetic.

"You have many prisoners," I reply in a bored tone, but my heart pounds and my gut clenches. This cannot be real. "How could a prisoner possibly escape? All of our magical fortifications are renovated. We've doubled the guards and completed repairs to the outer walls that were damaged from last year's winter storms. There isn't a single way in or out of the castle that isn't known about and constantly monitored." Except possibly the secret exit outside my mother's resting place. But only three people know about it; my father, Nero, and myself.

"Now isn't that the very question I've been asking myself," Tricella replies, her words laced with accusation as she leans forward in her throne, staring me down.

I laugh at the incredulous unspoken accusation. "What?" I wipe my hand over my mouth, clearing away all humor. "Who has escaped?"

"The very acquisition you brought to me just weeks ago." Tricella glares at me, attempting to pierce my heart with ice daggers.

I maintain a façade of indifference, masking the complex swirl of emotions beneath my stoic exterior. She is free. She is free... but is she safe? My mind races, conjuring all the possible places she could be. I force my body to stand still and maintain my regal posture, but all I want to do is run.

"Are you accusing me of helping her escape? After all I went through to retrieve her?" I bristle with demand at the unspoken charge. Cover your relief. Don't let her see. I raise my brows in disbelief.

"Well, I wouldn't have thought so, but then Kieran here informed me of an interesting encounter you two had last night?" She leans back in her chair, lacing her fingers as her lips curl into a wicked feline sneer. "From what I have heard, you were holding her in a very... protective manner," Tricella adds and I need to stop myself from unsheathing my sword and killing Kieran here and now. "I cannot even imagine what your poor mother would have said if she knew you were fraternizing with the very people that killed her!" Her words slice open an old wound and I can see my father flinch at the mention of her. I take another deep breath, my fists clench at my sides. I know what game she is playing, but she won't get the reaction she is hoping for this time around.

"Your prisoner would have escaped last night had I not stopped her running through the castle unsupervised," I spit in Kieran's direction, and vow that I will take my revenge when the time is right. "Can't Kieran just look for her once his little headache is over?".

"Kieran is working on other matters for me," she says dismissively. "You and Nero shall go and fetch the unicorn for me. I want her back. She belongs to me. This time, make sure she isn't able to escape." Her voice drops threateningly. She waves a servant over who hastens to bring her a goblet of wine, dismissing me. I ignore the tug in my gut, willing me to shout back at her that she is mine.

"What do you plan to do with her when we return?" I challenge her, my hand resting on the hilt of my sword. "Why are there countless shifters still locked in the dungeons instead of being sent north?" I fix my gaze upon Tricella, determination burning in my eyes and demanding the truth. I can sense Nero tensing behind me, his knuckles white on the marble floor, reading to intervene should things escalate. This is the first time I've openly questioned her, in complete disregard of the consequences. Even my father turns his gaze on me.

Tricella's cold, calculating eyes meet mine over the rim of her goblet as she sips her wine. "What did you say to me?" The tingle of magic fills the air as she slams the goblet on the arm of the throne, the ruby red liquid staining the cream sleeve of her gown and skirt.

"Don't fucking play coy now, Tricel—" I explode, no longer able to keep hold of my anger.

"How dare you! You impertinent boy," Tricella screams, and as she stands in protest, she unleashes her magic with a blast. The throne room trembles with ominous energy and panic ripples through everyone present. Their faces contorted with fear, unsure of what to do. The air crackles with an otherworldly power, but I do not yield. I square my shoulders in defiance, sword drawn. No more, I think to myself. Nero tries to reach me but with one swift hand motion, Tricella sends him flying across the room. Her magic pulsates in the air like a poison; draining the world of its energy.

"You have been a thorn in my side since the day I entered this castle." The queen takes a step in my direction and as she comes closer, I see dark purple veins pulsating along her forearms, but as I ready myself to confront her once more, a faint voice cracks my growing fury.

"Aramis." My father's voice speaks, rusty with disuse. He stands unsteadily and then lifts an arm and lays it on Tricella's forearm. "Enough. Do as your stepmother requests. You must stop the threats to our kingdom."

I watch as he wearily sinks back into his throne, a mix of

hate and sorrow clenching my heart. The sound of his strained voice echoes through the room. "I'll take you out for a ride when you're done with your studies," he then mutters, so silently that I question if I have imagined the words. His face contorts in pain, sweat glistening on his forehead, and I furrow my brow in concern. Can grief alone cause a man to wither this much?

Tricella's powers disappear as quickly as they have appeared. Pretending as if nothing out of the ordinary has happened, she sits back on her throne. "You're dismissed. Take your dog with you." Her eyes gleam, her grin feral as she waves towards the door.

My eyes, still fixed on her, have a newfound clarity. Feeling as if I am slowly resurfacing from the depth of an ocean of lies and conjectures I have cowardly hid under, I turn towards Nero and lead us both out of the throne room. I'm finding out the truth.

Once I capture myself a unicorn.

Again.

"That was…intense," Nero says, keeping pace with me as we make our way back to my wing of the castle. "What happened back there?"

"I am not entirely sure, but something isn't right." I slam the door open, startling a maid changing the sheets on the bed. "Leave us."

She quickly grabs her basket and leaves the room. I throw my magic out, closing the door and creating a barrier blocking prying ears from overhearing. Nero takes a seat by the fire, leaning back and crossing his fingers before him. He looks at me circumspectly, trying to ascertain what I'm not saying.

"It's just something Sybil said." Leaning over the table, I let my finger run along the aged parchment map. I trace from the castle down to Bellevue, where her house would be. Is she heading back home?

"I thought Sybil wasn't anything more than a shifter?" Nero's tone is casual, but when I glance up at him, both eyebrows are raised. He tosses his feet on a chair before him as he leans back in his chair. "Since when do ye believe anything that crosses her lips?"

"I don't know what to believe anymore." I reply grimacing and take a deep breath. "When I saw Sybil in the dungeons she told me things I refused to believe, but I am starting to wonder if that was a mistake." As the words hang heavy in the air, my shoulders sag under the weight of the undeniable truth that has finally breached the fortress of my denial.

How did you escape, Sybil? Where would you go? The questions come unbidden. I have to find her. I have to know she's okay.

"I have to find her, Nero. She knows the truth."

My finger lazily draws circles on the faded ink marks of the forest to the North. It would be suicide to be out there without shelter. There are no known villages directly North of the kingdom. Only thick forest that leads to the Mountains of Aldervora. Shadowvale winters are anything but mild. She is just as likely to freeze to death as she is to be eaten by beasts. A chill runs down my spine, leaving the hair on the back of my neck standing up.

"Ye think Tricella has a hand in it?" His chair lands on all fours with a thud as he stares at me.

"No—yes, I don't know." I sigh, glancing back up at Nero. "She seems to be desperate to have her. I don't think she would have allowed her to escape." She needs her.

"No matter how high they rise or how much they amass, those who lust for power will always have a ceaseless craving for control and more dominion." Nero grips the arms of the chair so tightly his knuckles turn white. I glance up at my best friend, concerned at his obvious anger.

"Nero, are you well? I apologize for not hearing you out earlier."

"Do nae worry about me, mate." Letting go of the chair, he stands up and knocks me playfully on the shoulder with a grin but his smile doesn't reach his eyes. "Where do ye want to search first?"

"Well," I muse. "If I was a prisoner in a foreign kingdom, I wouldn't seek refuge in towns that would sell me out. She likely doesn't know the territory at all, but knows we came from the South. I expect she's going to head north."

"That's what I was thinking. Unless she's that desperate to go back home?"

"Sybil is not a female to run back home with her tail between her legs." I snort with derision. "No, if I learned anything about her on our journey, it's that she's smart and resourceful." That beautiful, magical witch is too smart to go home. "Do you think anyone saw her escape? That could give us a clue."

"I could ask the servants and guards." Nero pushes up to stand.

I shift my gaze from my friend to the open window. I can see storm clouds hovering above, casting a dark gray hue over the room. The sunlight peeks through the covered sky, creating a dancing pattern of light and shadow on the table in front of me. The scent of snow permeates the air. I can hear the distant rumble of thunder in the distance. While thundersnows are not unheard of this far North, they are rare. And deadly.

"Be quick about it. Meet me at the North gate in an hour whether you've discovered anything or not. I don't want to waste the precious daylight. Or tempt a storm."

Sliding into his vacated chair, I bury my face in my hands.

What am I even going to say if we find her?

More importantly, what will I do with her?

SYBIL

et up. Get up. Get up!

Gasping in pain, I roll on to my stomach. My heart pounds in my chest at the sound of paws sliding down the steep slope at my back. The odds of fighting a wolf single-handed without a weapon, injured, and with my magic depleted, are slim, but it is better than dying a coward. I spot a large rock and grapple for it. Flashbacks of the chimera come back to me. I can do this.

I've not come this far to die this way.

"You fool!" A sharp feminine voice reprimands. Turning around, my jaw drops as I view the female behind me. Her deep, curly auburn hair bounces wildly around her head as she purses her lips and crouches next to me.

"Where did you come fro–" I ask, dumbly. Wasn't there a wolf here just a second ago that was about to bite my head off?

"I've been looking for you." She grins wryly at me.

"Me?"

"Yeah." She glances down at my bruised ankle and silently requests permission to investigate. At my nod, she gingerly prods it.

"Ouch!" Wincing, I pull my foot closer to my body. "Who are you?"

"Didn't Nero tell you?" Her laughter echoes through the air like the gentle jingle of wind chimes. At the shake of my head, she continues on. "No matter, my name is Kela MacGregor. Let's get you to the safe house before the storm breaks." Her blue eyes twinkle with mischief as she sticks her hand forward with a wolfish grin.

I have found the rebels.

I glance between her proffered hand and the cloudless sky. Rays of light stream above the tree line. Storm? I look at the wolf shifter with inquisitive eyes. Once again, I am forced to trust a stranger. I only hope that Nero knew what he was doing sending me here.

"I'm Sybil. Sybil Vandeleur," I hesitantly reply, taking her hand.

"Oh good. I was afraid I had found the wrong unicorn shifter running around the forest." Kela grins at her humor. At my blank stare, she rolls her eyes at me.

"Well, you scared me shitless back there, Kela. Thanks for that!" I respond to her joke with a dose of sarcasm of my own as I clean my skirts from the snow. "I thought you were one of those lovely monsters roaming the woods. Back home in Bellevue–,"I pause as my voice cracks at the thought of my house. My forest. I clear my throat and continue, "There are wild beasts who will attack without a second thought if you're caught alone."

Kela laughs kindly, picks up my mother's satchel from the ground and hands it to me. Who knows if there's anything left intact after the fall? She then slides an arm around my back to help me with my painful ankle. As I swing the bag over my shoulder. Lemon pops his head from the pocket he hid in.

"Well hello there, handsome," she crones as we slowly make our way up the opposite slope. "Nero did not tell me

196

you had such a lovely ramidreju. They are incredible creatures who seek out those in need. The cutest little guardians and protectors. I've only read about them in books, but my mother tells me my great-great-grandfather had one."

"A ramidreju?" Laughter bubbles up my throat. "Lemon is just a simple ferret."

"He's more than just a simple ferret." She pauses, glancing sideways at me.

"That's impossible," I scoff, glancing down at him. "If he was more than just a ferret, I would have sensed it." Wouldn't I? I'm beginning to realize there is more to my world than I ever imagined.

"Does he have an obsession with shiny gold and silver objects?" she asks.

"Well, yes. He does like shiny things." I admit reluctantly. He always collects lost trinkets and hoards them in his nest. Absent-mindedly, I spin my family's ring around my finger. How did he know to grab it all those weeks ago?

She reaches over and runs her hand along his back, his eyes close as he lets out a rumbling sound of contentment. "You've never noticed the subtle green sheen when the sunlight hits his fur? And how long exactly have you had Lemon?"

Glancing at him, I bite my bottom lip as I see the barely visible hint of green shadows in his white fur. I always thought it was a residue from his love of rolling in the grass. "I've had him for about twelve years."

"The average ferret only lives six to ten years," Kela states simply. The judgment I expect to hear isn't there, and we continue walking. "It would make sense that he was drawn to you. It is said their fur has healing properties and everyone knows you unicorns know a thing or two about healing. Have you not noticed how his canine teeth protrude more like small tusks?"

As if to prove her correct, Lemon bears a grin and

flicks his tongue up, licking his nose. My mind drifts to his peculiar moments of intelligence. Memories of how his and my intuition were the same, and how, despite my lack of understanding, he always seems to know me better than I know myself.

"How did you know?" I ask in awe. The dull throb begins in my left ankle, and I lift it up for relief, tenderly circling it.

"I pride myself on being a bit of a mythical creature expert. That and there isn't a book you could keep away from me." Her arm supporting me tightens as we crest over the ridge. A small house—more like a shack—is barely visible through the thick copse of trees ahead. "Ah, here we are. Let's get you inside, cleaned up, and fed."

Kela stands in front of a small fireplace, stirring a pot. The aroma of boiling potatoes, onions, garlic and bacon fills the air. The safe house comprises a single room, jam-packed with an assortment of odds and ends. As I glance around, my eyes settle on a small table by the bed, where a stack of books is piled high. It feels like a lifetime ago since I last had warm soup in the comfort of my home, surrounded by my books.

"How long have you been with the rebels?" I ask as Kela makes her way towards a large wooden crate next to me. Dozens of rolls of fabric, bottles of tinctures, and other assortments fill the container to the brim.

"Well, that depends." She gently invites me to take a seat by the table and carefully pries the shoe from my foot. I flinch as pain radiates from the movement. I dare a glance down at the swollen purple and blue flesh. Hopefully, it is no longer broken. Bitter disappointment coats my tongue as I think of the ease of which my father would have mended it, were he here.

"Kela, I am going to need you to keep talking to me if you're going to try to fix my ankle. I need the distraction," I say through clenched teeth as she gently prods my ankle. She pauses, the air between us falling silent as she lifts her gaze, her piercing blue eyes locking onto mine. The intensity of her stare makes me feel as if all my defenses have been stripped away, leaving me exposed and vulnerable.

Almost as if she can see to the bottom of my soul and every unspoken fear and doubt about myself.

"My mother and father are the leaders of the rebels, although we don't call ourselves that. They were among the first to work with Evangeline after she uncovered Tricella's plans. So, you could say I've been with them my entire life." She makes fast work, rubbing a salve over my ankle, placing two stiff rods from the box and wrapping them tightly with a roll of fabric. She pinches my toe and we both watch as the color changes quickly from white back to rosy pink. At least she knows how to check if she has cut off circulation to my toes. I'd very much like to keep them. I wiggle them, then test moving my ankle. It barely budges from the tight wrapping, but I can hardly sense any discomfort.

"What do you call yourselves then, if not rebels?" I ask, the flood of questions falling from my mind to my mouth. Now that I know my ankle will be fine, I am not disconcerted in asking them. "How old are you? And what was in that salve?"

"Whoa there, girl." She gently pats me on the shoulder before propping my foot up on two stacked crates. "Let's eat first, then I'll answer all your questions."

Kela pours steaming stew into two bowls, handing one to me. She swaps the pot over the fire for a kettle of hot water before plopping herself down on the bed.

The buttery flavor of the soup soothes my aching body. As we eat quietly, I take the time to examine the contents of the room more closely. Shelves line one wall of the room. Stacks of clothes, books, and tools line the shelves and are shoved in every possible free space. The corner is a mess of cluttered piles of moth-eaten and patched blankets, and in the midst of it all is a small basket of worn toys. Strings of dried herbs and vegetables hang from the ceiling above baskets of root vegetables and dried meats. Next to the fireplace hangs an assortment of pots, pans, and utensils. Their surfaces are dented and scratched with use. The entire room has the atmosphere of a hodge-podge mixture of anything someone on the run would need, no matter how old or young.

Kela clears her throat before taking my empty bowl from my hands. "I'm sorry it's not much, but it's the best I could do, given the circumstances." She shrugs as she walks to the kitchen to drop off the bowls and then pads back to me. Kela picks up a tin, giving it a little shake with a grin. "But how about a little tea? Do you prefer honey? Sugar? I'm afraid we don't have any cream."

"I would die for a cup of hot tea," I reply greedily. Saliva fills my mouth at the thought of fresh hot tea. "Sugar, please."

"Now don't go dying on me. I might be a wolf, but I'm not so feral as to not offer tea to a guest." She flashes me a wolfish grin while she measures a scoop of rich dried tea leaves into two chipped china cups, along with a heaping spoonful of sugar. As the tea steeps, I lean into the hard wood of the seat, trying to find a good place to let my ankle rest. Kela settles backwards into a chair next to mine, leaning her forearms across the back and cocks her head at me, her cup nearly overspilling at the movement.

"So, let's start with your first question. We aren't rebels so much as defenders of the people. From what I've been told, when Tricella married the king of Shadowvale about a hundred years ago, that's when the troubles began." Kela's history matches Aramis's timeline, at least. I muse on the thought as she takes a sip of her tea and continues. "People say that the problems between shifters and elementals started when Tricalla became queen but the truth is they started long before, during the fifty year war between Kallistar and Shadowvale. It was a silly war if you ask me, fighting for a strip of land! The conflict eventually ended with a peace treaty, but what the war truly caused was a divide within the people of my kingdom."

I nod in understanding. "You see," Kela continues, and I bite my lips as I hardly blink, not wanting to miss a single detail. "Shifters have lived in Shadowvale for centuries. My family was born and raised here and we've always felt welcome, but things changed during the war. Since the kingdom of Kalistar has always been considered a safe-haven for the shifter community due to their long reigning line of shifter monarchs, elementals started thinking that the war over the territory separating the kingdoms was simply an excuse. A pretext brought forth by the shifters to overturn the crown here in Shadowvale. It did not matter that my ancestors fought side by side with elements to defend Shadowvale during the war. Even after the conflict ended, many kept believing we were spies, secretly helping Kalistar, ready to backstab our neighbors to end the rule of elementals." I can hear Kela's frustration seeping through her words, but do not interrupt her. Aramis's prejudices against shifters is starting to make more and more sense.

"Things only got worse once Queen Rose was murdered and rumors started spreading that it happened by hand of a group of shifter rebels, attempting once again to put themselves on the throne and shape Shadowvale in the image of Kalistar. As you can imagine, it did not take much for elementals to blindly believe this lie and start pointing fingers."

"The war had had terrible consequences in Kallistar but nothing of this sort; neighbors at each other's throats. The towns and cities affected were rebuilt, and the crown had helped everyone get back on their feet. Every traveler passing through Bellevue often praised my kingdom for how welcoming it is to every species existing in Craeweth," I say.

Anger and sadness fill her voice and I can see her knuckles turn white as she clenches her fists. "When the King married Tricella things completely escalated. Entire clans of shifters were summoned to the castle to answer crimes of treason during the war and ties to these rebels. It was as if they all forgot we were there, that we fought next to them, and that we had lost our Queen too. Entire families were summoned and were never heard from again." She pushes over a stack of objects on the table before sitting down her empty cup.

The rage boils past my ears, my chest constricting as I think of the two tiger cubs locked in the dungeons with me. I had to find a way to free them. All of them.

"I am so sorry, Kela," I whisper, knowing it won't help make all these wrongdoings right but she gives me a faint smile in return. I think about my sheltered life at the cottage. How peaceful my life was in Bellevue, dictated by routine and the simplest pleasures in life. All the while, people like me had to fight for their right to live. "I imagine that's when Nero's mother came to find your people, to fight back?"

"Yes. The clan leaders all met and determined something was not right. We weren't the only ones. Some elementals of influence, including Nero's own mother, began questioning the trials. " She pulls a dagger from its sheath on her belt and I watch her wide-eyed as she starts tossing it up in the air, catching it by the tip of the blade.

My eyes cast down into my empty cup. I examine the pattern the dregs created at the bottom. I'm at a loss for words with which his story was told. Nero's eyes, full of pain, explaining with a plea to tell the story of his mother, and my peevish and petty demands of expectation for him to reveal his heart and pain, because I was too angry at his role in my kidnapping. My disgust at myself roils in my stomach, and the wave of anger is washed away. I could have been kinder. I could have been more generous and patient. How was I so

202

wrapped up in my own selfish concerns and needs?

"So, ironically, the so-called "rebels" didn't exist until the decree of the shifter rebellion came to be. We know Queen Tricella is behind all of this but we don't know her motivation, and we don't know what exactly she does with those she takes. All evidence shows it's not good. To say the least." Kela concludes and I shiver as memories of the queen's chamber with the dark stains surface come back to my mind. The fleeting hope of gaining my power full strength, only to have it wiped out by her touch.

"She wants our power," I say, voice cracking from the painful flashbacks. "Tricella drained me of my magic as soon as I arrived at the castle. I am not entirely sure but I think it helps her stay young. She said something about needing time." Kela's brows furrow in concentration. This must be new information to her and I hope it can help with the mission.

"We know she uses dark magic, although it is very difficult to prove. Dark magic is extremely dangerous as it drains one's lifeforce, maybe she is using our powers to replenish what she loses." Kela's gaze takes on a faraway look as she formulates a new theory.

"Suffice to say that regardless of what she wants, we will not give it to her," she says softly after a moment. "We are the defenders of the people," she adds, and the brush of bravery that swells in my heart brings emotion to my eyes. "We do what we can. Mostly it involves moving those that the queen plans to capture and house them with someone safe in our order. We thwart her plans wherever we can, but sometimes we can't get there in time. And the bitch of it all, is that she always seems to get one step ahead of us."

"I think I can answer that question too," I reply, grateful that I can be of such help to the cause. "The queen employs a seer whom she uses to hunt your people." When my eyelids grow too heavy, I blink multiple times. The stew is like a sedative to my exhausted body. A familiar warm tug wraps around my torso. I cast my eyes to the snow falling out the window but the sensation leaves as quickly as it came.

"Our people." She confirms, and I am grateful that she is including me as much as I've welcomed the plight of shifters and the cause into my own heart. It doesn't matter that I hail from Kallistar; shifters are family, no matter the kind. "We've long suspected as such. Nero even hinted that a seer was involved. He has to be cautious, but he tries to warn us where he can." She takes the empty cup from my hands, stacking it on top of hers before offering me a hand.

"As for my age, I'm a young shifter, barely 32.' She continues on steadily, happy to share news as much as I am to receive. She glances down at my ankle. "The salve is one that my grandmother taught me. Willowbark and ginger for numbing, calendula to speed healing and comfrey to decrease bruising. I'm not officially a healer, but knowledge is power. You never know when new skills will come in handy." I like her.

A yawn takes over my body in a shuttering inhale, and I gather my wits about me to exhale it out slowly. My ankle throbs, and I blink sleepily at her.

Kela grins. "Enough talk for now. You can barely keep your eyes open. I'll go wash these down in the stream and restock us on wa—"

I watch as her eyes take on a cloudy, faraway look, her arms limp at her side.

"Kela?" I ask, my voice squeaking on the last syllable. My heart beats frantically when she doesn't respond, worry pushing past my exhaustion. I reach out and grab at her wrist, but she continues standing, her body swaying slightly. Goddess help me, what can I do? I study her body, but overall she seems to be in good health. I snap my fingers over her foggy eyes, but get no response.

204

"Kela!" I call again, louder. I snap my fingers at her face one more time, and Kela shakes her head. Her clear blue eyes refocus on me.

"What in the name of the goddess, was that!?" I demand, standing. All pain in my ankle is forgotten as I curl my arms around my chest. I raise my brows, tapping my fingers on my thigh–

"Well, that's one more secret for you to keep." Kela interrupts my inquisition, grinning at me sheepishly. "I'm the clan's secret weapon."

ARAMIS

nowflakes drift lazily around us and Nero casts his eyes skyward. Following his gaze, I note the dark gray clouds, heavy with the promise of snow.

"If we don't find her soon, her tracks will be lost to the snow and we will have to turn back." Nero sighs as he lifts his ax and points down the path. Small footprints mar the soft soil, and a sigh of relief begs to escape my lips. "It looks like she went this way."

My shoulders release their tension at this first clue. I look back at the secret passage through the crypts that leads to this path. Someone must have helped her escape. A warm breeze caresses my face and moves my gaze back towards the thick of the trees. I close my eyes and for a split second the gentle touch brings back loving memories of my mother. Come back to me Sybil. "Let's get going, there is no time to waste," I say, voice full of unwavering determination as I follow the footsteps.

"She dinna ken these forests like we do, Aramis. We could spend hours and not find her. Especially if we're caught out during a thundersnow," Nero adds as he chops down a branch blocking our path.

"Then we need to pick up the pace. Her footprints won't

be the only thing lost in the snow if we don't find her first."
My stupid heart clenches at the thought of her lost in the
forest in a blizzard or worse, facing one of the many wild
beasts known to roam the deeper mountain passes.

After following what little is left of Sybil's prints for
what seems an eternity, they suddenly start to change into
hoofprints–hot hair expels from my lungs to fog in front of
my face.

"She shifted. This must mean her strength is coming back,
but also that she is able to run a lot quicker." I rake a hand
through my cold hair, contemplating our options. The icy wind
is slowly picking up.

Nero glances up at me and breaks the heavy silence. "Right.
If I were Sybil, I'd travel north before skirting to the east or
west to avoid any patrols from the castle." I keep my head
lowered, just to make sure I don't give away the built up tension
building in my chest. "Aye, Sybil is a smart lass. She could offer
her healing services in exchange for a warm bed from one of
the outlying farmlands."

"No," I shake my head in denial. The thought of others
reporting sights of Sybil to any guard is too terrifying to
contemplate. "That would be too obvious. She would know
we would be looking for a healer and a shifter, nonetheless.
People are greedy and would be more than willing to give up
her location for a few coins." I stare up at the sky, frowning as
clouds continue to darken the further we travel. Fuck!

"She would if her choice was between living and freezing
to death." Nero adds matter-of-factly.

As we reach the heart of the forest, I clutch my cloak
tightly around me and send a silent prayer to the Goddess,
begging her to hold the storm for a little while longer. Step
after step, I imagine Sybil in her unicorn form running through
these trees, wild and free, and wonder how that must feel. Nero
follows next to me, a worried expression on his face, but no

sign of him suffering from the cold. "I think this is the first time in my life I wish I had fire magic. I'm losing sensation in my toes," I say trying to lighten the mood.

"Mate, you'd be a terrible fire element–." As he lifts his foot to step over a fallen log, I quickly throw an arm out, stopping him in his tracks.

"Wait!" I crouch down, examining the snow. Hoofprints and footprints are mixed together everywhere. Not much further, there's an imprint of a body and something else, something different. I stop when I recognise the shape of large paws, like a wolf's, standing out following petite hoofprints. My heart races and my palms sweat as fear and hope intensify. The emotions are overwhelming, and I struggle to keep them in check. "Something happened here."

"It looks like she tripped." Nero points out, crouching beside me. "Are those wolf prints?" He asks, standing up and walking a few paces.

As I observe her prints, my chest constricts. The change is too obvious. It becomes apparent that she is injured and favoring her leg.

"We have to find her. She can't be far," I growl, quickening my pace along the tracks. The thought of her out there, alone and unprotected, makes me shudder. What if this creature took her by surprise and she did not have a chance to defend herself? My mind races with worst-case scenarios.

"Dinna fash; we'll find her. Be rational." Nero reassures me as he clasps my shoulder in solidarity, and the touch is comforting. "It will do nae good if we get injured searching for her in the process." The once serene winter landscape has turned into a blur of white as the snowflakes become larger and denser. The air becomes thick with the smell of wet earth and cold, damp snow that's seeped through my clothes, my hands and feet tingling and numb. Despite that, my mind is solely focused on finding her.

"She is clearly hurt, Nero. With Goddess-knows-what hunting her. I will not fail her." I turn in place, facing him, clenching my teeth. Panic rises in my chest as I realize that if we don't find her, she may be lost to me forever to a fucking storm. I grab Nero's wide shoulder and with extreme clarity open my heart to him, "I cannot lose her too."

My magic, my royal status, my kingdom will mean nothing if I won't be able to save her. My hands shake as I am consumed by the need to find her, to ensure she is safe, and it is threatening to unravel me. Mine. She is mine. The mating bond ripples through me at the thought, like raw power, and what I've fought for so long has been won over.

It's there. The undeniable truth I've been avoiding. The tension in my muscles releases, replaced by a controlled intensity. I have to beg her for forgiveness and tell her how I feel, but my heart wrenches at the thought of losing her before I have the chance to make amends.

I let my hands fall and shake my head in despair. What a fucking fool I am. How many opportunities have I missed? Will she even forgive me after all that has transpired? My jaw tightens, no longer in denial but in resolute acceptance of the connection that binds me to her. The wind shifts, blowing cooly against the back of my neck and sending a shiver of premonition.

Nero pauses, his face contorting in confusion. With a sudden jolt, his eyes widen as his eyebrows shoot up into his hairline. His hands grip my shirt and slam me against a tree. I gasp for breath as the impact forces the air out of my lungs. As he pins me down, I watch him pant, his nostrils flaring.

"Nae. This canna be." He lets go of my shirt and storms a few paces away before turning and facing me. "How long?" He demands.

Brushing down the front of my shirt, I silently meet his gaze, raising a brow in question. "How long, what?" Shit.

"Dinna play coy with me, lad. We've been friends for too long." Nero steps into my space, jabbing a finger into my chest. "How. Long. Have. You. Known?" Each word articulates the point with the jabs of his finger into my chest.

Pursing my lips together, I cross my arms over my chest. He watches me like a wolf sizing up a deer, as if he can see right into my thoughts.

"I can see it written all over yer face, ye arse. Fate has dealt us an interesting card my friend," Nero continues to ramble on. "I can smell it on ye. Yer mated to Sybil, aren't ye?" A laugh escapes him as he rubs his forehead and shakes his head. "What a fool."

I tense as I hear the words spoken out loud for the first time. Fuck. At his accusation, I turn on my heel to face him, old instincts kicking. "No, it's not what you think. It can't be."

Lies, lies, lies.

The words hurt. Why am I scared to tell him the truth? He is my closest friend. My deepest ally. He's a brother to me. If I cannot trust Nero with this, how can I even trust myself? The turmoil churning in my gut clenches. My head pounds. The truth is that as long as I keep this realization to myself, I can protect it. I can find a way to protect me and Sybil from the hate we will otherwise receive. An elemental mated to a shifter is unheard of, abnormal even. What will the kingdom say if they know their Prince's soul is bound to that of a shifter, inferior in status and the constant reminder of the enemy? What will Nero think after saving me from those shifter assassins the night they came for my life? Will he despise me as much as I already despise myself for letting this happen? I lower my gaze, trying to hide the fear that curses through me at the possibility of losing my brother.

"Do ye even hear yerself? You're such a pompous arsehole," Nero replies, grinning wolfishly at me. Had I not known my best friend as long as I have, I wouldn't have caught the glimpse of something deeper dwelling in his eyes—a flicker of pain and anger. "Lad, ye don't know what sort of trouble yer in now."

Anger roils in my stomach, his accusations building on top of each other. The condescension in his voice builds layers of fury, ready to erupt within me. "Fuck off Ne–"

"Don't ye dare try to deny it, lad," Nero shouts, getting in my face. "If ye do, ye'll go mad."

"Call me lad one more time," I growl at him, stepping so far in his space that we're nose to nose, fuming at each other. My hand rests on the hilt of my sword. The pent up rage inside me is beginning to fester. His words are the hard reminders of my own actions and thoughts.

"Or what?" He falls into a defensive crouch, circling me. Taunting me. "Would ye rather I continue telling yerself all the ways ye've lied?" Nero glares at me, outraged at my laughter. "Did ye nae think I wouldn't notice the stolen glances ye sent her way the entire journey back home? Or would ye rather—"

Fuck this. I lunge, slamming my fist out to connect with his jaw, but he moves at the last moment and I'm met with air.

"You know nothing!" I yell as I whip around to face him.

"I ken more than ye think. I know ye haven't been ready for the truth until recently." His punch lands on my shoulder, causing me to lurch to the left, but I quickly regain my balance.

"What truth?" I bellow, thoroughly outraged and confused. Nero easily jumps back as I crouch down to swipe out a foot.

"That not all shifters are bad. Just as not all elementals are good." Nero exhales, pausing for a moment. We're both panting as we face each other. Each heaving breath turns to misty fog in the air. "Not everything is as simple as it seems. I know what happened with your mother was atrocious, but it's not a reason to hate the whole lot of them."

"Wait. So you're not disgusted by the fact that Sybil is my mate?" I stare at him.

"Aramis." Nero states, calm etched on his face as he claps a hand on my shoulder. Heat radiates from his palm as fire dances in his eyes. His skin shimmers with magic, leaving metallic overlapping scales in their wake. "Not all shifters are bad." The words are repeated for emphasis.

"What?" My jaw goes slack as I stumble back away from him. "What trick is this?" My eyes rove from his head to his toe before stopping at the large membranous wings sprouting from his back. Other than the wings and scales, he maintains his humanoid features.

"This is nae a trick. It is time ye know the truth." Nero declares. His magic releases and the scales melt back into his skin, but the wings remain.

SYBIL

I awaken from my fitful sleep to a deep rumble accompanying the shaking of the windowpane. Kela sits in the single chair, staring deeply into a blazing fire with a book lying open in her hands. Lemon is curled up in her lap as she strokes his back absentmindedly.

The remnants of peculiar dreams cling to the edges of my consciousness like elusive shadows. A sense of familiarity lingers as if the dreams were connected fragments of a story I'm struggling to piece together. One moment I was running through the snowy woods, desperate to find someone, to make sure they were safe. A second later I'm in a cave, emotions of sorrow and anger so vivid tears prickle my eyes. A mix of voices and words play over and over in my mind like a riddle I can't solve, the most prominent one being Alapheia. I gently lay a hand on my chest, trying to convince my aching heart that it was only a dream but I am restless, almost as if I have left something that belongs to me behind.

Rolling over, I stare out the window. Darkness has fallen, leaving the world in shades of gray. Small pieces of hail and sleet pelt against the glass. A blanket of white covers the ground outside.

"How did you—" My brows furrow as I push myself up to a sitting position and turn back to Kela.

"How did I know it was going to snow?" Kela asks, a knowing smile curling on her lips. She closes the book and sets it to the side. "I just had a feeling." She grins mischievously at me and taps her temple.

"That's some power you have." Swinging my legs over the side of the bed, I gingerly test my weight on my left foot. My eyebrows shoot up in surprise as I hardly discern a twinge of discomfort. "How long was I out for? It looks like it's nearly nightfall outside."

"You sure do have a lot of questions." Kela teases. "You've been out all day and most of the night, it's almost dawn. It doesn't surprise me though. You used up almost all your magic between your transformation and attempting to heal your ankle. Didn't anyone teach you that your magic isn't an endless well?"

"I never had the chance to train beyond the basics," I grumble. This fact is the bane of my existence, whether I want to admit it or not.

"You're also lucky for this little guy." Kela grins, caressing Lemon's fur, just as he likes it. "He slept curled up around your ankle until just a few hours ago." She stands up, gently placing Lemon on the bed beside me. "Although you didn't heal yourself fully, I'm grateful you attempted. I can handle a sprain in a pinch. I'm not good at resetting broken bones and I don't know how powerful a young ramidreju's powers of healing are."

"I still can't wrap my mind around the fact that Lemon is a healer. He's always just been incredibly intuitive." I watch as he scampers across the quilt, chasing a small woolen ball Kela tosses at him.

"The healing you have, regardless of how much knowledge you possess, is better than nothing." Kela reassures me. "We have trained healers at the rebel camp that can assist you further."

"Unicorn healers?" My voice cracks with hope. Could there be others like me? Long-lost cousins? I think of the tapestry in Queen Rose's crypt. There were dozens of unicorns in the field of Shadowvale. I meet Kela's stare and watch as her expression falls.

"Sybil, you're the first unicorn healer my clan has heard of in over a hundred years. You might very well be the last unicorn. Unless you have family hiding somewhere you haven't told me about?" She raises an eyebrow and I see a spark of her infectious positive energy return.

"My father and mother died over ten years ago in an ambush. I have no other family that I'm aware of. We live for hundreds of years, but having offspring is rare." I pause, sniffing the air as the crackling of animal fat hitting the fire draws my attention. "What are you cooking?"

"Well, while you were tending to your beauty sleep, I stayed busy preparing. You need to restore your strength and your magic, especially if we need to transform to reach the rebel camp. The storm will not let up for at least a few days until we can travel, so I stocked up." She gestures to the new stack of wood piled by the fire, a bowl of freshly picked winter berries, and a few buckets of melting ice. "We can always melt snow for more water, but I collected what I could. As luck would have it, I snared a juicy, fat, wild boar that should last us for a couple of days, too."

"So, what's the plan while we are snowed in?" I muse, while picking up a book from the stand. I blow the dust off its cover. 101 edible roots in Northern Province. With a frown, I place the book back on the table.

"Oh my dear Sybil, we are going to have so much fun!" Kela says with a sneaky grin, and I can't help but worry a little bit. "I need to make sure you're fit and strong enough to make the journey to the camp where you can meet the others and tell the elders all you know about Tricella. Your information is going to prove invaluable, Sybil." I smile at her words. "Let's start off with some basics." Kela turns towards me and I watch in awe as her canines elongate, the tips of her ears lengthen and her nails sharpen into claws. "You know that shifter's have three phases?"

"Yes," I say as I roll my eyes. "I'm not entirely daft. The goddess blessed us with the power to shift between our animal and humanoid forms. But, she bestowed the gift of a demi-form, a half-form, that would allow the shifter to maintain the ability of speech while being able to access the full potential of their powers. Some shifters are blessed with healing, others with speed or strength. My father made me learn about the shifters and their forms in order to know the best way to heal a body."

"Good," she says. "Then you also know that even with goddess granted gifts, we have to train and practice to hone these gifts, lest they go to waste." Kela grins wickedly before poking me in the stomach. "How long did they keep you locked up in that castle? And how do you expect to help your people heal wounds and deliver babies when you're so frail? You look brittle as a twig!" She pinches my left bicep.

"Ow! You don't have to pinch me." I rub my hand against the pink flesh, but my lips are curled into a grin, knowing she's right. I was lean before they kidnapped me, but the time spent imprisoned did not benefit my health, strength, and endurance.

"I know that as a unicorn, your purpose is to heal and save, but I still believe everyone should learn at least a little bit of self-defense. You never know when you want to punch someone in the face. I've had my fair share of occasions in all honesty." Kieran's face comes back to me. "With my help, no one should be able to get past your defenses. Unless you want them too." She wiggles her eyebrows provocatively and I fall

back onto the bed in a fit of giggles at her antics. As much
as Kela and I differ from each other, these next few days are
going to be lively—to say the least.

"How is a few days of training going to help me?" I ask
exasperatedly as we quickly go to work, moving as many things
up against the wall as possible, stacking what we can in the
cramped room. I watch as Kela stretches her arms above her
head, her back arching and her feet lifting onto their tiptoes. I
stand, hands loose at my side, watching her.

"Even one day of training can put you in a better position
than you were yesterday," she says matter-of-factly.

"Warriors train for years before going into battle…" Just
as healers train for years at Nova Esther, or as apprentices.
But, look what I did for my village with the little training I had.
Perhaps the wolf is right.

"It's not about how much you know, but knowing enough
that you can trust your body in time of need. Plus, they all had
to start somewhere. The first lesson is about balance. Before
you can learn to hone your body to move with grace, you
need to learn how to listen to yourself." She moves through
a series of slow movements, her legs spread into a lunge, one
arm in front and one pointing to the back. "This is the first
step to move past your fears and delve into your inner power.
Connecting body, mind, soul and power."

"I know how to balance." I chuckle, crossing my arms
over my chest. "I thought you were going to show me how to
defend myself."

Kela swivels on her feet, my eyes barely registering her
movements; she is like living water. My heart speeds in my
chest as she moves faster and faster around me in the small
space. A cold steel blade caresses my neck, and I bolt in panic
as her other arm pins mine to my sides before I can blink.

"You were saying?" She lets me go with a small push and I
stumble, rubbing at the phantom sensation of the metal against

my skin. "It's all about routine. Every day I start by practicing. It helps build mental focus, concentration, determination and perseverance."

"When will we move onto more physical defense?" I rub my arms. The image of Aramis holding me in his tight grip as he takes me from my home and Kieran dragging me to the dungeon come back to me. I vow to never let another man take me against my will ever again.

"So eager for violence! Patience, my friend." Kela laughs and helps me into position as she begins to instruct my movements, her hands gently guiding my left foot and arm forward with my right back. "Finding physical balance will also help you hone onto your magical balance. You need to be able to assess not just your physical limitations, but your magical limitations as well. And in this, you can push on those limits."

This isn't so bad.

"Now keep your knee over your ankle like this, and sink down, lengthening through the top of your head. Imagine you're wearing a crown." She winks at me as I make the slight adjustments.

As if I'd ever wear a crown atop my head. Balancing a book would have been a better analogy. "Who taught you?" I ask, curious to know more about Kela.

"My mama. She's the most formidable fighter I have ever met. She can disarm opponents much bigger than her without a second thought! Being one of the leaders, I don't see her often these days." A glimpse of sadness crosses her gaze and my heart aches as I can feel her loneliness echo mine. "I've become a bit of a lone wolf since I started playing a bigger role in the rebellion. As a seer and shifter, they prefer I stay in hiding, as I'm too valuable to lose. I regularly send messages to the camp with updates, but I'm constantly on the move, from safe house to safe house, but that's okay. We're fighting the good fight and sacrifices have to be made. Perfect!" She claps her hands and a gleeful gleam shines in her eyes as I manage to hold the stance. "Now we will practice breathing."

"I know how to breathe. I practice with patients all the time as I talk them through their pain." I roll my eyes as I move to stand.

"Nope, back down in position. You're going to practice breathing. Without breaking your balance." Her lips curl back even further into a grin, her sharp canine teeth glinting in the firelight.

The days go by between training sessions, tasty meals and intriguing conversations, but when night falls, I am restless. My dreams have become incredibly vivid and most nights I run through the forest following a red thread, desperate to reach its end. Sometimes I see books of every color I can imagine hanging from the branches of trees, but every time I try to open them, someone whispers that it's not time yet. The ending of my dreams, however, has changed. I no longer hear Alapheia's call but Aramis' whispering. Come back to me, Sybil, and I have to force myself not to run through the cabin's doors.

The storm is gradually waning, its ferocity yielding to a more subdued force. At the same time, my magic is replenishing at a much quicker rate than it was at the castle, the lack of torture surely helping somewhat. Living with Kela so far has been like sharing the room with a ray of pure sunshine. She's been taking care of me as if she's known me her whole life, even if I'm nothing more than a stranger to her. Maybe we'll be friends someday.

With her help, I finally feel myself again, but I am not the same Sybil that lived in Bellevue. I have changed, marked by the challenges life has thrown in my path, and I cannot wait to get to know this new version of myself better.

Sweat drenches my body. My legs are on fire, my arms are like a bowl of gelatin as I once again try to maintain the posture. My breath comes out in ragged pants. I lose my balance after less than a minute the first few tries, but Kela encourages me to get back up.

"That's enough," Kela claps, bouncing up from the bed. I collapse into a heap on the floor, grateful for the cool wood against my hot flesh. Who knew holding one position for so long would be so hard? "Now we move on to squats. Up." Kela pokes my side with her toe, urging me back up.

"I am questioning what would be worse: being locked up in a tower or having to hold one more balancing position. I give up Kela." I peer at her from the floor and shake my head before resting my cheek against the ground. I don't even care that my sweat is mixing into mud with the dirt.

"What happened to the fearless unicorn ready to take on a wolf with her bare hands?" Kela nudges my side with the toe of her boots. "Get up."

With a groan, I push myself into a sitting position.

"So with a squat—"

"I know how to do a squat." I interrupt, wiping the sweat off my brow before squatting down and gesturing to my legs. My body curses at me as I position my knees in a bending position. Goddess grant me the strength to–

"You're doing it all wrong." She patiently chides as she walks to stand beside me. "Straighten your back, you're hunching."

"Am I though?" I look sidelong at her. "Squats aren't that difficult."

Kela rolls her eyes at me. "Well, you're doing this one wrong. Butt out unicorn. Straighten your arms–"

"My arms are straight!" I groan.

Kela pulls my arms out from the slight bend in my elbow. I groan, knowing that Kela misses nothing with those wolf

eyes of hers. "They weren't. Now hold those there while you
straighten your back and push into the ground with your
feet. Your feet–" She taps my toes with hers, "are the roots
that make you stand tall. Now pull through your core with an
invisible string–"

"Like this?" I ask, being aware of an acute difference in my
core and back. "Are you sure?"

"Yes girl! Like that!" Kela grins at me, wickedly. "Now, do
fourteen more."

"Goddess help me!" I groan. Through the repetition of
the movement, the power builds up in my thighs and backside
along with a comfortable burning heat. Sweat pours down my
body as I pant. By the time I finish my last repetition, my knees
are trembling and my thighs are screaming at me. "I don't think
I can handle anymore of your training."

"Then let's do a cool down." The gentle smile from Kela
makes me concerned. This training has thoroughly kicked my
ass. My eyes wander to the door as my thoughts stray to the
fluffy white snow banks slowly piling outside.

Another chuckle from Kela. I turn as she hands me a mug
filled with half melted snow. "Have a drink and then we will
do some stretches. They're made to bring your body back to
a normal pace. Plus, they help limit any soreness you'll have
later. You need to balance it with your breathing. Look inward
at yourself, at your power. Your breath can help channel your
power, gathering it up and then directing it where you want it
to go."

"You seem to know an awful lot about magic." I mimic her
movements with my legs spread wide before me on the floor.

"Tell me more about the shifters in Shadowvale. You
mentioned Nero's mother sided with the shifters. She even
married a shifter…" I reach for my mug, only to find it
knocked over in the bustle. The remaining water has soaked
into a thick green paste on the floor.

"It's true, we have many elementals who have joined our cause, or shelter shifters." She pauses, dusting herself off and stares at me. "Not all towns in Shadowvale are open to us though. Especially those closest to the castle who've been poisoned by Tricella's lies. Many of the shifters, or halflings like Nero, have fled to towns on the outer edges of the country and beyond. But not all have the means or the health to travel so far."

"What kind of shifters live in Shadowvale? Do other species live here too?"

"Oh girl, there are so many species of shifters; wolves, tigers, foxes, rabbits, chickens, snakes, otters, deer, and birds." She ticks them off on her fingers. "I'm sure there are dozens more. Most live in fear of Tricella and refuse to leave their humanoid form. There are a few fae and humans who live in some of the larger trade cities, like in Verdigris Falls near the northeastern coast. Then you've got the elementals. My grandfather used to tell stories about the great elemental rulers before the war who could become the living element themselves."

I take a large sip from my mug, the slushy, cold water sliding down my throat. The abrupt coolness is instantly refreshing, and I stand a little straighter.

"I've spent my whole life in a pack of shifters and elementals with different forms of magic." She lifts her arms high above her head before bending forward at the waist, her forehead nearly touching the smooth wood floor.

"If I try to do that, I'll crack in half. You'll have to carry the two broken halves of me back to your pack." I bluntly assess her pose, and a chuckle escapes my lips. Kela cranes her neck, an identical grin plastered on her face.

"Oh, I'll have you loving stretching so much, you'll be moaning in pleasure and begging for more." Laughing playfully, Kela quickly sits up.

Heat flushes my face, which only sends her into a fit of giggles. Kela falls backwards, knocking into the shelf behind her. A bowl wobbles precariously before falling upside down beside us. Fine dark green powder flies everywhere at the impact. The fresh, sweet, vegetal smell of matcha fills the air in the small room.

"Relax, Sybie. You're too easy to tease. You've got to toughen up if you want to stand a chance in the pack." Shaking her head like a dog, she sends hazy green dust clouds into the air.

Lemon shakes his body, sneezing. His fur is coated in a fine dusting of the powder giving him an ethereal appearance.

"Well, covered in green tea, you sure do look the picture of a mythical creature!" My hair clings to the sweat beading my forehead. "I'm sure I am not the picture of beauty myself; sweaty, exhausted, and covered in green tea powder."

"We should probably get cleaned up." Kela pushes herself from the floor. "Unfortunately, there isn't a big enough tub for us, but if you help me take this pot outside to fill with snow, we should be able to heat up enough water to both get cleaned up before it starts storming again."

ARAMIS

The forest is a wall of white as we trudge through the trees. My breath condenses in a fog with every exhale. Beside me, Nero pushes on steadily. Icicles cling to the tips of his hair, blown back by the headwind.

"She can't have gotten far, especially in this storm. We have to find her before she freezes to death." I yell over the noise of the ceaseless wind.

"We have to find shelter before we freeze to death, Aramis. We're wandering in circles." He yells back. "Look, there seems to be a small ravine. If we're lucky, we can find a cave to weather the rest of the storm in."

"I won't leave her alone in this blizzard." I wave at the snow blowing around us.

"While I love this recent change of heart, I don't want to explain to yer father how I let ye die. Who will save yer people then?"

The sting of his words sinks in.

"I'm sorry."

"Aye, I ken the urgency to see this through—and quickly, but Sybil is a smart lass. She would have sensed the storm coming an' found shelter." Nero briefly glances back my way before starting down the side of the ravine. I can't help but wonder if he's is hiding more.

Stones and shards of ice tumble down the slope with each step. I quickly follow after, the snow biting into my palms as I grip the side of the rocky surface for support. Glancing over my shoulder, I notice a thin ice covered stream at the bottom surrounded by rocks. Its surface appears smooth under the thin blanket of snow, but a fall from this height would be dangerous.

"Any luck?" I shout at Nero, the wind carrying my voice away.

"Up ahead, I see a darker shadow!" He throws out his arm to point and I watch as he slips from the ravine wall. His whole body leans precariously backwards as he scrambles at the rock and ice before him, wings flapping on his back. Instinctively, I reach out to the surrounding air and blast it against his back, slamming his head into the snow. His claws make purchase in the rock wall and he turns a grateful smile in my direction. A laugh erupts and I slam my fist against the wall before me at the sight of his face plastered with snow.

Nero grabs a fistful of it and throws it right at my face, faster than I can move. I'm blinded by white as I swipe at my face. "You ass."

"But at least I'm your arse," he replies, batting his eyes dramatically at me.

"Get moving before I let you tumble down onto your ass for goofing off. I am freezing and I am not in the mood to lose any fingers today." My teeth chatter as if to emphasize my statement.

"Yes, your royal highness. As you wish." He jumps down to a small ledge, his feet crunching in the snow. His massive frame disappears before he pops his head back out and says, "It's going to be tight."

"Better tight than being stuck out in the snow," I say

through clenched, chattering teeth, and I follow him along the ravine edge. "Do you think you'll be able to light a fire?"

"That's hard to say. With all this snow, any wood is bound to be soaked. Even with my powers of fire, it'll be difficult." He frowns back at me.

"What if I dry it out before you light it on fire?" Lifting my hand, I use my powers to brush away the piling snow, revealing more branches.

"We should be careful how much energy we use. You never know if we will need it," Nero says.

"All the energy in the world won't matter if we freeze to death," I grumble under my breath as I watch his body disappear into the rock face once more.

His head reappears with a sharp grin on his face. "Did I mention Drakes have exceptional hearing?"

"You may have skipped that part, and about a dozen other facts about your life." I retort as I duck and follow him into the opening. The cave is a small one, barely deep enough for the two of us to sit side by side. Nero tucks his wings behind him and braces himself on the floor, knees to his chest. He pats the ground next to him.

"It's nae the hot springs in the mountains, but it's dry. Well, at least until the ice you're covered in melts," he laughs.

"Me? You're one to talk." I gesture from his head to his toes, where the ice has already melted, soaking his chemise. I quickly brush off the layer of snow that has gathered in my hair, shoulders, and pack.

After slinging off my pack and cloak, I wedge myself between him and the hard cave wall. I am used to Shadowvale's harsh winters, but usually we are lucky enough to find a tavern or local to stay with if we are caught out in a storm. I pull my cloak over my body up to my chin, take a deep breath and try to relax my tense muscles.

"How long have you known?" I finally ask, my gut

churning, still trying to put the puzzle pieces together concerning Nero's true identity. I lean my head back against the rocky wall, my body exhausted.

"I didn't find out until years after we became friends. I started showing signs and my mother confessed my father was a shifter. I guess that makes me a halfling." He slides to the ground next to me. Steam rises from his snow wet clothes slowly drying from his warm body. "Didn't ye ever wonder how a boy of yer age could break down yer door and carry ye to the healers when even yer best guards couldn't?"

"Why didn't you tell me sooner?" I ask, unable to hide the hurt. "Were you ever planning to tell me?" Before Sybil came into the picture, my mind silently finishes the thought. Because, before Sybil, I might not have handled this so well.

Nero gazes solemnly from beside me. The silence weighs heavily in the air. I exhale, tense and unsure if I'm ready to hear his response.

"I was scared it would break our friendship." Nero sighs as he restlessly tosses a ball of fire back and forth between his palms. His fingers are tipped in sharp claws. "Ye were so consumed with hatred for shifters after yer mum's death. Ye still can't stand the thought of them. So much so that after a hundred years you deny yer own feelings towards yer mate." Silver lines his eyes as his words trail off. Sparks and ash fall to the snow as he clenches his fist.

"I—" The words die on my tongue as I watch the grief play across my best friend's face. How would I have responded a hundred years ago? Fifty? Twenty-five? The truth is that I would likely have arrested him and taken him back to the castle for treason.

But things are different now. My mate is a shifter, so I can certainly accept my best friend being one too. Is this what the spirits in the forest were talking about? My hand reaches to grasp the stone around my neck that seems to pulse against my skin since Nero's transformation.

Knowing how my entire existence has been shaped by my prejudices and hatred, can I really be angered that he feared for our friendship by withholding this information? With a sigh, I stand up, then reach down and help him to his feet.

"Nero, you've been my friend for over a hundred years." I begin, clapping him on the shoulder. He turns the gesture into a hug, and I accept it. "For too long, I've been looking for ways to seek revenge for my mother's death and needing to protect my people. But perhaps it's time to change."

"I'm surprised yer taking this so well, yer majesty." Nero jabs me in the side of the ribs and grins. "What an unprejudiced reaction."

"I'll give you an unprejudiced reaction." My brow raises in challenge and we both start laughing. I have a lot to process, but I am finally learning to not let pride and prejudices get in the middle of a century-long friendship. It will not shape my future, or the man I hope to become one day. With the hope of Sybil accepting me as her mate—one day—and with Nero at our side, surely all that comes after this is manageable.

"How long do you think the storm will last?" I inquire after a while, watching the wind blow furiously outside the cave opening. It is slowly filling up the space with snow. Hopefully, it will help keep our body heat in the small space.

"Ye and I both ken Shadowvale winter storms are unpredictable. They can be two hours or two weeks. But ye know, I'm nae very good at small talk and ye are very good at evading difficult conversations." Nero rubs his hands together before exhaling against them. The small cavern immediately warmed up a degree or two. He cocks his head and grins, a dimple appearing in his right cheek. "At least yer lucky I'm a fire drake, nae an ice drake."

"There are ice drakes?" I ask, my eyebrows shooting up.

"Maybe?" He shrugs before digging in his pack and pulling

out a flask and taking a swig before offering it to me. I drink deep, reveling in the burning sensation while it slides smoothly down my throat. My eyes water as the warm sensation fills the rest of my body.

"Whoa there. I know it's been a shocking afternoon, but we need to keep our wits about us." Nero takes the flask from my hand and returns it to his pack. "Ye ken better than anyone how potent this stuff is."

"What did you mean by, maybe?" My hand drifts to the crystal at my neck and I rub my thumb against its smooth cool surface, once again quiet.

"I don't see why there shouldn't be ice drakes. There are earth, water, wind, an' fire elementals plus all the sub-elementals. Why can't there be more than just fire an' earth drakes?" He counts off the types on his fingers, the tips of his claws making tiny clicking noises.

"Have you ever met other drakes?" I ask, curiously. I watch his face fall as he stares in his lap.

"That's one thing Sybil and I have in common. I've never known another drake in ma life, outside of the man me mum said was my da."

"Sybil has only known one drake in her life?" My heart speeds up at the sound of her name.

"Nae, ye dolt." He reaches over to ruffle my hair and I swat him away. "Unicorn shifters are as rare as they come. I inquired around, but besides Sybil and her parents, nae one has heard hide nor tail of them for over a century. Wouldn't ye think if she knew of other kin, she'd have moved to them after her parents' death?"

My mind travels to Edmund, the poor elemental child orphaned after the death of his parents. I close my eyes, my fist clenching. Sybil has no one. I had my father at least, although after the death of my mother—he was never the same man.

"Death of a loved one affects us all differently." I sigh,

grabbing a pebble beside me and tossing it to bounce off the hard stone floor. "Do you remember when we first found Edmund after that shifter raid?"

"Aye, he was a wee lad." Nero grins, lost in memories. "He followed us around like a pup after ye brought him home. If he wasn't on yer heels, he was my shadow constantly asking questions."

"That boy was an endless stream of questions; how does this work, what does it take to get on the king's guard, when can I go on a mission, when can I learn to wield a real sword, why why why…" I chuckle then sober up as I think about him at the castle waiting for us to return. But how can we return now? "How is he going to take all this?"

"The lad is smart and he trusts ye, and he trusts us. He took a shine to Sybil after she healed him. The world is nae black nor white, Aramis. He'll understand that not all shifters are evil, like the group that raided his city and killed his parents."

"Perhaps you're right. But what about Sybil? What am I going to say to her?"

"Tell her the truth. Tell her how ye feel. Yer fated mates, Aramis. Ye were nae the only one looking when ye thought the other's back was turned. She cares about ye, even if she hasn't admitted it to herself." He chuckles and nudges me. "Look how long it took ye to accept it.

"Yeah, but…" Guilt churns heavy in my stomach as I replay that night in the dungeons. Sybil standing defiant and proud despite her torn gown and bloodied head. How could I have been such a fool and not seen it? I should have been the one to rescue her that night.

"I'm nae saying she will forgive you right away. Ye've got some groveling to do my laddie, but I've seen the real you. I ken she will too, just be honest with her and give her time," he says solemnly.

"How about you tell me how you helped Sybil escape?" I ask, trying to lighten the mood and I am pleased when I see a shocked expression on Nero's face.

"I–" He pauses and glances at me. "Alright, ye've got me. I could nae leave her down there. Not knowing what I did about Kieran and the Queen's plans."

The words settle belatedly in my mind. The ones of plans that Kieran and the queen have. "What plans, Nero?" I ask, rage lacing my words, my entire body tensing.

"Easy there, Prince." Nero responds soothingly, but any humor is wiped off his face as he sees the expression on my face.

"No, you told me it's time to tell me the truth. I want to hear it."

"The Queen has been using dark magic for quite some time. You have seen hew power in the throne room. That is not normal magic, Aramis. It's dark, and it is unforgiving. As such, it asks for a price. We are not entirely sure what her ultimate goal is, but she is draining shifters' of their magic to counteract the effects of whatever evil she is manipulating. It helps her cheat time. The attacks are an excuse. She sends some sort of demons to raid unprotected villages, and then she sends us there to collect the leftover shifters."

"You fucking knew!" The words slip out of my mouth automatically. "Sybil told me all of this and I called her a liar to her face. Goddess-damn it, Nero." She is never going to forgive me. After all this time… after trying to protect my people, I have been unknowingly causing harm. Goddess above, no wonder people have torn opinions about me. "Fuck, Nero!" The words burst out, revealing the hurt I don't want to show. "Why didn't you say something earlier?" Fury rises in my gut. I have played a part in all this destruction: innocent men, women and children, not rebels.

"Would you have believed me? Would you have believed

any of it?" Nero asks, voice cracking after moments of silence, clearly reading my own. He leans his head against the rocky cave wall behind him as he runs his hand through his hair and takes a steady breath. Everything I've ever believed has been a partial lie, and it was I who was unraveling my kingdom one raid at a time. I press my lips into a line and sigh. I must make amends. To him, to my people. And, most importantly, to Sybil.

The light coming through the cave mouth has slowly become darker as the evening wanes and snow fills the entrance.

"Tis going to be a long night, Aramis." Nero cuts me off. "Ye ken speculate on what ifs until water burns, but ye will nae be any closer to the answers ye seek. Ye ken we need as much sleep as we can get if we're going to hike through the snow banks an' catch up wi' Sybil. We won't find her in the dark, even if it stops snowing."

I sigh again, knowing he's right. But this conversation isn't over, and we both know it. A long time passes as I sit in silence watching his small ball of flame dance before us until sleep claims me.

SYBIL

Kela pulls two packs from the shelf and tosses them on the bed followed by empty flasks, sacks of dried food, an assortment of cookware, and a tin of tea leaves. "The skies should be clear of storms for a few days, but it's going to be a journey. We will need to avoid Shadowvale's patrols as much as we can." She shoots me a knowing glance.

"How long until we get to the rebel camp?" I begin packing the bags and my healer's satchel. Luckily only a few bottles cracked during my fall.

"Well that depends," Kela replies, grunting as she tosses a heavy armful of thick winter clothing on the table. "They move around a lot to keep from being detected. Our progress is going to be slowed due to all that thick snow. Have you ever tried hiking through thigh-high deep snow?"

"I can't say that I have." Glancing out the frost covered window, a frown tugs at my lips. The snow had indeed piled up at least thigh-high over the last couple of days to my utter surprise. It snowed in Kallistar, but never more than a few inches at a time. The most I had to worry about were my toes freezing on my walk to the village. This will be a real adjustment to make.

"Well, if we didn't need these supplies and our magic at full strength, I'd suggest we shift. We'd both be faster on four legs but we need to be smart about how and when we use our powers." She turns away and pulls out the cast iron pan from the fire and places it on the table. "At least we will have warm, full stomachs when we leave."

Lemon slithers into the bag of food and pokes his head out, watching us. "Hey! You little rascal! Get out of there!" I scoop him up in my arms and plant a soft kiss on the top of his head. Of course he would try to slither into our food provisions. I shake my head in disbelief, giggling slightly.

Kela lifts the lid, the aroma of caramelized berries mingles with a buttery pie crust. Nestled in the bottom of the cast iron pan sit six small pastries.

"Those look and smell divine." My mouth waters as my eyes devour the perfectly browned crust and oozing baked berry compote. "Hunter, healer, and baker. Is there anything you can't do?"

"Hmm. I can't grow wings and fly. Boy, that would really come in handy. You don't happen to know a drake shifter do you?" Her eyes twinkle as she grins wolfishly at me with eyebrows raised.

"Nero?" I shrug as I pull thick woolen socks over my feet. I know he is part fire drake, but you'd think I'd remember him having wings.

"Pfft. He's a cinnamon roll that would do anything to help a damsel in distress, but I think I'd remember if he could fly." She bites into one of the pastries and groans. "Unless you know something that I don't. Here, try this."

Before I can answer she grabs another pastry and shoves it into my mouth. My eyes close in ecstasy as the pastry melts on my tongue; flaky savory crust mixing with sweet sticky jam.

"You've really outdone yourself this time." I say between bitefulls of her sinfully delicious pastry.

"Oh please," she says, nonplussed, waving a hand in my direction as she backs towards the fire, but I can see a creep of blush along her cheeks and silver lining her eyes. I try to make eye contact with her, but she doesn't quite meet my eyes.

"Kela, is something wrong?" I asked, worry creasing my brow. She doesn't respond, and her silence sits like a cold stone in the pit of my stomach.

"Was it something I said? I was being serious about your cooking being delicious." I cross the few remaining steps to her side and lay a hand on her shoulder. My movement brings on a fresh wave of tears rolling down her cheek. I don't know how to explain it but I can sense sorrow and loneliness rolling off of her in waves. Was this an extension of my powers? I had never been able to feel another's emotions before.

"No, it's not that." She sniffles and rubs at her eyes. "It's just, all my life I have not fit in with the pack. I was always the odd wolf out, especially since I started getting my visions from a very young age. Sharing the cabin with you for the last couple of days has been the happiest I have been in a long time. Thank you for reminding me what it's like to have a friend and not having to constantly look behind my back." I smile knowing very well what she is talking about.

"We were meant to find each other Kela," I say and take her hands in mind. "I will be your friend for as long as you'll have me."

"Oh Sybil," she embraces me in a tight hug that squeezes the breath out of me. I pound at her back until she lets me go.

"You are one strong woman!" I wheeze as I lean forward bracing my hands on my knees, catching my breath.

"Hah! Sometimes I don't know my own strength—" her words and then her body pauses briefly before she shakes her head. Her blue eyes meet mine. "It's time to go—something is coming. The vision was blurry, but we must make haste."

My breath puffs in clouds before me as we make our way through the trees. The snow, trapped by massive boughs above us, only goes up to our shins. I chance a glance behind us at the small cabin camouflaged between the snow and towering pines. A small stream of smoke rises through the chimney from our banked fire, the only indication that we were there.

"We don't have time to cover our tracks." Kela grabs my elbow and pulls my attention forward. "The best we can do is hope the snow slows them down. We need to head east. We can skirt around the towns at the base of the mountains to avoid the King's patrols."

"Who is after us?" I involuntarily shudder, pulling the borrowed thick fleece lined cloak closer.

"I don't know." Kela says dismissively as she lets go of my hand and breaks off a dry branch.

"What if it's Nero? Didn't you say he might be meeting us?" I jog to catch up to her long strides.

"I'm not sure, Sybil." She purses her lips in decision as she keeps breaking branch after branch until she finds the right one, thick enough and sturdy enough to walk with and hands it over to me. We continue another twenty paces before she breaks off an equally large branch and fashions herself another stick. "I'm not risking it. No one should know about that cabin except a select few in the clan including myself and Nero."

"So what if it's—"

Kela cuts me off with a hand to my face and signals for me to be quiet. The woolen gloves are rough and cold against the soft skin of my lips. Silence echoes around us only broken by the occasional thump of snow falling off trees and thudding to the ground.

"Let's go." She whispers and points to her left, further into the mountains. "It's not Nero. Or, if it is, he's not alone. I sense

236

another's presence—one I'm not familiar with."

My heart leaps in my chest. Could it be Aramis? What has Nero told him? "What if another storm blows in?"

She stops in her tracks and turns to face me. "Sybil, trust me. We're safe for a few more days at least before another storm hits. By that time, even if we have not reached the next safe house, there are plenty of caves we can camp out the storm in."

"What if Nero comes looking for us and we aren't at the cabin?" I inquire.

"I left a message only he will be able to decipher. If he doesn't find the message, he knows my first priority is to get you to safety."

We travel for over an hour, only stopping occasionally for her to sniff the air, shake her head and then point us in a different route. For every turn we take, there is a familiar tug in the opposite direction, almost as if she is purposefully keeping me from reuniting with whatever it is that is calling to me.

Lemon shivers in my pocket, occasionally poking his head out before ducking back inside. I use my free hand to reach in and scratch his head. Around me as we head further into the forest and higher up the mountain, the world is nothing but tall pine trees and snow. Icicles the size of my forearm glisten in the early morning sun.

The snow crunches under my boots as we crest another hill, the exertion of hiking making me sweat despite the cold winter. and my mind starts wondering.

"You know," Kela starts interrupting the silence, "once you've shared all the information you have about Tricella with the council, they will probably be able to help you go back to your village, should you wish to. This is not your fight after all." Her voice is full of genuine curiosity.

"I don't think that's a good idea. Tricella is desperate to have me. She probably sent some of her guards to Bellevue already. I'm also not entirely sure I want to go back there," I say between labored breaths. This is the first time I've admitted not wanting to return to my old life and I am surprised at how committed those words sounded.

"I am a shifter so this fight is as much mine as it is yours. I want to stay and help, if the defenders will have me," I continue, voice clear and full of determination. Kela turns back to me and nods with a smile. "I just wanted to make sure you knew you had options. They might have dragged you into this but you have a choice Sybil. No one can take that from you." My friend concludes and turns back to keep going. Step after step, I try to imagine what my new life could look like, helping the rebels free Shadowvale of Tricella. Surely they can use another healer on their side, even if just a half-trained one. Will I be able to have a place to call home or be constantly on the move like Kela? Will the shifters accept me even if I am from Kallistar?

Through the opening in the trees I spot a small valley glistening white, its surface undisturbed. It looks like it belongs in a fairytale, the way the sun sets the surface sparkling as if it's alive with magic.

Just then, the wind changes, and with it comes the scent of sweat, sulfur, and iron. I watch as Kela's pupils dilate before gleaming fangs descend from her upper lip.

"Run!" she growls before pushing me towards the slope leading to the valley.

I stumble, but find my bearing, digging my walking stick into the ground. My heart thuds wildly in my chest as my lungs seize up. They've found us.

My whole body is frozen. I can't move. I can't breathe.

"Sybil, run!" Kela screams at the top of her lungs. It's enough to break me from my panic. I begin racing down the hill as fast as I can, one hand braced against Lemon to keep him from bouncing out of my pocket. My leather satchel and pack pound against my back and side with every step. I'm halfway across the field before I realize I don't hear anything except the thud of my feet as they sink through the ground and the beating of my heart in my ears. I stop and turn around. My eyes scan the entire valley but all I see is the track my feet made in the snow. Kela is nowhere to be found.

ARAMIS

Ice bites into my palm, a fresh sting of pain against my already numb flesh as we dig against the packed snow. Overnight, the storm blew a dense mound of snow blocking the only entrance and exit to our cave. Small rays of sunlight filter through as we clear the entryway and crawl out of the small space. Glancing out of the tunnel, the sky above us is crystalline blue, not a cloud in sight.

"Fucking storms," I mumble under my breath as I kick at a pile of snow and send it flying into the air.

"Hey, at least we did nae freeze to death." Nero yawns and stretches. His large membranous wings glow shades of cobalt blue as the sun hits them. I reach out a hand in fascination to the wing closest to me.

"I don't know if I'll ever get used—" He quickly snaps his wings back, out of my reach, folding them gracefully behind him.

"It's rude to touch someone's wings without permission," Nero says, crossing his massive arms over his chest. "They're extremely sensitive."

"Sorry, I didn't realize you were so sensitive, you big baby. Can you blame me? My friend of over a century suddenly surprises me that he's a giant lizard." I throw my hands up in surrender and grin. He responds by punching me soundly in my left arm. "Ugh!" I grunt, rubbing the sore spot.

"Aye, and look who's the big baby now. And I'm no lizard, ye daft arse—I'm a drake shifter." He laughs, then jumps down the ledge below us, making his way to the bottom of the ravine.

I don't deign him with a response. Besides, we don't have the time. "How do you know we are going the right way?" I scramble down after him, my boots sliding on the loose rocks and ice. "Her tracks are bound to be completely covered after last night's storm, unless you're going to tell me you have an extremely heightened sense of smell?"

"Think with yer head, Princeling." Nero stretches his arm towards the sky. A thin trickle of smoke is barely visible above the treeline before the wind whisks it away.

My heart begins to speed in my chest, my mouth dry as I take off at a run to the other side. Only one thought in my head.

Mine.

"She's gone!" I yell, slamming my hand into the stone fireplace. The pain radiating from the impact barely registers as I turn to face Nero.

"She canna have gone far. The ashes are still warm." He attempts to soothe me as he crouches beside me, then places his bare hand in the half burnt logs and soot. "Maybe they left a note."

Rage boils inside me. To be this close and not find her makes me want to tear the world apart. The longer it takes us to find her, the more my agony deepens. Is this what the fated link does to us? Take over so all I can desire is her safety? I didn't know the physical pang my heart bears as it pumps harder, trying to reconcile the fact that she's not here. I thought this was it—that we would find her. I close my eyes, my hands clenching at my sides.

Where are you, Sybil?

"Aramis." Nero's voice is distant.

The guilt and the need twist into me, slowly pulling me apart. There are a million things I could have done differently had I not been so blinded by my own prejudices and fear. I should have listened to her in the dungeons, reasoned with her, freed her. What kind of man sees his mate thrown in the gutters and leaves without looking back. If Sybil does not grant me forgiveness I will understand. Why the fuck would a gentle and brave soul like her see past all my disgraceful flaws. I barely know if I can forgive myself, but I have to try, even if it's the last thing I do. The urgency to see her drives my every move. The desire to ensure that she is safe is the only thing working in my brain and in my heart.

I have to find her.

"Aramis!" Nero's voice is louder. A steady pressure grips my forearms through my leather gauntlets. Opening my eyes, I see we're standing in the middle of a small cyclone, the wind ripping the objects off the shelves and smashing them into the walls. Above us the roof shakes from the force of my wind magic. I pull my power back in and the wind slowly dwindles to a light breeze making the objects fall to the floor with a crash, except for one small scrap of fabric which floats towards the floor.

"I'm sorry." My voice falters as I turn away from my best friend and snatch the piece of fabric. I lift it to my face, inhaling deeply. It smells of rich lavender, vanilla, and black tea. I breathe in her scent. My mate's scent. "She was here," I say, my thumb idly caressing the worn fabric in my hands. Her cloak. The memory of clasping it around her neck the night we raided her house surfaces. Even then my senses tingled as my fingers brushed against the bare column of her throat. I sigh, suddenly aware of my indifference even when the truth was right in front of me.

"Of course she was here, ye dolt." Nero smirks, laughing at me. "And if ye want any chance of catching up with her, we have to leave now. She's with Kela, I can smell her all over this cabin, despite your destruction. She'll have Sybil halfway across the country by nightfall if she has her way."

"What are you talking about. Who's Kela?" I growl, my body tensing possessively.

Nero reaches over and grips my shoulder, staring me in the eye. "Calm yerself down, lover lad. Kela is a close ally. She's one of the good ones, like me." He points to his chest in emphasis.

"Where is she taking Sybil?" I ask. We pick up the pace as I spot the tracks leading away from the cabin. Two sets of petite boot prints in the snow.

"If I ken Kela as much as I think I do, she'll be taking Sybil to the Southeastern rebel camp. It's nae safe to tarry here in the woods, especially with Tricella in a rage. She's a seer, she'll have sensed her looking for the unicorn." I look at him wide-eyed at the news that the shifters have a seer of their own.

"That crafty little wolf." Nero grins as he points at the ground. "See how she doubles back and then heads off in another direction? She's trying to lead someone off to break their neck falling down one of these ravines. Ye would have kept walking and fallen straight through the snow, had I nae scented it."

Nero breaks off a branch and pokes directly in front of the path I was about to push through the foliage. The snow falls away between the roots revealing a downward steep slope to snow covered rocks below. He points to our left where another set of footsteps continues.

"Two more steps and at best ye'd have broken yer leg. At

worst, ye'd have fallen through and broken yer neck."

We turn and head into the direction of the other footprints. I'm more careful about where I place my weight, which slows our progress.

"This is taking too long," I complain after hours of hiking uphill. Each step is a struggle, the weight of the accumulated snow pulling at my boots like unseen hands determined to pull me down. Impatience simmers within me like a restless flame. "Can't you just use your dragon powers and fly above the tree line?" I grumble, pushing aside a branch in my way. A yank at my collar has me stumbling backwards. A large sharp icicle falls directly where I was just standing. I throw a grateful glance in Nero's direction.

"One: who would save yer ass? Two: I'm a drake, nae a dragon. It's different. Imagine how unicorns and horses are different—do you remember all of Sybil's protesting that she nae knew how to ride a horse?" Nero chuckles at the memory. "If I were to fly us above, we might miss their tracks. Kela is a great huntress and has more than one trick up her sleeve. Come, ye impatient arse, and follow behind me." He skirts around the tree and continues following the path. For being my best friend, he can sometimes be an asshole. I glance up at the sun as it rises further in the sky.

"Nero, you're lucky tha—" Cold steel presses against my throat. My body tenses at the blade biting into my skin. A collection of blood wells from its shallow cut.

"I'd stop, if I were you," a female voice growls in my ear. "And what is a princeling doing, gallivanting about my forest in the middle of winter?"

I slowly move to grab the dagger sheathed at my waist, but I pause as another blade presses into my gut.

"Not one more move, pretty boy, or you'll finally get to see that princes bleed out just like the rest of us." I freeze as the blade presses deeper against my skin. "Now, I'm only going to repeat myself one more time. What are you doing out here?"

The female's breath is warm against my cheek as I contemplate my options. Am I fast enough to detain her with my wind magic before she slices my throat open? If I tell her the truth, will she believe me?

"I—" Sweat perspires on my brow and palms despite the frigid winter air.

"Kela that's enough now," Nero chuckles as he turns around and sees my predicament. "Ye've had yer fun, lass. Let him go." Pain radiates down the back of my leg as she kicks me, forcing me to my knees. The steel blade never waivers or leaves my throat.

"This is not funny. How dare you bring one of them here, Nero Lockheed. Let alone their prince." She spits at Nero. "I thought you were one of us!"

"Where is she?" I growl, ignoring the bite of ice and rocks beneath my knees. I have to find Sybil. I have to tell her I'm sorry.

"Shut up, you elemental trash! She is none of your concern now." The blade cuts deeper into my skin, pressing against my windpipe. My heart pounds in my chest but that familiar tug stops me and I cast my gaze through the trees begging for a glimpse of her.

"Aye Kela, I understand your protective nature for Sybil." Nero cautiously steps between us, and this girl—Kela—tenses behind me.

"Let him go. He will nae harm her, as he—"

"—Nero, don't you dare—" I bark at him. That's not his secret to tell.

"Don't come any closer." Kela interrupts us. "Tell me why you've brought the fucking Prince of Shadowvale with you?" Her voice cracks on the last syllable.

Pounding footsteps catch my attention, my eyes scanning the forest. Nero turns, crouching into a defensive position.

Sybil breaks through the tree line, her hair streaming behind as she races towards us. Her hazel eyes jump from Nero, then to Kela holding me in a kneeling position on the ground. She digs her heels into the ground coming to a stop, chest heaving.

"KELA! You're ali–!" She exclaims but stops in her tracks as soon as her eyes settle on me, meeting my gaze. My pulse begins to race as I take in the way shifts of sunlight cut through the trees, illuminating her face. A glistening, twisted horn of white protrudes from the star at her forehead. I have the sudden desire to run my fingers up the side of her face and down its length.

"What's he doing here?" Sybil asks quietly, her cupid bow lips pursing in a grim line. She looks between Nero and Kela, but not back at me. Look at me, Sybil! Goddess knows, there is so much I want to say…

"That's exactly what I was just trying to figure out." Kela says.

"Kela, let him go. He's nae here to harm Sybil or take her back to Shadowvale." Nero sighs exasperatedly. He relaxes his position and sheaths his ax. "He's her–"

"Nero, goddess-damnit." I croak out.

Nero looks at me then back at Kela, silently pleading with her. "Here to help me."

"Why should I believe you?" she snarls.

"When have I ever given you, nae, the rest of the pack, any reason not to believe in me?" He opens empty palms towards her and hesitantly takes a step towards us. "I will nae harm you, nae will the Prince." Kela and Nero have a silent battle of wills, and after a moment of fierce debate I cannot decipher, she relents.

"Fine. One wrong move and next time I won't hesitate." Kela removes her blades and shoves me to the ground. I rub at my neck, blood smearing under my fingers as I push myself to stand. Sybil finally looks at me, and her eyes widen in surprise and she steps forward making my heart skip a beat.

"You're hurt." Sybils murmurs softly–just for the two of us. She raises a hand in my direction and briefly touches the wound, then turns to Kela, as if she just remembered something. "I thought you were behind me Kela. I thought I lost you, silly wolf!"

"And I thought I told you to run." Kela sighs exaggeratedly. "How did you end up here anyways? I told you we were going east," she adds, raising an eyebrow.

"I just followed… a feeling," Sybil says sheepishly, her eyes turning back on mine. Did she sense the bond as I do?

Kela flips a dagger in the air before pointing it at Nero. "Meanwhile, I caught the scent of this one mingling with this one." Her eyes narrow, the blue pupils glaring at me.

"Aye, and you ken we were coming to find you two." Nero interjects. "I told ye—"

"That wasn't the plan!" Kela responds sharply, pointing her dagger at him. "The plan was you would meet me and the unicorn alone and help escort her to the camp."

"Aye, Kela, and plans change." Nero grumbles as he crosses his arms across his chest.

"Does he even know?" She lifts an eyebrow at him pointing her dagger back at me.

"Do I know that my best friend for a century has kept his half-shifter life a secret from me?" I quirk a brow in amusement. Kela and Sybil's eyes widen with shock, clearly not expecting me to know the whole story. I laugh, just to spite them–well Kela, at least. "We've moved past that, and have made our amends. Now—please, would you stop pointing that dagger around before someone gets hurt?"

"You hate shifters." Kela accuses, still pointing that dagger open in the air, and to my dismay, it's pointing at me. "Your whole family hates shifters and wants nothing but to steal our powers and send us to work in the mines." When I begin to protest, Sybil steps in, narrowing her eyes at me.

"She is not wrong," Sybil says, confrontationally. I open my mouth to protest again, but Sybil almost sneers at me. "Don't deny it, Prince. It's a mercy that I actually survived this kidnapping let alone what the queen did to me. What you let her do to me. You have always made it abundantly clear what exactly you think of me, and what you think of shifters, no matter how many times I proved you wrong," her voice catches and she drops her gaze to the ground. I glance at Nero quickly, and the expression on his face only seems to tell me, Easy there, Aramis, you arse. Be. Careful.

"I–" the words caught in my throat. How do I explain the sordid history, and the way that Sybil has quickly captivated me and haunted my every moment? How do I tell her I was falling for her so fast on that trip from her small village to Shadowvale that I didn't know it was happening? How do I tell her that I have no excuse for how I behaved but that I will spend whatever is left of this lifetime winning her trust back? I exhale slowly. I don't need to tell her everything–yet. I steady myself as I make myself focus on Sybil. She's been in my dreams, upsetting the very foundation I stand on.

She's my mate.

I exhale once more, and when Sybil finally locks eyes with mine, I tell her just a little of the story. "I did–I mean, I have hated shifters since the night they murdered my mother." Sybil's eyes widen, but it encourages me to go on. I clear my throat and begin again. "I know now, that I have let that anger color my judgment of your people–of you–before having the chance to truly know them, and–to know you."

She stands watching me and it takes everything not to cross the space between us and crush her to me.

"I'm sorry. I know I've done you a disservice–as well as all shifters of Shadowvale." I continue, expecting bile to rise in my throat, only to discover that I feel a keen sense of relief, sharing this aloud—at last. "I cannot expect you to forgive me, but I hope you will allow me to get to know you. I just want a chance to mend this rift that I created. I am sorry, Sybil. For all my mistakes, my fear, my ignorance. I have been a fool. I should have ripped those fucking bars off of that cell and carried you out myself. You are the reason I stand here today with eyes wide open. You never gave up on me so I will not give up on you. There will only ever be you, since the moment I laid eyes on you."

Sybil casts dubious eyes on me and I wait patiently for her reply. My heart beats wildly as though it will burst from my chest of its own accord. What will I do if she denies my olive branch? If she denies me forgiveness, there is no opportunity to right my wrongdoings.

The silence that hangs between us is my undoing, and I unravel falling to my knees before her, desperate for her to understand everything that's happened in the weeks that have passed. "Goddess—Sybil," I plead, thankless in my begging. "Say something." I take a deep breath, like a man awaiting his death sentence and let my eyes tell everything I am not ready to say out loud.

"Aramis." My name is a breath on her lips. Sybil pauses, gathering her own thoughts. My name on her lips is a cocktail of lavender and honey. I close my eyes and hang my head, anticipating her rejection and the very undoing of my soul. It is eternity waiting on bated breath before the cool pads of her fingers trail along my throat, followed by a warm tingle of magic. "We cannot choose the life we are born into, but we can rise up to overcome our prejudices. Without bearing great sorrows and burdens, greatness goes unnoticed."

Opening my eyes, I stare in wonder at her hazel ones peering meer inches into my own. I've laid my soul at her feet and she hasn't stomped it out of existence. I exhale with relief.

I'm sorry. I tell Sybil with my eyes. I'm so sorry I hurt you and put you in this terrible situation. The only consolation I have now is that I can begin the work of fixing all of my mistakes and become the man she deserves.

Kela clears her throat behind us and Sybil shakes her head as if waking from a dream. I watch as she slowly backs away from me, curling a lock of hair around her finger absentmindedly. Exhaling quietly I meet Nero's glance who lifts his chin up in acknowledgement and praise.

"While this moment of clarity is truly inspiring," Kela says with mocking patience, "We can't just sit here all day." She turns to Nero, flipping her daggers in the air again until she points it once more in my direction. Goddess, she really has to stop it. "He's your problem. The elders are not going to like this, draken."

"The elders will just have to deal with it—" Nero interjects with a pointed look in my direction but interrupts himself when Kela's eyes take on a faraway look. "Kela. Kela!" Kela's body relaxes, then sways side to side. I have seen that look hundreds of times before. She's having a vision.

We remain silent during the long minutes that pass before Kela's eyes open and immediately glance from me to Sybil. Her body trembles before she lifts a hand to her forehead and falls to her knees.

"What is it?" Sybil asks, rushing forward. "What did you see?" She grabs her face between her hands.

Kela's eyes slowly focus on her and then glance back to Nero and I.

"I saw the queen. There was a male with her, I've never been able to see him before." Her hands tremble as she braces herself on Sybil's arm. When she is composed, Kela stares accusingly at me. "He told the queen that you were hunting the unicorn, not for her, but for yourself. He told her that you want her power for your own purposes," she growls.

Fuck! "Kieran." I growl under my breath. "That no good son of a bitch."

Does Kieran know about the mating bond?

Kela looks at me disbelievingly and sneers, "Kieran. The queen's seer. They tell no lies—we tell no lies."

"It is a lie!" My teeth grind together, heat rising up my neck. I turn pleading eyes to Sybil. "It's not true—I swear. You've met that slimy two-faced deceitful ass and know him for what he is. You have to…"

"He must have seen our plans to come find you, but not take you back, then twisted his vision." Nero interjects, always the diplomat—always the peacemaker. "He's always trying to find ways to worm into her good graces from the day he set foot in the palace. I'm surprised he's not warming her bedsheets already."

I watch emotions play across Sybil's face. She's been so quiet and contemplative.

"That's not all." Kela's voice is low and serious. "The queen replied that if she can't have her, no one will. He told her where we are. She's sending something after us. We have to go."

"That's preposterous!" I exclaim. "My father would never let her harm me. I'm the sole heir to Shadowvale."

Kela turns mournful eyes to me, her mouth softening into a frown. "I did not see your father in the throne room, Prince Aramis. His chair was empty." For once, her tone is not ironic or sarcastic.

SYBIL

or hours we silently head northeast through the forest. Snow glistens on every surface. The crisp, cold air smells of evergreen. I barely take in the scenery, as my head is full of so many thoughts.

How can the four of us take down the Queen of Shadowvale? When the time comes, what side will Aramis be on? Can he really give up over a century's worth of prejudice? I can see him struggling, visibly torn between wanting to avenge his mother and wanting to be the protector of his people. But the shifters are just as much an integral part of his people as the elementals, and now he knows shifters are not the perpetrators of the rebellion. The silence of the forest unnerves me. It's too quiet.

"If the queen is sending forces after us, wouldn't it be unwise to lead her directly to the rebel camp?" I finally break the silence with the thought that's been plaguing me all morning.

"Yes, which is why we aren't heading directly to the camp." Kela replies. She points up ahead of us. "If we can make it to the mountains, there are secret passages that tunnel through them. They haven't been used in hundreds of years, but they

252

are warded. Our people were offered sanctuary there in the last war by the clan of the white witches. If we can make it there before the queen finds us, hopefully they can offer us shelter until it's safe to continue or allow us passage through the tunnels."

"White witches?" The ghostly scent of jasmine fills my senses as the memory in the tomb returns along with her words.

Seek your training with the white witches in the forgotten library of Harpalyke.

"Yes, they are a lost clan who's dedicated themselves to protecting some forgotten library and the Shrine of the Goddess Al–"

"Alpheaia." Aramis finishes, cutting her off. His hand drifts to his neck where he grasps a chain. Kela stops, her body slowly turning and stares at him.

"How do you know?" She asks quietly. The tone in her voice is edged with danger, but my heart is racing at this new information so much so that I have to know more.

"Do you know how to get there?" I interrupt, stepping between Aramis and Kela. "To the library of Harpalyke?"

"Wait, how do you know its name?" She eyes us both speculatively.

How do I tell them that a ghost, possibly Aramis's own mother, visited me in the tombs of the kings of Shadowvale and told me to find the guardians of Harpalyke to free my people? I am not even sure Nero fully believes me and he was there.

"Well, let's just say it's complicated," I start.

"Aye, tis my own doing. I took Sybil through the catacombs to escape Shadowvale," Nero interjects. He twists his hands nervously before him. "When we passed through the tomb of Queen Rosalind, goddess bless her soul, Sybil went into a trance."

"My mother's tomb?" Aramis asks with wonder.

"She spoke to me," I clarify. My hand goes to my pocket, where I nervously brush my fingers through Lemon's fur. "She called me child of Alpheaia and told me that I needed to seek training with the white witches of Harpalyke."

"I don't know why she came to me, but I know her words were true when she sent me on this quest," I reply, trying to shove down all the twisted emotions that attempt to escape my control. Aramis is looking at me with such intensity I shy away from his gaze. I wish he could see his mother again, even if only for a second.

"We have to find those tunnels. I know this sounds ridiculous, but I need you all to trust me." I beg Kela, a frown crossing her features.

"Alright, unicorn, but it'll be a long shot. No one has been to Harpalyke for at least a hundred years. The only thing I know is that the tunnels that lead to it are located in the mountains. If we find the tunnels, we find the library."

"What direction do we go?" I ask with a tone of urgency.

"The stories say to enter the mountains of Aldervora seeking wisdom and look for lichen to show you the way." Kela quirks a curious brow at me, as well as Aramis. My stomach tugs at his gaze. Goddess—the intensity.

Lichen. The word interrupts my spiral, and my heart drops at her words. "You're telling me that to find this lost library of Harpyalyke we have to look for special lichen, in a forest full of lichen to show us the way?" I raise my own brows in question.

"What were you expecting? A detailed map? A magical unicorn to prance through and show us an enchanted portal?" She asks, a smile tugging at her lips as she teases me. Kela pulls out her daggers and begins nervously tossing them in the air.

"Well then," Nero says with more enthusiasm than needed. "Let's find these magical lichen, shall we," and rubs his hands together in excitement.

"How about we also hope the queen's soldiers don't get to us first?" Kela responds with a serious look that puts Nero back to his place and starts heading towards the mountains. I watch as Aramis tucks the chain back under his shirt. He's hiding something. I can see his struggle plainly on his face, despite how much he tries to disregard it. I only hope the love for his people and country outweighs his lifelong prejudices.

SYBIL

Three days pass as we make our way further into the mountains. There has been no sign of pursuit, but we continue on high alert. The cool air seeps into my bones, eyelashes encased in frost.

"Wh-why d-d-oes it ha-have to be s-s-so colddd?" I stutter, willing my teeth to stop chattering. I'm grateful for the layers of warmth Kela piled on me before we left the cabin but despite the thick woolen socks and scarf, the chill wind still cuts through the layers.

"Aye, I'm sorry lassie, but the winters are always like this. Ye'll get used to it." Nero shrugs, his breath coming out in large white clouds.

If I live long enough.

"Our summers, though beautiful, are nothing on the Autumn harvest." Aramis flashes me a knowing look. Lemon nudges my hand from the pack, and I look down with confusion. He blinks at me, clearly telling me something I don't understand.

"Warm apple crisps," Nero groans, his tongue licking out to moisten his lips.

We all moan in unison—though I've never had one, the

vision of the warm flakey crust mixing with melting sweet apples and cinnamon taunts my tastebuds, making me anxious to know if I'll ever have an apple crisp made from Shadowvale's renown pomme d'argent.

Aramis' secret smile for me is a reminder that he often thinks of the time we journeyed together. Warmth flushes through my cheeks remembering the endearing way in which he stood up in his saddle to let me taste one of the sweet, sacred silver apples. And while I don't quite smile back at him, I acknowledge the memory with a hint of entertainment in my eyes. It's a comfort to see this acknowledgement from him. The sun finally breaks through the trees, warming my face.

"What are we going to do if we can't find the lichen?" I ask, idly twisting my family ring around my finger. We've been traveling for miles and have yet to see anything beyond pine trees, rocks, and snow.

"We will find it. We have to," Aramis says and I nod grateful for his support in this fool's errand.

My magic has returned to full capacity as I healed over the last week. It hums quietly under my skin, a comforting buzz acknowledging my strength and agility. As we pass further into the mountains, the intensity of my magic increases. The land, the sky, and winds, all connected to my power, as if they share the same energy, like I belong here. This simple thought grounds me and keeps me going despite my growing aches

Continuing on what feels like a fruitless walk for ages, I shift my head to the side and observe an old tree, thicker and taller than any of the others surrounding it. Its dark red bark is a vibrant contrast to the snow that clings to it.

"Look!" I rush towards the tree and brush away the snow with my gloved hands. Beneath my fingers clinging to the bark is thick dark green lichen. Ordinary lichen. My shoulders slump, my heart dropping with them as my companions rush up behind me.

"What is it?" Aramis asks.

"What did ye find?!" Nero exclaims.

My retinue crowd around me, asking questions with such hope that I just sigh, pulling my gloves off in frustration to study my discovery.

"Just a false alarm," I groan as I start turning to show them the false evidence but I stop when the lichen in my hand starts glowing an iridescent teal color, pulsing rhythmically.

"Your ring" Kela says in surprise, and I notice how my family heirloom has taken the same hue of the lichen. "I don't under–," my voice breaks when I see Aramis pulling the chain from around his neck, the small crystal pendant glowing just as much as my ring.

"What is that?" I whisper, my gaze moving from his hands to his face.

"The night in the forest when we were ambushed, I spoke to the attackers. They were curious creatures, I have never seen anyone like them. They said they were guardians of Alpheaia." His words trail off as he stares at the crystal around his neck.

"You nae told me that," Nero interjects gesturing at his neck. "What else did they say?"

"Not much." Aramis shrugs his indifference, but slides a glance at me. "They asked me about my intentions with Sybil, and they said I was the tipping point. Then they disappeared into smoke and gold dust."

"After stabbing Edmund?" I purse my lips. "That doesn't sound like a reassuring ally." My thoughts start racing once more and I can't stop thinking that we're all pieces of a much larger plan. Maybe our paths were destined to cross.

Goddess, why in the wide world does he keep looking at me like that!?

The look sends unbidden shivers down my spine and into my core. I reach for Lemon in comfort, and he nuzzles my fingertips.

"I didn't say they were an ally, but there is more to them than we—"

A heavy crunch in the snow, followed by a deep bellied laugh catches our attention. On the right, two hundred feet away, stand eight massive creatures. Large tusks protrude from their mouths, their dark hairless skin only covered by a leather loincloth and large black claws the size of dinner plates tip their protruding beefy arms. The scent of their putrid unwashed bodies hits us as the wind changes directions. My body seizes up in terror.

"Fuck." Nero says as he throws his pack to the ground giving voice to my thoughts.

"What are they?" Aramis asks, turning to Nero for confirmation as he draws his sword and unfastens his cloak.

"Shouldn't you know?" Kela shouts while she drops her pack to the ground, then begins tearing off her layers, her face already starting its transformation. "They're your stepmother's creatures, I'm presuming. Haven't you ever seen damage that is so atrocious that it doesn't add up?"

Aramis grimaces, like he has.

I wonder...

I break from my moment of panic before following Kela's lead. I have a better chance of fighting at my full strength as a unicorn. The world seems to move in slow motion as I watch one of the creatures leer at us, slowly scratching its belly with the tip of its spear. I toss my pack besides the others before stripping to my undergarments. The icy wind bites at my skin, but my magic is already humming. My muscles contract and grow as heat replaces the cold; limbs lengthening with sharp hooves replacing my hands and feet. My horn glistens in the sunlight as I toss my head and whiny. Beside me, Nero uses his wings to propel himself up into the branches of the tree, his skin covered in amethyst scales. Aramis crouches to my left, sword poised in his right hand, a shield of shimmering blue air

forming on his left. I give him one last look, and he offers a
smile I don't know how to interpret.

One of the vile creatures roar, and my heart hammers
in my chest as we all charge. I veer to the right, my hooves
pounding into the ground as I pick up speed, throwing snow
up behind me. We have to keep the skirmish away from the
packs so Lemon doesn't get trampled.

Nero jumps from tree to tree above me. His powerful
muscles flexing under his scales. He lets out a roar that echoes
around us and the creatures start rumbling to life, swinging
an assortment of swords, axes and spiked clubs. They look
unnatural. A mix of limbs and features of different creatures
collated together to give form to an abomination. They have
short flat snouts like pigs, beady eyes and thin sprouting hair,
but stand as tall as ogres. Saliva runs freely from the corner of
their mouths as they menacingly stalk towards us. They look
greedily at Kela and myself, making my blood boil.

With a growl, Kela launches herself at the smallest one's
feet, biting deep as Aramis slices at its chest. His blade scrapes
along the thick leather chest plate, nicking the underside of its
armpit. It wails in pain as hot red blood seeps into the snow at
its feet, steam rising into the air.

Wind whistles in my ear as a spiked club swings millimeters
from my face. In my momentary distraction, one of the
creatures snuck into my space. I prance to the side, avoiding
a second swing. I can smell the stench of rotting fish breath
this close up; its teeth crooked, covered in thick slime. I snort,
steam rising from my nostrils as I rear up then strike with my
sharp hooves. The creature grunts, the breath knocked out
of it as it loses its balance and topples to the ground. Kela
pounces on top of the creature, sinking her muzzle over its
throat before ripping it out. My nostrils flare as the smell of
iron fills the air.

"Sybil!" Aramis yells out as a sting of pain slices along my right flank.

Prancing to the left, my eyes narrow on the creature laughing. The sword held high in the air, its edge glistening with my blood. I buck and knock him slamming back into the tree behind him, knocking the grin off his face. Aramis jumps, slicing his sword gracefully through the air. The creature's head falls from its shoulders and rolls towards my hooves as its body slumps to the floor.

"Are you okay?" Aramis assesses quickly, and I nod my head in reassurance. "Good." His face and chest are splattered in dark blood, but his focus is on me, concern etched deeply on his features. I assess his well being quickly and rejoice in seeing he is not hurt. We are both safe. We turn in unison as we hear Nero roar. His ax is embedded in the chest of a creature twitching on the ground. His wings flair above him as he stands on the back of another.

Seven bodies lay on the ground. Where is the eighth?

A howl of pain pierces the air and I turn in time to see the final creature slice its sword into Kela's abdomen. My vision clouds to red, my muscles move of their own accord as I push myself the distance between us and slam my horn through the creature's back, right through his heart. His life force immediately drains from his body at the impact. I toss my head, dislodging him.

I transition into my demi form as I drop to my knees, quickly assessing my friend. My hands clutch at her abdomen as red stains across her tunic.

"Kela!" my voice is hoarse as I scream her name. She coughs, blood bubbling from her lips. I will my healing magic to knit her wound closed, but she's losing blood faster than I can repair and I have used a good dose of my magic during the fight. Behind me, Aramis and Nero slowly approach.

"Sybil." Kela lays a hand on top of mine, glowing as I pour every drop of healing magic I possess into her. "There is a lot I need to tell you."

"Hush. Let me heal you." I interrupt, pleadingly as tears start running down my face. "You can't leave me," I whisper but as my magic enters her body, I soon discover that she sustained more than just an abdominal wound.

"Sybil." Kela lets out a wet cough, as she begs my attention. "I had a vision, long before we met. I knew my fate was to meet you. I knew what was coming."

"What do you mean?" I beg, trying to make sense of her words.

"We were always meant to be great friends. I knew it, despite the short time we had together." She coughs, her body spasming. Kela smiles grimly at me as she lifts her free hand to my face, her blood mingling with my tears. "It's been worth every second, no matter the time, but I need you to listen to me, yes?"

I nod dutifully, unable to speak as tears keep cascading down my face.

"There is to be a great battle between our people and the false queen." Kela's gaze is steady, and my heart breaks as I listen to my friend's final words. "The king is not yet dead but he is in grave danger." Kela glances at Aramis, her chest quickly rising and falling. "Do you hear me, Princeling?" She demands his attention, and he honors her with his full focus. "She has cursed him with her dark magic. He's sick, you have to brea–' Her breathing becomes more labored as she starts coughing blood. Kela grabs my hand once more, keeping her gaze steady on me."Break the curse and you'll free us all, Sybil. The library, the witches, they know how. It has to be you. You are the key."

"I am no hero," I exclaim, sobs burst through my body, thoroughly wrecking me. I summon every drop of magic I can muster to save her–praying to the goddess, or anyone to hear me and help save her. "I can't do this Kela."

"A hero is not the extent of their training." Kela grins her last sardonic grin at me. Blood spills through her guts and over my hands as she laughs. "A hero is a hero because even when hope is lost, even when everything you do amounts to nothing and shows no promise, you keep trying. You fight," her voice is a whisper and I brush a strand of hair from her forehead, in an attempt to bring her comfort.

Nero and Aramis are silent. Their eyes, once filled with the vibrancy of camaraderie, are now loaded with grief. Shoulders slumped in shared despair over the scene in front of them. Kela's weakened frame trembles under my touch, her gaze fixed on mine. Her fingers clutch at the fabric of my dress. "Free us all, Sybil." Her voice falters, and I can sense the effort it takes to summon the strength needed for this farewell. "Keep him close," she whispers, "You will need each other." As her eyes lose their focus, a profound stillness settles over the woods.

"No!" I whisper. "Kela! Get your bloody ass back here." Her body is limp as her head lolls to the side, supported by the tree behind her.

"No!" I scream. "Fuck! Kela! Come back!" The last of her life force slips out of my fingers like grains of rice. I lower my horn to her wound, tears dripping onto the open flesh. "You aren't allowed to leave. Do you hear me!?" I cradle her neck into my hands and pull her close, attempting to heal a useless body, unreceptive to my powers.

"You can't leave me!" Kela's body doesn't respond; her flesh refuses to knit back together.

She's gone. Tears streak my face and fall down my neck as I hold her tight to me. No matter what I will—what I demand of the goddess, she remains limp in my arms. I'm at a loss for words. I'm utterly useless in my sobbing, shaking, weak body.

I failed Kela.

ARAMIS

ero and I gather wood from the clearing whilst Sybil takes her time cleaning Kela's body in a nearby lake until she looks peacefully asleep. Seeing Sybil and Nero so lost in their grief over the death of the wolf shifter had nearly brought me to run back to the castle and kill Tricella with my bare hands. Until Sybil announced she would not leave until Kela had a place to rest and Nero promised her they'd give her a pyre worthy of a princess which made me realize that my place is here, comforting the people I love.

Sybil brushes and braids Kela's wild hair into a crown around the top of her head and places her hands together across her chest, her favorite dagger nestled against her breastbone.

With a nod at Nero, she steps back.

My friend slowly approaches the pyre we've created with Kela nestled in the middle. Blue flames lick from his mouth, igniting the fire. It quickly eats through the dry branches, fueled faster by the beating of his wings until the entire pyre is alight.

As I watch the flames mount higher, smoke twisting up into the sky, something inside me cracks. I can't return to the castle. Not until Tricella is dead or until we have everything we need to kill her. If I truly want to save my kingdom, my people, and my father, I have to help Sybil find a way to break his curse. Returning now would only lead me to my death, I am sure of it.

We stand together, an odd trio; an amateur healer, a halfling drake, and a now outcast prince, remnants of a short alliance of a worthy cause. I didn't know Kela well enough to truly grieve her, but she was an important female. I'm sorry for the loss of integrity, of independent thinking, and true nurturing care for her people, friends and family.

"Aye, Kela was a grand warrior," Nero says from beside me as he creates a miniature wolf of flames in his palm. He sends it running towards the flaming pyre and up into the sky until it's mere sparks. "She had nae fear since I met her the first time as a wee pup, always defending the weak to her last breath."

"Kela was a true friend to me," Sybil solemnly speaks up, her eyes never leaving the fire and I notice how her posture has changed. "She believed in the strength that she saw in me; believed that I would join the shifters and be a force of great change. I just—I never imagined I'd be doing it without her by my side." Gone is the insecure woman I took to Shadowvale. I had seen a glance of this version of Sybil in the dungeons but here, with the glow of the flames reflecting in her eyes, it is crystal clear. Sybil demands revenge, and she is ready to bleed for it.

I cross my hands behind my back and decide it's only right that I say the truth I understand now, after death. "Kela and I were not friends. But she had integrity, passion, and loyalty to a cause I am only beginning to understand. I'm sorry for the loss of such a worthy warrior." A single solitary tear slips down Sybil's cheek. I step forward to lift my hand and brush my thumb against the delicate skin.

Her hazel eyes are rimmed with red as tears fall unbidden.

"You'll do her justice. I see her spirit in your eyes." I run my hand down to Sybil's chin, turning her face towards mine, pulling her closer to me–as close as I think I can get away with. "I did not know her long, although I wish I had. She knew her fate before any of us did. You honor her memory and sacrifice by fighting on. You don't falter. You don't lose resolve–do you understand me? That was her last request."

"I will honor it," Sybil says solemnly, closing her eyes, and the weight of her head leans into my caress. Tears cascade silently down her cheeks, grief etching her whole body. She needs me. A great sigh carries over my body, and relief wraps around me as I bury my hands in her hair and hold her close.

"Listen Sybil darling," I begin. "Will you?"

Sybil stiffens slightly at the term of affection, but nods with agreement. Thank the goddess. "We both know loss is never easy, and the pain never goes away," I murmur, brushing the tendrils of her hair gently. I send a wisp of wind to brush a stray tear away and she shivers into me.

She softly exhales against me, and it's a breath that taunts my dreams. "We carry it like a badge of honor. Grateful for the time we had with them," I say. Sybil exhales hard but nods.

"Please consider," I ask one last request, taking advantage of the moment to wrap my fingers in her hair. It's as soft and thick as I imagined. "That whatever Tricella has done, that I am here for you. I support you, and I will do everything I can to make it right." Rubbing at my chest, I glance again at the fire, which has dimmed considerably. Sybil looks up with a shy smile and, seeing where my gaze falls, she pulls away from me.

"Thank you, Aramis." Sybil offers me a sweet smile and I watch her walk away from me, the distance heavy between us.

As she kneels before the fire, she tends to it with a furrowed brow. I send a wind her way, letting the fire grow, and she looks back to me and gratefully nods her head, sadness still etched in her eyes. We remain at the pyre, watching the flames burn down, only leaving the remains of ashes on the ground.

Nero and I make quick work disposing of the bodies of the creatures while giving Sybil space to mourn her companion. We collect our packs and make a small meal of dried bread, cheese, and berries before refilling our cantines from a nearby stream.

"Aramis?" Sybil's voice is tentative and unsure as she kneels at the remnant of the pyre. I immediately gravitate to her side. I want to tell her. I need to tell her, but she is grieving, and now is not the time. She needs a pillar of support, not another complicated emotion. "Will you do me a favor?"

I move to sit on the ground next to her left as Nero crouches beside her on her right. I hand her the cloth I've wrapped the food in and nod as my eyes drift over her face, memorizing every curve. "Anything."

"Will you send her ashes across the mountains? I think she would want to be free to roam and protect this sacred area." Sybil nibbles at her bottom lip, hands twisting in her lap. "Then I think we must be going. The queen has to know by now that her creatures failed, and will send others after us."

"Aye, tis wise," Nero says as he clasps a hand to her shoulder. My eyes are immediately drawn to the contact, my lips pursing involuntarily before I meet her gaze.

"It would be my pleasure. She deserves nothing less." I reach down and squeeze her hand before pushing up to stand. Running my fingers through my disheveled hair, I inhale deeply before reaching deep for my magic. I overspent more than I usually do during the battle to ensure we were protected, but it wasn't enough. Tapping into the wells of my magic, I sensed it waning, and towards the end of the battle, I was slowing down. Could I have prevented Kela's death if I had been faster? Stronger? Guilt clenches deep in my stomach as I lift my hands before me, guiding the wind to swirl around the ashes, lifting them higher into the air as my power swells inside me. One powerful gust, and my magic sends the ashes outward across the mountains and tree tops.

Nero's strong arms catch me as I'm propelled to the ground. I rest my forehead against my knees, breathing deeply, my body trembling from the exertion of the remnants of my power.

"Thank you," her quiet words cause my chest to constrict as she rests her head against my shoulder, gazing up into the mountains before us.

"Always," I whisper back, closing my eyes and imagining for a brief moment a vision of our future.

As we pack our belongings and plan our next move, I think about what lies ahead of us. Is this the beginning, then? Have we started something by identifying the lichen with her magic and the necklaces the goddess' warriors handed to me? We have to find this magical path or Goddess knows where we'll end up. Sybil goes back to the tree she first identifies and as soon as she is near it the lichen starts glowing. "Let's start from here," she says, raw determination lacing every word, and I follow her command.

You'll need each other. I exhale hard as Kela's final words still echo in the wind and I wonder if she knew the truth about us. She seemed to know a lot about Sybil after all. What a peculiar twist of fate that this shifter with her deep hazel eyes was the bane of my existence for a while, is the answer to all my prayers and now the solution to all our woes. I pray to the Goddess to grant me the strength I need to make the amends I must make so I can be the male by her side to support her and her power, whatever it builds into.

SYBIL

As the sun sets between the mountains in the west, the forest is illuminated by thousands of clusters of lichen clinging to the trunks of trees. The path is approximately twenty feet wide and stretches endlessly into the mountain range for as far as my eye can see. Small groups of luminescent mushrooms glow in the nooks and roots of the trees in neon colors. We pass a large bush covered in glowing purple berries the likes of which I haven't seen before. While I should be overjoyed to see our path and the magical wonders that accompany it, my soul aches with an empty hollowness.

I let Nero and Aramis walk ahead of me. Lemon scrambles up my cloak, curling around my neck, his little head nestled against my collarbone. He lets out a low rumble of content as I scratch behind his ears.

"We're a long way from Kallistar, boy." He nips playfully at my fingertips. I sigh deeply as my hand drops to my side. My eyes draft towards Aramis' form, a gravitational pull to him as I trace the outline of his back and neck. The man in front of me is not the same one who captured me all those weeks ago. My heart is desperate to talk to him, let him know that a part of me understands where his prejudices came from and that he should not let his past determine his future. My mind however, reminds me of all the pain he's caused me and urges me to be cautious. I cast my eyes skyward where I can see the beginnings of stars twinkling in the amethyst sky and nibble on my lip in anticipation.

"I'm nae familiar with these woods this far into the mountains." Nero turns around as he explains his thoughts. "I'll scout ahead to see if I can find a place for us to camp for the night. I dinna know how far the entrance to the tunnels Kela mentioned is."

At the mention of her name, we all fall silent. My chest tightens painfully, and tears pick at the corner of my eyes. Her loss weighs heavily on me, on all of us. Even Aramis has surprised me with his compassion. My breath hitches, recalling how intimately our bodies mingled together as he held me from falling apart over her loss.

You are brave. You don't falter. You don't lose resolve. I repeat the words in my head. Pieces of wisdom given to me by people who saw past my shortfalls and made my strength shine. They remind me of who I can be. Goosebumps rise on my arms at the memory of his lips whispering against my skin. His hardened tone was the only thing familiar about Aramis, but it was coated with patience and generosity. Am I pathetic for eagerly drinking up any sort of kindness, or is it just as meaningful as my gut tells me it is?

"Be safe," Aramis says as he nods to his friend, taking his pack. "We will continue following the lichen path and meet you in due time."

We watch, side by side, as Nero flexes his wings before shooting up between the trees. Our fingers barely brush against one another, and electricity shoots up my arm, putting me on edge. I glance towards Aramis, but his face is focused on the sky, watching his best friend in his shifter form scout the territory to keep us safe. There is no hatred or disgust on his face, only worry, and my heart clenches at the thought of how far this man has come.

"He'll be alright. He's cunning and strong," I say, offering a shy glance which he slowly returns. His gaze is a thorough caress as his winds sweep across my cheek. Aramis's icy blue eyes, once guarding a fortress of anger, have thawed into an azure expanse that mirrors the ocean. As I look into them, I see his transformation—no longer the gaze of a man barricaded behind walls of disdain, but a revelation of vulnerability. Goddess help me. We stand there in silence, neither willing to interrupt this moment and I realize this is only the second time we've been completely alone. There's a clarity in his eyes that transcends words and reflects emotions he can no longer conceal. I gently place my hand on his cheek, a silent plea for connection. The light stubble is coarse against my palm but before I can return the same honesty he is offering me, I panic, overwhelmed by what this could mean so I step away and continue walking.

"I wish I could have seen your face when Nero told you he was a shifter. That must have been a shock for you," I say snickering, trying to diffuse the tension between us.

"It certainly was a surprise but I've known him my whole life, he's practically a brother to me. Nothing can come between us." Aramis sounds assured, unhurried even. His eyes return back to the sky. "I can't imagine a life without him."

"Even though he's a shifter?" I ask, unable to help myself as I study his face.

The corner of his lip pulls up into a grin. "Even as a shifter."

"People often keep secrets to protect loved ones or keep them safe," I reply, keeping a wary eye on him.

"I've never seen this many stars at the castle," he says after a moment. "My mother used to love painting the night sky. She believed the stars were guardians, holding the secrets of the world." His gaze wanders across the night sky, desperately searching for something. I smile because I know how it is to wonder at the majesty of gazing into the skies. How many nights did I spend after packing my bags for Esther Nova, only to spend the evening under the stars wondering what it would be like, but too afraid to leave?

"The sky is a thing of wonder." I sigh, looking for my favorite constellations. "This far north from my home, the stars are shifted in the sky."

"Navigating by the stars is a skill. I can teach you—" Aramis pauses and the tips of our fingers brush again, sending tiny sparks up my arm. "—If you'd like." Every stolen glance becomes a fleeting caress, each word carries an undertone of something more profound.

I smile shyly at him, seeing the thoughtful male I had begun to know all those weeks ago. "I'd like that very much, Aramis."

We continue trudging along in silence, my eyes constantly returning to him. Apart from this small conversation, he has been so quiet, barely speaking a word to me. Even the nature around us seems to hold its breath, waiting for the moment when the unresolved tension between us unfurls. Aramis remains close to me, despite his silence. There are so many things I want to ask; so many things I want to know. What is on his mind? How is he dealing with the loss of identity after leaving the Kingdom?

My boot snags on a hidden root in the snow and I careen forward, arms pinwheeling at my sides as I attempt to regain my balance. In a heartbeat, Aramis' arm snatches out, catching me around my waist and preventing my fall. He braces me against his chest, his fingers flexing around my hips. The heat of his fingertips burn through the thin fabric of my gown, making me gasp at the warmth and my reaction to it. His eyes mere inches away and locked onto mine, hold a question I don't know how to answer.

My breath catches in my chest from a desire so intense that it pools in my core. My body flushes with heat as our breath mingles in white puffs. I tremble, and Aramis' grip tightens on me before I can move too far, desperate to prolong this moment.

"Sybil," he whispers, staring deeply into my eyes. I tilt my head to the side in concern and that tug in my stomach intensifies. In this suspended moment, with the stars shining bright above us, the pull becomes irresistible and righteous, as if letting go is the easiest and simplest decision I can ever make. Aramis's gaze drops to my lips, and a shared understanding passes between us in this moment as if blessed by destiny itself.

What would it be like to kiss those lips? How would I feel if he kissed down the soft flesh of my neck? The heat of his hands on my waist is almost too much to bear. The wood around us seems to retreat in the background, leaving only us to make sense of our emotions. My body yearns for more, to fill this void that has been growing inside me. Aramis drinks me in like I'm the sunshine to his flower.

"What are you thinking?" I ask breathlessly. My heart beats faster in my chest; I can hardly perceive the cold chill around us, only the burning heat spreading throughout my body. I nibble my lip in anticipation. His eyes watch every moment with that intense, thorough investigation.

"I'm thinking..." He takes a step forward, a wicked smile on his lips. When my back brushes up against the trunk of a tree, luminescent lichen sprinkles down over our heads, dusting us in a fine glowing powder. "I am thinking that I will follow you until the end of time itself, Sybil. I am thinking that I have been a fool for letting you slip through my fingers and I am thinking that, if you'll have me, I will never let you go again."

"Oh?" I gasp, unable to help the twist of desire sweeping through my body. Whatever is gathering in my stomach is sinking down to my core.

Aramis places a forearm against the tree, caging me in. "Every time I close my eyes I am haunted by the vision of you." Wind teases my neck, making me gasp. "You are my greatest torment, and my sweet awakening, Sybil Vandeleur," he whispers the last words in my ear. His fists bunch in the fabric of my skirts, his forehead pressing against my own. He closes his eyes, breath ragged, hands trembling as he slightly loosens his grip. His wind brushes up the inside of my leg and I gasp.

Goddess help me. Mine. The word crosses my mind and it feels sweet like a prayer. I lift my hands to his chest, the pounding of his heart under my palms in a wild rhythm with my own. With a tilt of my chin, my lips gently brush against his own. It's a tender collision, the culmination of a journey marked by countless obstacles, stolen glances and a sprinkle of fate.

"Ah, Sybil, my pomme sucrée. You taste so sweet," he says in between kisses. The dam of emotions explodes within me. My magic sings as he deepens the kiss, gently coaxing my mouth open. Our tongues meet and dance; a spark of heat shoots through me. His hands slide down my hips, pulling them forward to cradle against his own. My softness caresses his hardness. His winds sweep my hair out of my face, stroking down my sides, and I groan.

"Aramis," I gasp.

Stop it with the winds. Please–

Aramis' fingers cascade down my back, making me arch into him as he slides a hand up my spine. He kisses down to the slope of my neck, rough stubble scraping against my delicate skin.

Aramis' other hand slides up, gently cupping my breast. I gasp, pressing further into his touch as he runs a thumb over my nipple through my chemise.

"I love the way you smell." Aramis inhales deeply, continuing to trace lazy circles around my nipple with his thumb. "Lavender, vanilla, and a hint of black tea." His other hand makes its way up my back to my scalp. Shivers run down my spine, a low moan escaping my lips as he fists a handful of hair and gently tugs my lips to him. His winds brush my ankles and up my calf, and I bite my lip in resistance to cry out once more.

"I am yours Sybil," he whispers as a delicate slide of air caresses my inner thighs. His kisses become more intense. Deep. Dominating. Our teeth and tongues clash in an erotic dance.

"And I am yours," I answer, knowing that it is the truth as raw energy rushes through my body. This is where I am meant to be, in his arms, in this kingdom, fighting this war. Aramis growls in approval and my body shudders in response. My lips are swollen and tender from our kisses.

"It's about time this happened." Nero crouches on a tree branch not far from us, bursting our little bubble. His big hands cover his eyes in a feeble attempt to pretend he is disgusted, even though his huge grin says otherwise. My cheeks blush from the embarrassment but also notice Aramis's hand on the hilt of his sword. It must have been his instinctual reaction at our rude interruption, always ready to protect me.

"Thanks Nero, perfect timing as usual," he says with a wicked spark in his eyes.

"Aye mate. I'd say you two should get a room but we're scarce on that at the moment. The path ahead is clear, come find me once you two are presentable," he continues, takes a big jump and lands on the snowy ground. As Nero disappears in the distance, casually whistling, Aramis lowers his forehead to mine, the smile on his lips is so bright it matches the stars above.

"He is going to taunt us with this for the rest of our lives," he says snickering.

"Good, because I want to remember this moment for the rest of mine," I vow and he kisses me once more with the reverence deserving of a goddess.

SYBIL

ramis and I walk in silence, loosely holding hands as we make our way towards Nero. My body still hums from his touch, yearning for more. I turn my head, studying his profile. His sharp angular jaw clenches every time he glances towards the sky with worry. But the corners of his eye crinkle with entertainment any time he looks my way.

"What does pomme sucrée mean?" I ask as I lace my fingers through his.

I can't explain the draw I have to him. It's like I have only now taken my first real breath.

"Ah." The corners of his eyes crinkle as he smiles softly down at me. "It means sweet apple." Aramis grips my hand tightly then releases it gently. The absence of his hand enfolding over mine makes me look up. He winks at me, and there's a promise in that gesture. Leaning forward he whispers, his breath a tickling caress, "Because you, Sybil darling, are my new favorite dessert."

Goddess help me.

Aramis tilts his chin up, breaking his gaze to scan the trees. The power of emotions courses through me and I am torn between leaning into the pureness of this moment, and trying to understand how this is going to change everything. There is also Kela's death still clinging to me like a relentless shadow, casting even the happiest moments into darkness.

The snapping of tree branches precedes Nero landing in front of us in a crouch. "Took ya some time," he says, a sneaky grin on his face. Splatters of iridescence coat his wings and body. Aramis doubles over in laughter, clapping his friend on the shoulder while helping him to stand.

"What fairy bush did you roll in?" He flicks at a gooey glob stuck to Nero's wing.

"What did I tell ye about touching ma wings, ye insensitive arse?" Nero growls, flapping his wings and splattering Aramis.

"Hey!" Aramis's eyes widen in shock as he glances down at his now glowing body. The tall, regal princely air is shattered and I bite back my entertainment. "That was uncalled for, you know. I carried your pack this whole way while you have been gallivanting up in the sky." Aramis pulls a glob of iridescence from his hair and throws it at Nero. It lands with a wet splat in between his brows dripping down his cheekbones.

"Gallivanting?" Nero growls, swiping at his face, smearing the goo.

I can't hold it in anymore. Glancing between the two of them squabbling like old housewives, covered in iridescent goo, I burst out laughing. I double over as I cackle at the sight of them. Nero grumpy with defense and Aramis trying to seek more information.

Splat!

Warm lavender goo obscures my vision. I wipe away at my face clean, revealing the two of them, fallen to the ground, doubled over with flushed faces from their laughter. "Who did that!?" I command an answer, but they continue laughing at me, denying me. I toss my bags on the ground.

"Get up, the both of you!" I kick at their boots. At their refusal, I lean down and pack a ball tight of snow, and throw it at Aramis' pretty face. I lean down, gather another one, and throw it at Nero. The snow around them glows faintly from their antics, but my attack has officially stopped their laughter.

"That's it." Aramis' tone commands, full of steel, and sends me a calculating look.

Ooooh boy. What have I just started?

Whilst Aramis gathers his own snowy ammunition, I let instincts take over, and dash off running as far away as I can from him. The heavy, wet impact of the snowball hits my back, sending me sprawling. My face hits snow, and Aramis laughs with triumph. I lean on my forearms, sputtering snow out of my mouth, and brush my hair out of my face.

"Aye, Aramis, that was a low blow," I hear Nero say over my muffled ears and turn around to see Aramis getting pelted by snow from waves and waves of Nero's wings. The image is so absurd I burst into laughter as the crown Prince of Shadowvale is slowly turning into a snowman, and as my stomach cramps up from joy, I realize I am not lonely anymore."Right." I begin as we all recover from our little snow fight.

I step around Aramis, ready to grab my bags, but slip over a root. I land in a pile of glowing mushrooms that let out puffs of iridescent powder coating all of us. This only causes the two males to burst into more laughter as I sit up, completely drenched and resplendent in fairy powder.

"Ye. Look. Ridiculous." Nero pants out his laughter.

"We all look ridiculous," Aramis agrees and offers me another hand up. His wind blasts the worst of the iridescent dust off my face, then gently brushes my lips. Lemon pops out of my pocket and crawls up to my neck, licking at my cheek.

"You didn't happen to find a stream on the way to the tunnels, did you?" I ask eagerly. "As much as I love looking like a firefly, I'd rather not draw unwanted attention to ourselves."

Nero flashes me an amused grin as he claps his hands

together and grabs his pack from Aramis's hands. "Even better, I found a small hot spring and some caves to stay in overnight."

Thank Goddess.

34

SYBIL

The steam curls into the air from the two small pools of water. The teal water glows faintly, spilling from the larger pool into the smaller one, until it dribbles down the mountain in a small stream. A sense of peace and calm fills the air as tiny fireflies dance, flicking in between the trees.

"The caves are just another two hundred feet up the path," Nero points out where the lichen continues to glow illuminating up the mountain.

"This is all so–" I inhale, the scent of minerals and pine filling my nostrils. "–magical."

I shed my pack, my boots, and overdress on the ground. I'll wash it later. Lemon scampers from my overskirt pocket and dips his paws into the water before curling up at the edge of the steaming pool and closing his eyes. Without a single care for the men behind me, I follow suit, undressing down to my chemise before submerging myself to my neck. All I care about is getting some warmth back into my cold body. My feet barely touch the rocky bottom, but the warm water soothes my aching muscles. The white muslin gown clings to my body and I slowly move to the other side and settle on a naturally formed rock bench.

Aramis watches me from the shore as he slowly removes his layers down to his undergarment and slips below the water. The semi-translucent water comes up to his chest. Nero follows behind, causing the water to rise and spill into the next pool as his weight displaces it.

"So, what now?" Aramis asks, his eyes meeting mine. He doesn't touch me but I can feel the need to gravitate in his direction.

"We should get rest for the night, then explore the caves in the morning," I reply, keeping that heady gaze upon me. I glance up at the moon cresting above us and sigh, hoping the Goddess is watching over us now that Kela is no longer here to guide us. "One of them has to have the answers we seek."

"Sybil, what do we do if we dinna find them?" asks Nero, concerned. He sinks further into the water and groans in delight at the warmth.

"We meet up with the council." Aramis glances towards Nero, eyebrow lifted for confirmation. "We can't go home yet."

Nero grunts his agreement, lips pursing as he stares up at the sky. We continue enjoying the warmth of the hot spring in silence until water splashes behind us as Nero pulls out of the pool. "Right ye two. I'm going to find a nice place to rest, deep, deep within that cave," he says, pointing to the smaller of the two caves. "Deep enough to not hear a single thing if ye get me," he adds, and I can see Aramis roll his eyes. "Yer majesty wake me when yer ready so we can take turns on lookout."

Once Nero disappears within the cave, I close my eyes trying to ground myself as the bubbling warm water caresses my skin. When I open my eyes again I see Aramis watching me intently as he moves through the water to sit next to me.

"Merry solstice," he whispers, his fingers entwining in mine under the water. "I know it's not the solstice you've imagined, but I'm happy to be spending it with you."

"Merry solstice." I smile at him, and tug our moving hands

closer to me, so that we're inches apart. With everything that has happened in the past few weeks, I forgot that the holiday was so close. It feels like eons ago that I was preparing for Bolide.

The moon illuminates his figure, giving him an unearthly glow making me gasp at how beautiful he is.

"It's the first solstice I haven't spent alone in years." I lift my hand and trace the outline of the moon's reflection in the water. "When I was younger, my parents and I would stay up late drinking milk tea and eating dried fruit biscuits while we came up with outlandish stories. After they died—"

The words fall away as I consider all my losses. I stare into the water, tears pooling in my eyes as I wonder what my parents would think of me now. I am not the successful healer they wanted me to be, and even though I had made their dream my own for many years, I am not sure it is still what I want. The replica of the moon shatters as I break the water's surface, unable to suddenly take the stillness offered. I back away from Aramis wide-eyed without explanation, looking for a place of solitude. I need to breathe, and I need the space to think. My movement quickly takes me to a quiet rock edge where I can take my time to sort out my thoughts. Turning away and resting my forearms on the rim of the pool, I take a deep breath and sigh.

"I lost my mother when I was young too, you know." Aramis moves quietly in the water until he settles next to me, the movement of the water gently pushing his body against mine. "Sybil?" Aramis turns his attention on me—that beautiful, thorough gaze. "What can I do for you? How can I help?"

I smile, appreciating his offer. "It's just taking me a moment to adapt to all these changes" I say, unable to better explain my inner turmoil. "My whole life I've only ever wanted to be a healer, make my parents proud, but I now realize that maybe I just wanted to help people." Aramis's fingers gently brush my arm, his gaze full of unspoken understanding. "And I don't have to be a healer to do that. I can still do that. Freeing the shifters is my way of helping, my purpose."

A smile appears on his lips as he says, "you are such a marvel, Sybil Vandeleur." I move a few inches closer to him, cup his cheek and brush a kiss of thanks on his forehead.

"The experiences of our past shape us into who we are today." Aramis whispers and takes the opportunity to intertwine our bodies. Before I know it, my arms are wrapped around his neck, his hands braced protectively against my waist. "I believe in you. I don't know what our future holds, but I vow I will be at your side every step of the way."

He pauses, as if holding something back, unspoken words lingering in his gaze. I shake my head to clear the thoughts as I hug him tight before lifting my gaze up at the stars, breathing slowly. They twinkle brightly between the tree branches, a living celestial dance. Letting out a sigh, I slip through Aramis' embrace and dunk under the water, letting its soothing touch caress my body. I surface moments later when my lungs begin to burn, gasping for air.

As I stand in the water, a cool wisp of air brushes against my body, my nipples becoming taunt at its touch. I don't need to look at Aramis to know that it's his winds caressing me. I turn around to see Aramis' steady gaze slowly travel down the length of my body, from the crown of my head down below the water's surface. His gaze is as hungry as a starved man when he slowly approaches me. Heat coils in my gut as I step backwards, the stone wall of the springs hitting the back of my legs.

"I think you need some help cleaning up, my pomme sucrée." Aramis' voice is a deep rumble as he lifts my hand out of the water, gently massaging in between each finger before kissing my palm. The touch sends sparks down my body as Aramis sends a wind up my arms. Goddess help me, my nipples harden more. A small whimper bursts from my lips, but I desperately shut myself up. I can do this.

"Thanks, but I can clean myself." I weakly protest, darting my tongue out to lick my lips. Aramis' touch turns to a gentle caress as he pulls me closer to him.

"Oh really? Because you missed a spot, here." Aramis trails a finger up my arm, then over to circle around my right breast. I gasp at the light touch.

"Oh?"

"And here." He kisses at the hollow of my neck. I exhale long breaths, trying to engage my core. My legs tremble but I shall not falter.

"And you, Aramis?" I manage, as I look him in the eyes. "What about you?" I lift my other arm to try and get an edge on him, but he grabs my wrist pinning both arms against the rock edge. His body presses into me, and all of his hardness molds into my softness. I tilt my hips up—just to drive him as wild as he's driving me crazy. He groans, returning the favor as his body presses back against mine.

Aramis' blue eyes pierce into mine. "You are going to drive me past my restraint," Aramis growls.

Good. I grin at him salaciously, and Aramis leans down to kiss me, but it's savage. He nips my mouth and I open, kissing him just as hard. Our tongues dance together, eliciting groans from both of us. Aramis sucks my tongue and I cry out, grinding my body against him.

"Sybil darling," Aramis growls in my ear. "You little minx. Put your hands on the pool's edge and don't let go."

I laugh in delight at how tortured he looks. Aramis looks the way I feel; insane with desire. The unfinished business between us is slowly driving me mad.

"Why?"

"Don't you know?" Aramis sends a torturous wind across my breasts, and I groan. "You need tending to. Now, do as

I ask." I obey, my hands gripping the edge of the stone. He
begins his ministrations, gently cleaning my skin and hair
free of glowing goo and lichen powder. His touch lingers
everywhere on my body. My thin gown clings to my body
under the water, the slight luminescent glow leaving not much
to the imagination.

"Do you want your reward for being an obedient, good
girl?" Aramis brushes a chaste kiss against my lips.

The prince has completely surprised me. As much as a
logical part of my mind screams to take caution with how fast
things are moving between us every fiber of my being acts as
if it belongs to him, is drawn to him. With his every touch,
my magic sings in my veins. Is this what love is like? Or is
there something magical and intoxicating about these cerulean,
luminescent hot springs?

"Oh, I get a prize?" I lean into the kiss, grinning as I
completely give in. "Something better than a kiss?"

"You want this reward." Aramis promises. I hum in
agreement as Aramis presses me against the pool's edge. His
hands lift my legs around his waist, and we're aligned perfectly.
Aramis groans as our bodies press together, and then moves
his hands up, sliding a hand behind my head and crushes his
lips to mine. I wrap my arms around his neck, clinging to him.
Aramis' other hand trails lazy, slow, tantalizing circles down
my chemise until it reaches my waist. He kisses down to my
earlobe, nuzzling against the side of my neck. I writhe against
him, my skin buzzing and sensitive between the lapping waters
and his caress and I gasp. I need more. So much more.

"Aramis," I plead as he pauses and pulls back, eyes roving
my face. The side of his lips curling up as our bodies shift and
he slides a leg between mine. I push down on his leg, just to
chase the sensations of pleasure building inside me.

"Not yet," he says, tugging at the back of my head until I
arch towards him. The cool air brushing against my chest as

it breaches the surface. He leans forward and flicks his tongue against one sensitive pebbled nipple before turning and giving attention to the other. Hands travel further towards my core, gently stroking me. A moan escapes my lips as I arch further into his touch. His whisper is a rumble against my skin. "I want the moment I finally take you to be perfect, Sybil, because that's what you deserve. Not here in the middle of nowhere. I want you splayed in front of me on the softest of beds worthy of you," Aramis whispers like a prayer but despite his promise, the wicked grin on his lips tells me he is not ready to let me go. His fingers stroke my core with newfound intensity and I flex my hips a bit more, grinding against his touch as pleasure keeps rising within me. Aramis groans, flicking a tongue in a tantalizing circle around my nipple. "You are so beautiful when you lose control," he says as our lips crash back together and I realize I have never felt more in tune with my body or more alive.

"Oh Aramis," I cry as his fingers slide inside.

"That's it Sybil, let go my love," and as those words leave his lips, the crescendo reaches its peak and I fall into a sea of pleasure that washes over me, wave after wave. I hold onto Aramis even after my heartbeat returns to his normal rhythm, scared of what my body will feel like away from his warmth now that he's imprinted on my soul.

Aramis moves a wet strand of hair from my forehead and I start blushing when he gently kisses my cheek. "You stunning creature," he says with adoration and I hide my gaze from him. "Let's get out of here before we get a cold." As I nod in agreement, Aramis pulls himself out of the water. My eyes rove his muscular body and the way his undergarments cling to his wet skin. He swipes my cloak off our pile of bags before holding it out to me.

"Thank you," I accept gratefully, wrapping it around my body as the chill air immediately seeps into my skin, gooseflesh prickling my body.

"Here, let me carry you so you don't get your boots wet."
Aramis says as he sweeps me off my feet. I lay my head in the
crook of his neck, inhaling his deep rich scent. The warmth
of his body radiates into mine. My skin radiates with sensation
everywhere that it touches him. When we reach the cave's
entrance, Aramis sets me down on the ground near a fire. Nero
must have predicted our needs, he even brought my bag in
and set up my sleeping roll. The stone is warm from the fire's
radiation.

"Where will you sleep?" I ask meekly, rubbing my hands
together before the flames.

"Sleep will be a long time coming for me." Aramis stares
out the opening of the tunnel to the forest beyond while
adjusting his pants. "Nero and I need to talk, then one of us
will stand guard while the other comes to warm up and sleep
here by the fire. Don't fret, we will return soon. Make yourself
comfortable." He kisses my brow gently before crushing my
body to his. As soon as he lets go, he turns and walks out the
entrance. I immediately feel the weight of his absence. I can't
get over how my body yearns and calls to him. The loss of his
physical touch around me hurts. I temper my yearning with the
practical settings surrounding me.

I peel my wet chemise from my body and pull a fresh clean
one from my bag as I lay the other to dry.

What is happening between Aramis and I? There is now a
sense of safety and content building within me when I'm in his
presence. Mine, I think again and the word rings true.

The flames crackle and pop cheerfully, casting shadows that
dance on the wall in the cave. It is a deep one and I can't see
the end of it from where Nero has set up the fire. He seems
reassured that it is safe. Are there creatures that live in the
mountains of Shadowvale like we have in Kallistar? Do these
creatures steal naughty children out of their beds at night? I

shiver at the memory of the night stories my parents told me to ensure I was a good child. Then I sigh, sad at the thought of their loss once more.

I roll onto my back staring at the stone ceiling. Lichen and luminescent mushrooms grow in the cracks and crevices like a star filled sky. A muffled whumph sounds from outside of the cave mouth. I perk my ears in with listening as the expansion of the cave grows, a glittering light in the distance enticing me.

"Hello?" I call out as I roll onto my stomach. Nothing but the crisp night air and sound of crickets chirping replies.

Another whumph precedes the sound of pebbles hitting the ground, and my curiosity has officially gotten the best of me. I glance at the front of the cave, hoping for a line of vision that shows me the two males who have quickly become lines of comfort to me.

"Aramis? Nero? Is that you?" I call out as I stare at the peaceful night. Lemon starts hissing, the fur on his neck and back standing on end as he runs further into the tunnel. I step behind the fire and scoop him up into my arms, as I scramble for my dagger.

Another whumph and then snow starts falling in clumps before the cave entrance, obscuring the opening within seconds and extinguishing the fire. I clutch Lemon tightly against me as he squirms with discomfort. The cave immediately descends into darkness, and I begin to fall.

I scream.

ARAMIS

I trudge back down the mountain, my boots crunching in the snow as I make my way to where Nero sits with his back propped up against the trunk of a tree. The tips of his membranous wings catching the glint of moonlight. I shake my head as I think only weeks ago we were hunting down rouge shifters. Now look at us. Outcasts of the kingdom, hunted by my very own stepmother. A prince without a throne to call his own.

And with a shifter as his fated mate.

A deep tug pulls in my chest and I glance back towards the cave. Should I tell her? Does she suspect?

"Dragon got yer tongue, mate?" Nero drawls from the ground as he stretches his arms behind his head and casts his gaze to the sky. "Have you ever seen anything so majestic?"

"Haha, funny," I scoff, kicking loose snow at him with the toe of my boot.

"Hey! Don't pick a fight ye canna win." He protests. Nero looks at my crestfallen face and instantly sobers. "But seriously mate, what's on yer mind?"

With a sigh, I sit on the ground next to him, razing my hands across my face and through my hair. "What do I tell

Sybil?"

"About yer obsessive need to match yer tunics to yer undergarments?" He waggles his eyebrows at me and I punch him in the arm. "Ow! Ye dinna have to do that."

"Don't be an ass. I am talking about the mating bond." My heart races in my chest at the thought of telling her. "Do you think she knows?

"She's smart. I wouldn't put it past her to suspect," he says. "The bond has snapped into place for sure then?" He picks up a rock and tosses it, skipping across the small pool of water.

I rub at my chest. If I reach inside, I can discern an almost palpable thin golden thread that is alive. It thrums with her essence, and I swear I can feel her emotions if I concentrate on it long enough. "I... think so. The night after the battle, when she fell into my arms, I felt this energy connecting us. It's like an invisible thread connecting our souls."

"They say powerful emotions push the deepest magic," he replies.

"What if she—" I pause as dread clenches at my chest "— denies the bond?"

Nero raises an eyebrow at me before glancing at the water and back at me, causing heat to rise in my cheeks and groin.

"A moment of physical interaction does not equate to her agreeing to be bonded to me for life as my mate." My heart jumps into my throat in hope.

"She'd be a fool then."

"I have treated her terribly. I abducted her from her home, from everything she held dear only for her to be tortured, thrown in the dungeon and now on the run for her life after losing the one friend she's made."

"Aye, but ye also saved her. Ye put everything ye have ever believed in yer whole life to the side for her. There is good in ye, Aramis. I have seen it since we were wee lads. It is up to ye to decide what side ye fight from now on."

With a sigh, I clasp him on the shoulder. "You're right. I have to tell her. Everything." I rub at my chest as an odd sensation takes form.

"Are ye okay there, mate?" Nero's body tenses, his brow furrowing.

"I don't–" but my words are cut off as the ground beneath us shakes violently and a loud whumph fills the air.

"What was that?" Nero and I are on our feet in an instant, grabbing our bags and heading up towards the caves. A loud scream pierces the air.

"Sybil!" I yell. I run as fast as I can, dodging branches as I head directly to the cave. My chest burns from the exertion, but it doesn't matter. I have to get to her.

"What is that?" Nero and I come to a sudden stop, breath heaving. Before us, where once was the opening to the cave, a giant mound of snow blocks the entrance. I immediately begin digging at the ice with my bare hands. I gather the winds around me to blast the snow away when I'm abruptly grabbed by the back of my collar and yanked into the air. The beating of wings is overshadowed by another whumph as a cascade of snow covers my progress.

"Let me go!" I yell, feet dangling in the air. I have to get to her. I have to free her! There are so many things I must tell her.

"Aye," Nero grunts under my weight. "As soon as ye calm down and think with yer head. Ye nearly brought the whole mountain down on us." He slowly lowers us both to the ground but maintains a grip on my shoulder.

"You don't understand!" I growl.

"I ken more than ye think, lad." Nero steps before me, meeting my gaze. "We can't risk causing a cave in and injuring Sybil."

I close my eyes and concentrate, reaching for that tiny golden thread tying us together. I mentally send my power across it and feel it hum in return, full of life and curiosity.

"She's alive," I say in wonder.

"Aye, and I suspect she feels you in kind," he says.

"What do we do now?"

SYBIL

My eyes slowly adjust to the darkness as the lichen glows brighter. My chest constricts as I stare at the thick blue-white wall blocking the entrance to the cave. Unable to contain Lemon, he runs down my neck, along my body, and leaps onto the ground. He chitters at me in approval, but I can't begin to contemplate what it means—his excitement and being lost underground. He scampers away from me, investigating into the cave, while I look at the closed entrance before me.

"Fuck," I swear, frantically scrambling at the wall.

"Aramis! Nero!" I scream, pounding against the blockade of snow, but silence echoes back. My heart starts to race as I grab my dagger and start stabbing the snow. A small chunk breaks free, and I sigh with relief. I continue to dig and stab, creating a small tunnel. All I need is to create enough space so they can hear me. They have to be alive.

A warm thread tugs deep in my core, then a phantom wind brushing along my skin.

Aramis...

He has to be alive. I don't know how, but I can feel him, sense him. I hear Lemon chittering further along the path, in what almost seems like a beckoning call, but I'm too distressed to pay attention.

Another rumble above me causes me to pause, counting down the seconds. Is that another avalanche?

"Aramis! Are you there?" I shout out, one more time.?
"Nero! I'm here—on the other side! Can you hear me?" The earth surrounding me shudders and I frantically dig again until I'm forced to step back as a large pile of snow falls in, pushing me further back into the cave and filling into the small progress I had made.

"Fuck fuck fuck!" I yell, throwing my dagger at the other end of the cave. Lemon pops back at my side, chittering as if his life depends on it. He wraps his little body around my legs and pushes the back of his head against my leg. Go. His movements seem to say. Come on! The flash of dagger gleams bright in the darkness until it skids down the stone floor, out of sight. The sound of scraping echoes off the stone, forcing me to finally look up. "What—"

I grab my bag and satchel from the floor and sling my coat over my shoulder. They don't look worse for wear, but I tug a little harder than anticipated because they nearly got trapped by the snow. I make my way to the end of the cave, Lemon at my side, chattering nonstop. "What is it, Lemon?" I finally ask. He's never been this chatty his whole life. The pathway narrows and curves, then continues into a tunnel. My fingers trace the wall, faintly lit by the lichen in glowing hues of blue, purple, and green. What is the lichen doing down here in the cave? I furrow my brow and look more closely at my surroundings. Lemon takes a running leap up my leg and then curls himself around my neck, finally at ease.

Faint symbols etched into the stone glow under my touch. My heart leaps in recognition. "Lemon look!" I exclaim. He looks at me as if to say, I told you so. I read the message etched into the wall, heart stumbling with anticipation.

The journey precedes the destination.
If one seeks the knowledge of healing, look inward.
Let go of all your expectations, all your beliefs,
and embrace your inner self.

Is this it? Truly? I look around the vacant, dark space and only see stone. Yet, when I look back at the carving, I know it in my bones: I've found the witches.

Thanks to the countless individuals who have offered their encouragement and support, the dream of bringing Sky of Thorns to life has become a reality. Their unwavering belief in me has fueled my determination to infuse our world with a touch of magic.

I am filled with immense gratitude towards my friend and fellow author, Charlotte Mallory. Words cannot express how thankful I am for her tremendous support and friendship. Charlotte is an amazing person who has not only been a wonderful supporter but also an incredible friend. She played a crucial role in bringing the cover for Sky of Thorns to life, and I am thrilled to announce that she will also be designing the covers for books two and three! I highly recommend checking out Charlotte's work as she is an exceptional storyteller. Her newest book, The Secrets of Jane, is a must-read among her collection of captivating stories.

I would like to express my gratitude to Dana Lee as well. Ever since I first shared with her about the world of Craeweth and Sybil, she has been my cheerleader. Her constant support and encouragement have pushed me to step outside of my comfort zone and discover my true voice.

Thanks to my co-author Johnna Dee, the Calpa series, my first published novel became a reality. Her unwavering support and encouragement gave me the courage to share my stories with the world. Without her, Sybil's tale would have remained a mere collection of scribbles on spare papers, only shared as bedtime stories with my daughter, recounting her thrilling adventures.

Finally, the magic of my world would not be possible without the unwavering love and support of my husband. Throughout our journey, he has consistently pushed me to pursue my dreams and follow my passions. I am beyond grateful to have him as my true bonded life mate.

BOOKS BY FLEUR

The Vandeleur Trilogy
Sky of Thorns
Secrets of Thorns (Summer 2024)
Succession of Thorns (2025)
To Scorch a Quartz Thorns (novella
Spring 2024)

The Calpa Series
co-written with Johnna Dee
The Clan of Mist
The Clan of Luna (Spring 2024)
The Clan of Deception (novella)

Fleur DeVillainy is an American fantasy author. In the realm of imagination, where love and enchantment intertwine, she crafts tales of extraordinary adventure interwoven with romance, internal growth and found family. By day, she brings healing to little hearts as a pediatric nurse practitioner. By night, she lets her pen dance across pages, weaving magical worlds and captivating characters. When not weaving tales, she finds solace in baking, sewing, and gardening. Join her on the many whimsical journeys through words and discover the wonders that lie within. Check out her series The Vandeleur Trilogy, her comic series Wolf and I, and her co-written Calpa series today!

If you want to know when Fleur's next book will come out, please visit her social media and website. Tiktok- www.tiktok.com/@FleurDeVillainy
Twitter- www.twitter.com/FleurDeVillainy
Facebook- www.facebook.com/FleurDeVillainy
Instagram- www.instagram.com/FleurDeVillainy

TRIGGER WARNINGS

Sky of Thorns is a new adult romantic fantasy and may not be suitable for all ages.

This book includes the follow trigger warnings:
kidnapping, violence, blood, profanity, open door sexual scenes, alcohol/drugs, slavery/imprisonment, death, war, mental health (depression/anxiety), starvation, and fire

- please note many of these trigger warnings are only touched on/light in content.

Milton Keynes UK
Ingram Content Group UK Ltd.
UKHW020701271123
433342UK00010B/91